Linda Sealy Knowles

# The Gamble

**Forget-Me-Not Romances: Winged publications**

Copyright © 2020 Linda Sealy Knowles

Forget Me Not Romances, a division of Winged Publications

All rights reserved. No part of this publication may be reproduced, stored in a retrieval system, or transmitted in any form or by any means, with the exception of brief quotations in printed reviews.

This book is a work of fiction. The characters in this story are the product of the author's imagination and are completely fictitious.

All rights reserved.

ISBN: 978-1-952661-07-5

Other books by Linda Sealy Knowles

*<u>The Maxwell Saga (Five books)</u>*
*Journey to Heaven Knowles Where*
*Hannah's Way*
*The Secret*
*Bud's Journey Home*
*Always Jess*
\*\*\*
*Kathleen from Sweetwater, Texas*
*Abbey's new Life*
*Sunflower Brides*
*Joy's Cowboy*
*Trapped By Love*

*Linda Sealy Knowles* is an historical western-romance writer who brings her love stories and characters to life. She gives God the glory for her talent that has given her much joy. Since 2012, she had written eleven novels. Linda is from the Satsuma/Saraland area in Alabama. She presently resides in Niceville, Florida, near her two children and three beautiful granddaughters.

# Dedication

Lauren Christine von Eberstein

To my wonderful granddaughter.

She's a happy-go-lucky, young girl with a heart of gold. She's willing to help anyone, especially me, with my spelling and grammar. I don't know what I would do without her.

# Acknowledgment

## Judith Griffin

I want to express my gratitude to my friend and reader of my book. She is dedicated to my story line. I am blessed to have her friendship and the time she spends on my pages before they go to my editor.

# Chapter 1

"Pa! You'd better not raise your bet using my Betsy or my chickens. I raised them from babies, and they're the only thing that keeps food on our table," Mary Grace Winters screamed at her foolish gambler of a father.

"Now, Honey, git your sore butt out of this here room before I lock you upstairs. A man's gotta do what he's gotta do when he has a hand as good as mine."

"You gonna up the ante, old man, or chew with that gal of yours? If you wanna make this pot enjoyable, why not put your gal up as collateral? I don't need a dried-up milk cow." Luke Tyler, the owner of the biggest gold mine near Crooked Creek, Colorado, leered at Mary Grace.

"You crazy. I'd never put up my gal, even with this winning hand I'm holding," said Moon, her father and also owner of the stage depot and café.

"Pa, what are you doing? I told you not to lose my Betsy. If you do, you'd better not close your eyes because you won't be able to open them in the morning." Mary Grace slammed a platter of hot doughnuts on the pile of money in the center of the table.

"Dang it, gal, if these doughnuts weren't so good, I'd take you outside and dump you down the well. You're worse than a boil on a man's behind," Luke Tyler shouted and scooted his chair back from the table.

Mary Grace stormed back to the stove and poured more batter into the pan of hot grease. She'd like to pour the hot oil over that handsome, cocky gold miner's head. All the same she was pleased to get a retort out of the handsome cowboy. He'd stopped by more than a few times to play a hand of poker but never said anything to her before tonight.

***

"You know, Moon," Luke lowered his voice, "I sure could use a cook up at my mining camp. How about letting your gal come and cook for my men? She'd have her own room, and I'd pay her a wage each week."

"Are you trying to distract me, sonny boy?" Moon peeked over his hand and glared at his opponent. "What would I do for a cook here? Her good cooking is what brings my customers in this place. I can tell you now it ain't my watered-down liquor or these card games."

"You can always hire someone to keep coffee on the burner and cook bacon, eggs, and toast for your so-called customers. T'ain't more than a dozen men who come here to eat. I bet you haven't ever paid your girl a dime for all the hard work she does around here."

"Hey, I don't have to pay her. She's got a roof over her head, and she gets all the food she can cook. Mary Grace don't want for nothing."

"Are you going to play cards or keep on jawing about your wager?" Jeffrey Sumter glared at Moon. "It's getting late, and I'm tired."

"Eat another doughnut," Luke said and continued to stare at Moon.

"I'm out, but I'll take them hot treats with me." Jeffrey tossed his cards on the table and stood while stuffing doughnuts in his jacket pockets.

"See you back at the mine, boy." Luke shuffled his five cards in his palms. "What's it going to be, old man? Are you raising your bet with your gal as collateral? I'm not accepting that cow."

"Hold on thar a minute. I gotta think. Thar's at least one hundred dollars in that pot." He stared at the money in the center of the table.

"Yep." Luke counted in his head and said, "One hundred, two dollars and sixty-five cents to be exact."

Sweaty beads collected on Moon's upper lip. He rubbed his

bald head and viewed the three aces and two kings. A winning hand for sure. There was only one ace out, and surely no one would be lucky enough to have that one black card.

"Time's up, Moon. Show me your hand or toss them on the table." Luke smiled at the old man who had been winning all night. "Lady Luck has been with you tonight and you still have a 50-50 chance of winning."

"All right, all right. My gal is my wager," Moon said as his daughter stood behind her father for their final play.

"No, Pa. You can't do that. I'm not a thing you can use as collateral. You can't just up and gamble me away. I will never forgive you for this—win or lose, I will hate you forever." Mary Grace whirled around and stormed outside the building. Neither watched her leave.

Several men had gathered around the table for this last turn of the cards. A big pot of money and a woman was the most intriguing wager most of them have ever witnessed.

"Now or never," mumbled Luke to Moon.

Slowly, Moon showed one card at a time. "Three aces," Moon said with a big smile, "and a pair of kings." The men mumbled amongst themselves, one patting him on his back.

Just as slowly, Luke spread his five cards on the table. "A royal flush." Luke leaned back in his chair and grinned as the blood drained out of Moon's face.

"You cheat! You can take all the money, but you'll never take my gal." Moon jumped up from his chair, which caused it to slide back and slam into the wall.

The men moved away from the table as Luke stood. He leaned over the table, pocketed his winnings, and glared at Moon. With a smile on his face, he said, "I won fair and square, and you know it, old man. Now, this money is mine, and so is your daughter. She will be going with me to my mining site and be my cook. Nothing more. I will see that she is taken care of and she'll get a good wage for her work."

"She'll never go with you," Moon said, watching the men file out of the place. He wished he had somewhere else to go because his daughter was never going to speak to him again.

"She'll go, but I want you to tell her what my plans are for her. I'll be by in the morning to pick her up in the supply wagon."

# Chapter 2

Early the next morning, Luke walked into the miner's dining hall and found Harry Jamison, an older man with a peg leg, sitting on a barrel. His wooden leg stretched out in front of his thin frame while he drank coffee from a tin cup.

"What are you doing here before breakfast?"

"I'm trying hard to stand and hop around, but I'm having a bad day, and the sun ain't even come up. Sure glad you hired that youngster, Jimbo, to help me out. He's out in the chicken house, gathering eggs."

"I come to tell you that I have hired a young lady to help out with the cooking. She'll be coming back with me today. I'll let her stay in the room that I built for myself."

"Well, boss man, she'll be a welcome change around this place. A girl, that's nice. The men will be happy to have someone else's cooking besides mine."

"You might have to help me make her feel at home here. You see, the gal's pa put her up as collateral during a card game last night. She might not be too happy to be here, but she will stay, even if I have to hogtie her."

"What? Did you gamble? You can't win a woman in a poker game. Have you gone loco?" Harry's eyes widened at the thought. He tried to stand, but the upper part of his thigh had been rubbed raw. He flopped back on the barrel.

"Don't get your drawers in a wad. The girl's not my woman. I want a cook and nothing else." He sat down on a barrel next to the counter where Harry served food. "This young gal has been working for her pa at the café and stage depot. He doesn't pay her and she don't look like she has anything nice. I'm going to pay her a fair wage."

"Guess I understand now. But, you'd better not do anything to that young gal. You know what I mean? If you do, boss, you'll be standing in front of that old preacher who drops by here once in a while."

"Gosh, old man. All I want is another cook. Just wait until you taste her food. You'll never want her to leave."

\*\*\*

Luke's first stop in town was at the dry goods store where he dropped off his list of supplies for the mining camp. He drove the flatbed wagon to the café and stage depot, then jumped down and entered the café. It took a minute for his eyes to adjust to the dim light of the room. "Why is it so dark in here, Moon?" Luke asked as he looked around. Over in the corner was a carpetbag and a shotgun lying on the floor. Moon didn't answer.

"Is your daughter ready to go to my mining camp?" Luke had hoped that the girl would be eager to go with him.

"Afraid not, Luke. I went upstairs this morning and packed her things, but she said that she would die before she leaves her room and goes anywhere with you."

"Does she understand that I want her to cook for my miners and nothing else?"

"I explained that to her, but she ain't being reasonable. I told you last night that she wouldn't go with you." Moon failed to hold back a smirk.

"Which room is hers and what's her name? I don't believe I've ever heard you call her anything but Gal." Luke placed his foot on the first step of the stairs.

"Mary Grace. She's at the top of the stairs. First door on the right."

Luke took the stairs two at a time and stopped at the first door. Sobbing came from the other side. He called to Mary Grace, and the crying stopped.

\*\*\*

Mary Grace clamped a hand over her mouth and wiped her

eyes and runny nose. She whirled around in her plaid shirt and tight denim. Her crying had stopped, but she was having trouble controlling the hiccups. She turned a thoughtful look at the front window, the only way to escape the room with him standing in the doorway.

"Miss Mary Grace?" Luke spoke gently. "Your pa has given you permission to work for me at my mining camp. I need you to help me out by cooking for my men. I am going to pay you a fair wage, just like I do my men. What do you say?"

Mary Grace opened the door and said in her politest voice, "No, thank you." She slammed the door in his face.

\*\*\*

Luke pounded his fist on her door. "Mary Grace, open this door and let's talk about the wager your pa lost to me last night."

The door flew open and Mary Grace stood with her palms on her hips. "You go and talk to Pa about the wager. I had no part in it, and I wouldn't cross the street with you. Now, leave before I make you sorry that you came up here." The door slammed in his face again, and the sound of a piece of furniture being moved against the door reached his ears.

Not to be outdone by a young whippersnapper of a gal, Luke took his pocketknife and removed the screws that held the door on its frame. Once he gained entrance, Luke stepped around the dresser that she'd pushed up against the door. The lovely gal stood across the room glaring at him with hands posted on her hips. Luke did the same, took two steps toward Mary Grace, and gave her a triumphant smile.

Before he could say anything to her, something hard as a brick hit him directly between the eyes. The room went dark and his head spun. He felt himself sliding downward, and he tried to steady himself by reaching for the girl. The walls closed in on him, and he lost all consciousness.

\*\*\*

Mary Grace eased over to the mine owner. Her big toe pushed on his shoulder. He didn't move, but she could tell he was breathing. He wasn't dead, but he'd sleep for a good while. That would give her time to leave on the next stagecoach. She stole enough money from her Pa's secret box to travel to her Aunt Louise's small farm in Wildwoods, Colorado. Her pa's sister had begged her to come now that she wasn't in good health. Mary Grace never wanted to be a nurse, but it was far better than being a kept woman.

Her pa was making coffee when she entered the room. "Where's your new boss man?"

"I told him I refused to work for him like I told you, so he left. Didn't he tell you what I said?" She peered up at her pa with the best innocent eyes she could make. Mary Grace picked up her carpetbag and shotgun and headed to the back of the café. With a glance over her shoulder to make sure her pa wasn't watching her, she hurried out into the alleyway and ran to the stagecoach that would be leaving soon.

# Chapter 3

Luke's eyes fluttered open to a wooden ceiling. A giant black spider was creeping in and out of a hole in a piece of wood. His head was killing him. The knot on his forehead was as large as a goose egg. He grabbed onto a rocking chair and pulled himself up off the floor. Dizziness vanished after a minute. He took in a deep breath of fresh air at the window. Turning to leave the room, he saw a large club of oak wood lying on the floor. That's what that vixen, Mary Grace, had used to knock him senseless. The gal smacked him right and proper, and now he was going to retaliate.

He struggled down the stairs to the café. Moon jumped up from a table. "Where have you been? Mary Grace said you left an hour ago. What happened to your head?"

"Your daughter and I disagreed about her working for me."

"You'll need ice on your face to make the swelling go down," Moon studied him like a doctor. "Did she do that?"

"Yep, I woke up on the floor in her room, but she's not there. Do you have any idea where she could be?"

"Afraid not. Mary Grace told me you had left and she went out into the kitchen, but she ain't nowhere around, and I need her to fix food."

"She'll return, and when she does, I'll be waiting. I need to pick up my supplies and head back to the mine."

As Luke entered the busy dry goods store, he overheard one of the men say something about Mary Grace hightailing it out of town on the stage. "Hey fellows, did I hear you say Moon's daughter left on the stage?"

"Yep, she sure did. Man, that little gal has a temper. I asked her why she didn't dress like a lady if she was going to travel, and she told me to mind my own business. Of course, she didn't say it so nicely. That gal has a mouth on her. We decided it was best not to bother her since she was carrying a shotgun."

"How long has that stagecoach been gone?" Luke rubbed the knot on his head. It hurt like the dickens.

"It got a late start. Maybe thirty minutes if that much," one of the men answered Luke.

In less than fifteen minutes, Luke had paid for his supplies, hired a man to drive the supply wagon out to his mine, and rented a fast, sturdy horse from the livery. Luke rode the rented horse as fast as he could for a while, and then slowed him down to a trot. With each pounding of the horse's hoofs, his head felt like a drum inside his skull. After traveling only about five miles from town, he saw the stagecoach stopped in the center of the hard-packed road. Two men were struggling with the back wheel.

Once the men spotted Luke, the driver grabbed his rifle and pointed it at him. Luke jumped down and held his hands in the air. "Hold on fellows. Can I lend you a hand?"

"Shore be obliged. Three pair of hands will shore make it easier handling this confounded wheel." The stagecoach driver snorted.

While working on the wheel, Luke told the two men that he had to remove one of the lady passengers. "She's a young runaway, and her pa wants her to return home. I came to get her. Hope you understand."

"Here we go on the count of three. One, two, three." The three men placed the wheel back on the coach, and it was ready to roll.

"Now, mister, which one of the ladies have you come to take home?" He opened the door of the stagecoach and peeked inside. "Hey, look yonder," the driver yelled. "A girl is running out through the woods."

"How about tossing her carpetbag down, and I'll go get her. Thanks, fellows." Luke caught the bag and gave chase to the girl. He didn't turn around, but he could hear the stagecoach leaving. Mary Grace was hiding behind a large bounder. "You might as well come out from your hiding place because I can see you."

***

Mary Grace took a deep breath and stood. She was mad at herself because she didn't have her shotgun with her. The driver had taken it away from her because it scared the other passengers. She stepped away from the big rock and glared at Luke as he sat on the horse. "You'd better be glad I don't have my gun. I'd do more damage to your body than I did with a piece of wood."

Luke's head was hurting so bad he could hardly keep his eyes open. "Get your raggedy tail over here and let's be on our way. I'm not in the best of moods since you nearly knocked my head off my shoulders."

"Where's my horse?" Mary Grace looked all around and didn't see another animal. "I'm not riding behind you, mister."

Luke rode his horse slowly over to Mary Grace. She stood with her back turned to him. He jumped off the tall animal, grabbed the waistband of her denim, and flipped her double when she struggled to get loose. He lifted her frame over the horse's saddle with her face staring at the ground and her middle lying on the saddle horn. Her feet dangled on one side while her arms hung over the opposite. Luke leaped upon the saddle and pushed the center of her back down. "Stay still or you'll be sorry."

"Put me down on the ground this instant, you mule-headed varmint. I'll kill you when I get off this horse." The man's horse sidestepped and stomped his front hooves from her wriggling and screaming.

Luke raised his hand and slapped her rear so hard that dust flew from the seat of her trousers. She screamed several nasty phrases, and he slapped her bottom again and again. "Keep it up, missy, and you won't be able to sit for a week. I can't tolerate young ladies spewing ugly words, understand?" When she didn't answer, he slapped her behind again, harder than before.

"Yes, I understand," she mumbled. Mary Grace bit her bottom lip to keep from crying. Her pa had never laid a hand on her, even though he threatened to do so many times. Her backside was on fire and she couldn't reach back and rub it. Oh, how she wanted to hurt this man some more. His face looked terrible. She hadn't intended to hurt him so badly, but now she was glad she had. The dirty lowdown polecat deserved everything she gave him.

As they traveled toward the mining camp, Mary Grace grew

dizzy from the blood rushing to her head, and the saddle horn was about to drill a hole in her stomach. "Let me sit up and ride for a while. I feel sick and my stomach hurts," Mary Grace demanded.

"Do you promise to sit still and behave yourself? Before you answer, let me tell you that I detest liars."

"I promise." Mary Grace said, crossing her fingers. If and when she got the chance, she'd be gone in a flash, and this time no one would find her.

"You promise what?" Luke asked.

"I promise to sit still and behave," she repeated slowly.

***

Luke stopped his horse and leaped off holding the reins tight. He wasn't going to trust this gal one minute. He lifted her off the horse and held her up until she felt her legs again. Luke got back in the saddle, then gripped her hand and pulled her up behind him. "One good thing about you wearing denim pants, it makes riding a horse a lot easier." As he moved the animal, he warned her. "Best be placing your arms around my waist and hold tight."

The ride to the miners' campsite was less than a mile away. He thought this was a good opportunity to speak with Mary Grace about what he expected of her while she lived at his miners' camp. He guessed now was a good time. "Mary Grace, I want you to be happy working at the camp. We have needed a good cook for a while. My cook can prepare simple, filling meals, but my men are tired of beans, meat, and cornbread. They deserve better food. I have twelve hardworking, crude-talking men working for me. I'll have them clean up their language around you. There's a room beside the kitchen that will be your home away from home while you're working for me. I promise you will be safe, and no one will bother you. You have any questions so far?" Luke waited for her to respond to her job description.

"Pa said that you was going to pay me. How much and when?"

"Payday for the week is Friday. So, I will pay you at the end of every week just like I do the men. Your wage will be seven fifty a week to begin with. After one month, if you're still with me and I am satisfied with your cooking, I'll give you a raise."

"How much?" Mary Grace asked.

"Ten more dollars. Forty dollars a month. Good wages." Luke

couldn't see her face, but he felt the tension go out of her body.

"I ain't gonna work as a prisoner who can't take a break when she needs it. What are my duties, and will I have time to myself occasionally?"

"You will cook breakfast and prepare the men's lunch buckets. While they are at work, you'll prepare a nice hot meal for dinner. Once the kitchen is cleaned, you'll be on your own time. You'll have two men working with you. Harry, my cook now, and Jimbo, a young man who's a hard worker. Both of them will be a big help to you. They will do whatever you ask, and if they don't, they'll answer to me."

\*\*\*

"Who makes the menus for the meals, and how do I get food to prepare?" Her voice had lost its anger; she was interested. She never had two dimes to call her own. Sometimes, a stranger would come to town and give her a nickel for bringing his food to him, but mostly her pa collected all the money. To be able to go shopping and buy anything her heart desired was like a dream come true. "I will stay at the campsite for a week to see if I like working for you. If I hate it and want to leave, I can. This is my deal, take it or leave it."

"You must know that I did win you lock, stock, and barrel, but I only wanted a cook. If you don't like cooking, my men, or your room, please feel free to leave. I will personally take you back to your pa."

## Chapter 4

They rode into the center of The Gypsy Lady mining camp. Mary Grace's eyes followed the painted sign until it was out of sight. Luke's horse knew the way to the reddish board building. They passed a square building with two large brick chimneys coming from the roof. Dark smoke floated from one of the stacks. Luke mumbled that Bear must be drying more deer jerky again. He rode between two big boulders. A larger building with several windows in the front and two on each side stood all alone.

Luke reached for her hand and helped her slide off the back of his horse. He leaped down and tied the reins to a hitching post that was ten feet away from the front entrance. "This is your home away from home. I hope you'll like it." Luke said, as they stepped on the front porch.

Jimbo, a tall, lanky young man, opened the front door and stepped onto the front porch. "Howdy, Mr. Luke. Harry said you'd be bringing us a cook, but I never thought you'd be bringing a gal. Golly, the men are gonna be surprised." He removed his hat and slapped it on his knee.

"Mary Grace, this young man is Jimbo. He will be one of your helpers."

"Hi." The boy's face reddened. She hoped she wasn't going to have a problem with him. She had to knock a few young men in the head back at the café to make them leave her alone.

"Gosh, Miss, can I take your carpetbag to your room?" Jimbo asked as he picked it off the ground.

"No, Jimbo, you can't do anything for the Miss right now. Chop some wood and place it in the bin outside the front bedroom door." Jimbo stood staring at Mary Grace as if he hadn't seen a girl in years. "Go," Luke said louder.

"Follow me, Miss," Luke said with a grin. "I will take you to your room, then I'll have some water brought to you."

Mary Grace followed Luke into the spacious dining room and stopped in her boots. Rows of long tables and benches filled the room. The glass windows were dirty, and the curtains were lopsided and pulled up on the rods. Food scraps and bones covered the floor.

Luke stopped to allow Mary Grace into her new room. She was still standing at the entrance to the dining room. "What's wrong?"

"This is where the men eat their meals?" She asked.

"Yep. The men have plenty of room to spread out and enjoy their meal. Do you like the room?" Luke's face beamed as he scanned the room. "Built this room myself."

"It's a pigsty." Mary Grace hurried to the kitchen area. "My Lord, this place is filthy. I can't cook here until it's cleaned."

"Look here now. I agree the place could be a little neater, but I wouldn't call it a pigsty. That's pretty bad." Luke scanned the room with new eyes, and he guessed maybe it was a mess.

"I hope my room is cleaner than this." Mary Grace followed Luke into her new home. She gasped and covered her lips. The room was one of the nicest places she had ever seen. The walls were scrubbed clean, sunlight was coming in the windows, and the wood floor had been waxed and partly covered with a colorful rug. A four-poster bed stood in the center of the room with a heavy quilt covering the mattress and fluffy pillows positioned at the headboard. A small wooden table and a chair set near one of the windows, while a rocker was near the fireplace. A curtain hung in one corner of the room for privacy.

Luke lit the lantern that sat in the middle of the table. "If you need another lamp, just put it on the list of supplies. You'll be responsible for keeping enough supplies stored in the kitchen, but if you need anything that will help make your job easier, place it on the list."

Mary Grace walked around the room, lifting the edge of the

scarf on the mantel, and then pushed the rocker back and forth. "This is a lovely room. I hope I'm not putting someone out."

"Well, to be honest with you, this is my room. I had it built for me, but I'm happy to give it up to you. This mining camp is important to me, and I don't want any more men leaving because of the food. Several have left to work for another mining company. You'll soon find out that men are serious about their food." Luke's serious expression changed into a big beautiful smile that made her knees go weak.

\*\*\*

Luke left Mary Grace and circled around his mining camp, but after a traumatic day, he had dinner in the bunkhouse. He decided to go to bed a lot earlier than usual. His head still hurt, and he was exhausted, but his dreams were about a wild, beautiful girl whose arms wrapped around his waist for hours today.

\*\*\*

Mary Grace was tired, but after taking a bath in her new room, she dressed in one of her older dresses, heated a bucket of water in the fireplace, and carried it in the kitchen. She placed the wood in the stove, and after it was warm, she put another bucket of water to boil. With rags she found in the pantry, she scrubbed the stove, the counters, and the serving bar. Finally, she felt that she could cook in the kitchen in the morning, but little by little, she would make it perfect. She found a broom in the pantry and swept the large floor clean. Tomorrow after breakfast, she would have Jimbo mop the floor. The glass panes needed to be washed with vinegar water. She would wash the curtains, but until she could do so, she removed them from the windows. Mary Grace worked until she was bone-tired, but she couldn't rest until she cleaned the kitchen.

In the few hours before morning, she had tossed and turned in the big four-poster bed. Mary Grace woke up with a thumping headache, but a good cup of coffee would help soothe it. She jumped out of bed and dressed in another pair of denim pants, then tucked her shirt into her trousers and tied a large white apron over her clothes.

Hurrying to the kitchen, she put two large pots of coffee on the stove, sliced four loaves of bread, and spread them with butter, cinnamon, and sugar. Later, she'd place them in the oven long enough to melt the butter. Mary Grace found a smoked ham hanging in the pantry, so she sliced off pieces and placed them in a heavy skillet she could hardly pick up. While the meat was cooking, she heated another pail of water for oatmeal. Tomorrow, she would fry potatoes and scramble eggs with homemade biscuits.

Mary Grace found a dozen lunch buckets sitting on a counter. Hm. What to prepare for the men's lunches today. She decided to boil a few dozen eggs and make fried apple pies. As she rolled out the dough, Harry and Jimbo came in the kitchen at the same time. Both gasped at the dining room and the clean kitchen.

"I'm happy you're both here this morning. Grab yourself some coffee and then start preparing sandwiches for the men's lunches. I know you can make jam and butter sandwiches, but they need some meat sandwiches. Harry, slice the roast beef that was left over from dinner last night and there's some cold fried chicken. There's enough for the men." Mary Grace gave Harry her sweetest smile.

"Those fried pies smell wonderful. The men will love them," Jimbo said.

"Good, because I want them to like my cooking," Mary Grace responded.

The men began filing into the dining area. The oatmeal was ready, the buttered bread toasted, and the ham was sizzling. The men oohed and aahed at the amount of food on their plates. Mary Grace instructed Jimbo to circle the dining room with the big pot of coffee and refill the men's cups.

Several of the men thanked her as they filed out of the dining hall, while others made comments about how nice the room looked. Mary Grace beamed at the men's appreciation.

Luke walked into the room as several men were leaving. They smiled and rubbed their bellies.

"That new cook is great. Don't let her get away," one of the men said, while others mumbled something similar and smiled.

Luke scanned the dining room and took a big whiff. "Someone's fairy godmother came last night and cleaned this place. The coffee smells wonderful, and those fried pies are calling my name," he said.

"Good morning, boss man," Harry grunted while stumbling over to a barrel to rest.

"How's the leg?" Mary Grace perked up at the older man's

response. She'd been watching how hard it was for him to move from one place to another.

"Don't fret over me. I'm fine. Just need to get off of it for a little bit." Harry picked up a fried pie, broke it in two, and took a big bite. "Damn, if this ain't the best thing I've ate in many moons."

Luke poured himself a cup of fresh coffee, chose a pie, and sat down at the nearest table. "Have you had breakfast, Mary Grace?"

"I have too much to do right now. I'll eat later."

"Nonsense. Grab a plate of food and come join me."

"You deaf? I said I'm busy."

"Have you already forgotten I'm the boss? Please come and eat with me." He stared over the rim of his tin coffee cup at her.

Their eyes locked. Mary Grace sighed, poured coffee, and selected a small fried pie. She flopped down on the bench in front of him.

"Why are you wearing those pants?"

"What does it matter to you what I wear?"

"I want you to look like a lady in my dining room. Those britches are fine for riding or working in the garden but not in here."

"I have this apron on over my clothes. The men can't tell what I'm wearing." Mary Grace had too much to do to be sitting here quarreling about her appearance.

"You had on a dress before you went to bed. Do you have any more dresses to wear?" Before she could answer, he held up his hand to stop her from speaking. "Write day dresses on the list, about five of them, and I'll pick them up for you when I go back to town."

"Are you out of your mind? I'm not spending my hard-earned money on dresses when I have good trousers to wear."

"The dresses will come under necessary items, and the company will pay for them." Luke gave her a hard stare. "No more discussion—no more britches after the new dresses arrive."

# Chapter 5

Mary Grace had asked Jimbo to help her peel potatoes for the evening meal. While he was busy in the kitchen, she worked in the back of the dining hall. With Harry's help, she stirred a big pot of hot soapy water that contained the dining room curtains. After rinsing them, she hung them on a long clothesline with a tall tree limb bracing it up in the middle. The air was fresh and crisp, and the material was light, so the curtains should dry in an hour or so.

As she was entering the back of the kitchen, an enormous blast shook the room, powerful enough to make a person lose their balance. She gripped the door handle and steadied herself. "What was that?" Mary Grace hurried over to Jimbo. He had tossed the knife down and was heading out the front door of the dining area.

"Wait. I'm going with you." He didn't stop and wait for her. She rushed out behind him, followed him through the pathway and down the trail to the mine. Clouds of black dust flowed from the entrance of the tunnel. Men were coughing and trying to catch their breath as they rushed out and fell to their knees.

\*\*\*

Luke had been taking a nap, but the shaking woke him up. He grabbed his boots and slipped them on while strapping on his gun belt. Grabbing his Remington rifle, he raced out the door. After he arrived at the front of the mine, several men were sitting on the ground, covered in dark brown dirt. "Is everyone out?" Luke yelled.

"Think so," one man said between coughs.

"You're not sure?" Luke grabbed a lantern, lit it, and hurried inside the mine entrance.

Mary Grace tugged on Jimbo's sleeve. "Where's he going?"

"He gotta make sure the men are safe and counted. After a blast, someone has to check on the condition of the mine before others can re-enter."

"But he's the boss. How come someone else doesn't do that?"

"Don't know for sure, but it's his mine. Guess he feels responsible." Jimbo walked over and sat down on a big rock and waited.

Mary Grace slowly made her way back to the dining hall. She couldn't just sit there waiting for the news about the condition; she'd stay busy. Back at the place, her wash was blowing in the breeze.

Mary Grace went inside, headed to the flour barrel, and dipped a large bowl full. Might as well get busy kneading bread. As she readied the dough, her search discovered only six loaf pans. "Something else to add to the list," she said out loud to herself. She could use at least six more pans because bread was needed at every meal.

After setting the bread to rise, she poured bags of dried beans into hot boiling water to simmer most of the day. Memories of how much her pa loved her cheese cornbread came back. After cutting slices off a block of cheese, she diced them into smaller pieces and added them to the large pans of cornbread batter.

Every so often, she walked to the front door of the dining hall to look and listen for the men. Mary Grace prayed that no one was hurt. She'd give anything to go look around the campsite, but she'd have to wait until Luke gave her permission.

Harry stumbled in the side door of the kitchen, carrying a large pan of pork chops. "Would you like to fry these babies up for today's meal? Luke has several barrels of meat down in the cellar. Think he forgot to tell you."

"They look wonderful, but what would you say if I baked them instead of fried them?"

Harry's eyebrows pulled together at first, but then he smiled and said she was the cook.

"Baking is easier, and we have to fry so much of the meat as it is. Baked chops should be a welcome change. If the men don't like them, then next time I'll fry them."

Harry sat down on his favorite barrel. "Did you hear the blast?"

"Yes. Do you know if anyone was hurt?"

"Not yet." He moaned as he rubbed his stump.

"You know, Harry. You should let me look at your leg. I can make a better bandage for you. Let's go into my room, and I'll fix you right up."

"I'm not too sure. Are you a doctor?"

"Do I look like a doctor, you old mule?" He grinned at her, and they both laughed. "Come on now, while we have a few minutes." Mary Grace opened her bedroom door and went into her room. Harry limped in behind her.

"Don't close that door," he said.

"Why? Afraid I might compromise you?" She gave him a sassy smile. Mary Grace pointed for him to sit in a chair next to the table, and he followed her instructions.

She removed the strap that held the wooden peg leg onto his thigh, then pushed his pant leg up, giving her a view of the stump. "Gosh, no wonder you have been in such pain. You've got a pretty bad sore in the center of the thigh. I'm going to doctor it before I put clean padding on it." As Mary Grace bent over Harry's leg to apply some whiskey, she sensed someone standing behind her. She whirled around almost spilling the pint of whiskey.

Luke stood in the doorway wearing a smirk. "So, am I invited to this party?"

"Oh, I'm so glad you're back," Mary Grace said. "Was anyone hurt in the blast? I've been so worried."

"No, not really. Scared and dirty but no broken bones. We were lucky this time," he said and came in. "What are you doing to Harry?" His eyes darted around the room. He smiled at the Bible sitting beside the bed and her hairbrush lying on the mantel.

"I'm making him heavier padding for his leg, but he has a bad sore in the center. See? Right here." She gestured with her head because she held the whiskey in her hand and a cloth in the other.

"What you gonna do with that good liquor?" Harry eyed the full bottle of whiskey in her hand.

"I'm going to disinfect the sore area. The alcohol in the liquor will help with the healing, but it's going to burn." Mary Grace poured a small amount directly on the wound.

"Damn it, woman! That hurts like you know what."

"Harry," Luke called, "watch that foul mouth of yours."

"Sorry, Miss." Harry rubbed his rough hand over his mouth and tried to sit still while Mary Grace placed the soft material over his sore stump and tied it tight.

"Can you use a crutch and hop around without the wooden peg?"

"Shore I can, but why?'

"The sore needs a few days to heal. After it gets well, you'll be able to walk around much better." Mary Grace gave Luke a concerned glance.

"You can still help in the kitchen, but I want you to stay off that leg. Once you get better, you'll start earning your money." Luke gave his old friend a grin and walked out of the bedroom.

"Hey, boss man. Can the men work in the mine?"

Luke stopped and turned to look at his old friend. "No, I'm afraid not. I'm going into town to purchase a wagon of new lumber. Some of the men can go kick up their heels in town for a few days, but others will help me repair the entrance of the mine. I want it to be safe before they continue working."

## Chapter 6

Luke drove his flatbed wagon directly to the sawmill. About a dozen of his men went straight to the saloon. Mr. Russell, the mill owner, came out to meet him. "Where're your men headed?"

"We had a small explosion in the mine, and I need some of your sturdy lumber. A whole wagon load should be enough to make the repairs."

"What about your men? They ain't gonna help load it on your wagon?" Mr. Russell frowned.

"Fraid not. Some of my men haven't been in town in several weeks. They're eager for some fun."

"Guess I ain't too old to remember those good old days," he said, laughing. "I'll call Mick to come and help us load the lumber."

Luke, Mick, and Mr. Russell worked up a good sweat by the time the lumber was loaded onto the wagon. They used strong ropes to secure it. Luke glanced down at his dirty clothes and used his hat to dust off his pants. "I should have done my shopping before I loaded the wagon. I'm a mess."

"Ain't nobody important in town? Besides, why should you care since you've got the prettiest gal at your camp?"

"She's only my cook, Russell. Nothing more," he muttered. "My men are enjoying her good meals. That's the plain truth." Luke felt the hackles rise on the back of his neck. "I'm heading over to the dry goods store. We'll settle my bill the first of the month, like always," Luke growled and brushed particles of sawdust off his clothes.

Luke entered the store and gave Mr. Rockwell, the owner of the store, his list. He glanced around the room and saw a rack of Stetson hats. Stopping to admire them, he tried on several and finally chose one that fit well. At the back of the store, he spied dresses of different styles and colors. After making his selections, he laid them on the counter.

"You wearing dresses, Luke?" Mr. Rockwell chuckled.

"My cook needs something to wear beside trousers. Add them to my list." Luke noticed several new canned items on the shelf behind the counter. "Give me about a dozen of those canned peaches, and is that corn packed in those jars?"

"Yep, something new from the peddler who stopped by yesterday."

"Give me a dozen jars, and if it's not good, the pigs will eat it."

"You got pigs?" Rockwell raised his eyebrows.

"Well, a couple of big sows. Jimbo found them wandering in the woods and brought them to the camp. No one has come asking about them, so he's already made pets out of them. Craziest thing I've ever seen."

"So, don't reckon you'll be eating them anytime soon." Both men laughed.

Luke walked back to the lumber yard and placed his packages under the front seat. Before leaving town, he decided to stop in the café and reassure Moon that his daughter was fine and doing a good job.

"Hey, Moon," Luke yelled toward the back curtain of the café. Moon came out and froze in his tracks. He peered over Luke's shoulder, causing Luke to turn and look behind himself.

"You didn't bring my girl home?" Moon stormed around Luke and opened a bottle of whiskey. He held it up to Luke, but he declined with a shake of his head.

"No, she didn't ask to come with me. The gal knows she can leave whenever she wants. I just wanted to tell you that she's doing fine and seems content. She hasn't complained or mentioned anything about leaving. She's already made changes to the place. My kitchen and dining hall never looked better. The men are enjoying her good, hardy meals." Luke turned to leave and stopped suddenly. "You're welcome to ride out to the camp for a meal and visit with Mary Grace."

"I'll do that," Moon said, looking disappointed that his gal wasn't with Luke. "Didn't realize how much work she done around here." He downed a glass of whiskey and swore to himself.

\*\*\*

Mrs. Rockwell stood at the big picture window of the dry goods store and watched the handsome mine owner drive out of town. "So, how many dresses did Mr. Tyler purchased for his new cook, that sassy mouth gal of Moon's?" She stood with her hands on her hips.

"Why do you care? You get busy and order more dresses from Tiny. I know she'll be happy that her dresses all sold at one time." Mr. Rockwell watched the devious expression on his wife's face. "Woman, you'd better keep a civil tongue in your head about what our customers buy. You may not like the mine owner, but he pays good money. We need his business."

\*\*\*

Luke drove the wagon near the front of the entrance to the mine. Several men came out of the bunkhouse and began unloading the lumber. "Just stack it over there and be sure to cover it good. A storm is heading this way. Dark clouds followed me from town," Luke said to the men. "What the hell?" Luke's hat went flying off his head.

All the men dove onto the ground and many took cover inside the mine. Luke raced to the wagon to grab his Winchester. With his rifle, he ran to the place where the bushwhacker had fired.

The men had recovered their rifles and were ready to face a battle, if necessary. The gunfire from strange men wasn't something new. Since Luke had owned the mine, there'd been two attacks. There were many claim jumpers, but most of them knew that it wouldn't be easy to take Luke's claim with so many men working for him.

Luke returned to the center of the camp and looked around at his men. "Whoever fired that gun was trying to kill me. He only fired once and then rode off into the hills. I can't imagine who wants me dead—now. If he had wanted to overtake the mine, he would have brought more men with him." Luke rubbed his hand through his hair and glanced down at his new black Stetson. "Damn, I just bought this. Jeffrey, post several sentries to stand guard for a couple of days. Place one on that high rock so he can see the road clearly and another man outback. They can take turns."

A significant drop of cold rain hit Luke on his arms. "Hurry, fellows, and get the lumber covered. Don't worry about unloading it. Tie the cover down with the same ropes that you took off. Once it's covered, get inside the bunkhouse until dinner is ready. Harry will ring the bell in a little while."

***

On the outskirts of Luke's land, a man and horse stood under a big scrub oak to escape the torrential downpour. "We'll get the good-for-nothing, cheating gambler next time, boy," Wally Moore said to his horse. "He'll not get away with stealing all my money and causing me to lose my farm." He dropped to the ground to settle under a tree and tucked the horse's reins around his wrist.

***

Mary Grace sprinkled the pork chops with spices and placed pieces of potatoes and onions in the pan. Once she had it ready, Jimbo put the pan in the oven. She slid in three large containers of bread dough. In just a few minutes, the dining hall smelled terrific.

"Hi, boss man. Who was shooting their gun a few minutes ago?" Jimbo asked, as Luke entered the front door. Luke jerked his hat off his head and tossed it over in a chair. He shushed Jimbo, not wanting Mary Grace to see that someone had taken a potshot at him. "One of the men just fired his gun at a rabbit."

***

Jimbo gave Luke a hard stare. He was smart enough to know that no man would shoot his rifle close to the mine, but he would question one of the other men later. Luke didn't usually tell a lie, so it must have been something.

"Jimbo, put on a rain slicker and go get the box under the front seat and bring it inside. I have some canned goods and other things for Mary Grace." Jimbo hurried to do as Luke requested.

***

Mary Grace poured Luke a cup of coffee and set it in front of him. "The men can eat when the bread is ready."

"What's smells so good besides the bread?"

"Pork chops. I'm baking them." She slid into the bench in front of him.

Luke glanced around the room. Every time he came into the dining hall, it looked better. The windowpanes shone, and the curtains were clean and ironed. How well-groomed Mary Grace was with her hair pulled back from her face and her house dress washed and ironed. She was a pretty young woman. Yep, he thought, I sure won a great hand against Moon. "I saw your pa today," Luke said. "I assured him that you were doing a good job. He was disappointed that you weren't with me. He misses you. I invited him out for dinner anytime he wants to come and see you."

"You were wasting your breath. Pa probably wouldn't walk across the street to see me, much less ride out here from town. Now, if he thought I was ready to return and work for him, he'd probably send someone out to get me."

"I'm sorry you don't have a good relationship with him." Luke looked around the room, remembering his pa and mama. The good smelling dining room certainly made him recall his childhood home. His mama was a great cook, and she enjoyed cooking for pa, his brother, Butch, and him. "I miss my folks," Luke said.

She peered up at him. "Why did you leave home?"

He studied the coffee grounds at the bottom of his cup. "Oh, opportunities, I guess. A young man like me wanted to see something besides the hind end of an old mule. A cattleman came to our farm and needed to purchase hay for his horses. After we loaded a wagon and carried it out to the open range, he said that he could use a few more wranglers to work for him. He was driving his new herd to Denver. The man paid his men a dollar a day. That was a lot of money for a youngster like me."

"So you left home with this stranger?"

"You could say that. Pa made me promise to come home once a year and said that I always had a home with him and Mama." He drummed his fingers on the table and glanced at Mary Grace. "I kept my promise at first, but as I got older, I didn't go home as often. It was hard. Mama cried every time I left, nearly breaking my heart."

\*\*\*

"I miss my Mama." Mary Grace jumped up. "I need to get dinner on the table." She hurried behind the kitchen counter, opened the oven, and pulled out the golden bread. She placed a spoon of butter on the hot bread and allowed it to run down the sides.

"Mercy, Miss, that smells wonderful. Watch out while I pull out the pork chops." Jimbo placed the pan down and laughed. "Here come the men. They ain't waiting for you to ring the bell."

Mary Grace watched as Luke strode out of the dining hall. He had a sad expression on his face. Did something happen in town that he wasn't telling? The rain had stopped, but it was still cloudy and dark outside. She would save a plate of food for him.

## Chapter 7

When the rain had stopped with only a light drizzle remaining, Luke lit a lantern and entered The Gypsy Lady. He studied all the fallen boards and eight-by-eight planks. Someone had set the dynamite, but thank goodness it had only damaged the front of the mine. Luke concluded that whoever planted the blast was smart enough to use only a few sticks of dynamite.

He bent and picked up a stick of dynamite without a fuse. "Thank goodness," he mumbled to himself. He tapped the damaged stick on his leg and surveyed the fallen wood. *Could it have been the same man who shot at me the other day? Sure wish I knew who hated me bad enough to kill me.*

***

Jeffrey was headed to the dining hall when he noticed a light glowing inside the cave. "How does it look in here, boss?" He glanced at the rock walls and then looked closer. "Look here, boss. I believe I see something red sparkling at me."

"Red? Let me get a gander." Luke climbed over the giant plank and stood beside the young man. Jeffrey placed his hand in the crack while Luke lit a stick of wood and held it up to the rock wall. He passed Jeffrey the light, took out his pocketknife, and scraped off a bit of the shining rock area. A small chunk of gold fell into his hand. He held it closer to the lantern.

A smile like Jeffrey had never seen spread over his boss man's face. "Jeffrey, I believe we are standing in the center of a honey hole."

"Whoopee!" Jeffrey tossed his hat in the air.

"Quiet." Luke slapped his hand over Jeffrey's mouth. "I have to be sure before we tell anyone. We'll need to get this area repaired, so it's safe to work in. Then we need to dig as much out as we can and hide it. Once the men in town hear of our strike, we'll have all kinds of claim jumpers coming out here. It could be a war zone. Maybe Sheriff Lambert will help us by arresting anyone who tries to jump my claim."

"If we can't celebrate right now, can we at least go eat? I'm starving," Jeffrey said. "Let's go before the men eat it all. Since it's been storming all afternoon, the men have been ready to eat for hours."

"Remember, stay silent about this find. After we eat, we'll come out and secure the front entrance. I'll tell the men it's for everyone's safety. Jeffrey, wait. I just remembered something important. I need to go into Crooked Creek and send a telegraph to a friend of mine at the First Bank of Denver. He has a lot of knowledge about gold miners. He's told me many stories in the past about how small miners have lost their claims because they didn't handle them correctly. We must keep this quiet until he advises me what to do next. Promise me you'll keep your mouth shut about this. We don't want to do something wrong and have a war on our hands with other claim jumpers."

"You can count on me. What will you tell the men about why we aren't going to keep working?"

\*\*\*

Before Luke could reach the food counter, Mary Grace placed a large plate of food on the table. She smiled at him, and he strolled over to stand beside her. "Is this for me?"

"Yes, I thought maybe you wanted to eat later, so I saved you a plate of food."

"That was mighty nice of you, and I am, as Jeffrey just said, starving. May I have a cup of hot coffee to go with this delicious meal?" Mary Grace gave him a sweet smile. He could get used to this little gal taking care of him.

Jimbo ambled by with a fresh cup in hand and poured Luke some coffee. Jeffrey hurried over and took a seat beside him. "Man, these pork chops smell wonderful. Harry said that they were baked instead of fried."

"Save room for some hot peach cobbler that will be out of the oven in just a few minutes." Mary Grace eased back into the kitchen.

"Golly, can that pretty girl cook. I might have to toss my hat into the ring and try courting that sweet gal." Jeffrey's eyes followed Mary Grace wherever she went.

"You don't have time to be thinking about women," Luke growled and his face reddened. He wanted to bust Jeffrey in the nose. *But why? Why do I care if he wants to court Mary Grace or any other woman?* Luke thanked Mary Grace and Harry for a delicious meal and headed out of the dining hall. Before he reached the door, he stopped to hurry Jeffrey along. "I'll see you in front of the cave when you've finished eating," he said, then strode outside.

\*\*\*

"Wonder why he's in such a big hurry? It's too nasty outside to do much." Harry limped over to the washstand and began washing the dishes.

"It seemed to me he was trying to get away from here, or me," She mumbled to Harry.

"Must be something important, that's for shore. I'll find out soon enough." He smiled at her and continued washing.

Mary Grace dried the dishes and placed them on the shelves, while Jimbo wiped the tables clean and swept the floor. After one man had tossed a pork chop bone over his shoulder onto the floor, Mary Grace stormed over to him. "Did you not see the pan I've set in the middle of the table for your bones, sir?"

"No, ma'am," he mumbled. "I'm sorry. I'll pick it up."

Jimbo would never have to sweep bones off the floor again.

Mary Grace set several pots of dried beans to soak and made sure there was enough bread to make the men's lunches the next day. She would prepare flapjacks, bacon, and eggs for breakfast. After whispering good night to Jimbo and Harry, she went into her bedroom to prepare for bed. It had been a long, dreary day, and she was tired.

\*\*\*

After breakfast early the next morning, the men stood outside the front of the mine entrance and saw the boards nailed across the front. Luke came out and instructed a few of his men to uncover the lumber on the wagon to start replacing the fallen boards and planks inside the mine. Jeffrey and another man then removed the boards from the entrance. "Men, I want the entrance of the mine to be ready to withstand a lot of traffic and big heavy wheelbarrows filled with rocks. I want a sturdy pathway built so the wheelbarrows will roll easier."

"Are you expecting piles of gold in the mine?" one man said, laughing. When Luke didn't laugh, the man said, "Well, damn, let's get it done."

"Wait," Luke said. "Grab your rifles because horses are coming." All the men rushed into the bunkhouse, then scattered and hid behind the wagon, boulders, and inside the mine.

Luke was standing on a rock when he held his hand in the air. "It's our men, fellows," he called out to the men that were hiding "Welcome home," Luke said. "How come you all came back so soon?" A closer glance at the men showed some of them sporting black eyes and busted lips. "I'd like to see the other men." Luke laughed.

Finally, one of the men spoke, "Some of Calhoun's ranch hands started calling us cacklers. We had to show those fools that we weren't lazy, no-good miners. Later, we lost all our money and the gals, well, you know—" He turned bright red when he noticed Mary Grace standing on the porch listening to them.

"No matter," Luke said with a grin. "I'm glad you're all back in one piece. Go get cleaned up, and if you ask nicely, Mary Grace will cook you some grub." He turned just in time to see her hightailing it back into the dining hall.

"Come over to the dining hall, fellows, when you get cleaned and bandaged. We got plenty of black coffee," Harry yelled, then followed Mary Grace back inside.

The men worked long and hard all day, removing the damaged timbers and replacing them with new ones. Large planks propped up the ceiling. The men smoothed a pathway by laying bales of hay and sturdy boards.

Luke stood at the entrance of the tunnel and was satisfied that the men could work safely inside. He wished the old prospector, who sold him the mine for a hundred dollars and two mules, was here to witness his find. The older man had worked for years, carrying buckets of black dirt and mud out of the side of the mountain in hopes of discovering gold. After he had dug so far, he placed timber on the walls to keep them from caving in.

Luke remembered the day he'd ridden by the older man's mine to ask if he could water his horse. A banked stream of water flowed across the front of the property so a person could use a sluice to help wash the mud and rocks. Luke found the older man sitting up against the wall of the mine.

The old man had fallen and smashed his right arm and couldn't work the mine anymore. He told Luke that he trusted no man to help him with the mining, so the prospector made Luke an offer he couldn't refuse.

# Chapter 8

After breakfast, Luke called all the men together for a meeting. Once everyone was inside the dining room, he stood and stared into all of their faces. "Fellows, some of you have already guessed that while you were in town, we discovered a wealthy vein of gold."

A rumble followed his announcement. Some were surprised while others smiled and patted their neighbor on their back. To get the men's attention, Luke banged on a pot. "Men, this is exciting news, but we have to keep this as quiet as possible. Of course, people are going to learn that we struck red, but they don't have to know how big until we have carried it into town."

"I need to notify a banker friend who works with many experts that have discovered gold. Finding gold is a hard job, which you all know, but it is essential to find out what to do, now that we've found it. We don't want to kill ourselves bringing the gold out of the mine and have others try to steal it away from us."

"Sometimes the bank will buy the gold mine and have their experts come here with equipment to retrieve the gold. They will have a cavalry of men to help them, so they aren't worried about claim jumpers. I hope that this will happen here. All of you know that I intend to sell this mine because I never wanted to be a miner. But since I am, I want to do what's best for all of us." Luke's eyes darted around the room as he rocked back and forth on his heels, trying to read the men's expressions.

"I will be riding into Crooked Creek at first light, and I'll wait in town for an answer from my friend. When I return to the camp, I hope to have an answer to your questions. For now, I want all of you to take turns standing guard. We need to have this campsite surrounded at all times, day and night."

"After you sell the mine, how are we going to get paid?" Jim Black, a short, bald man, stood as straight as an arrow and raised his voice loud enough to be heard a mile away.

"Men, you know that you can trust me. I have always paid you well. I want you to know that I'm going to share the profits with all of you—equal. But, if any of you go into town, and run your mouths about what we've discovered, we'll all be in trouble, and that man will be left out of the shared money."

The men stood and closed in on Luke. "We'll place guards around the clock and shoot any strangers on site," one of the men said.

"Now, I don't want anyone becoming trigger happy. We'll protect this mine, but we aren't going to be a bunch of killers. Is that understood?" Luke saw that he had taken some of the anger out of a few hot-headed men. "Men, I'm planning on taking Mary Grace back into town. I don't want her to be in any danger. If any one of you can cook, maybe you could pitch in and help Harry and Jimbo."

"Shoot fire, Luke. That little lady knows about the gold strike. Aren't you worried that she'll tell her pa and then everyone will know."

Luke stared at Jeffrey, but he didn't comment. He might be right about her telling others about what they'd discovered. Would he be able to trust her to keep her mouth shut? "All right, I'm placing Jeffrey in charge of scheduling you to stand guard. We will be on guard twenty-four hours a day. Any man caught sleeping on the job will be sorry. Remember, after I hear from my banker friend, we'll know what to do."

\*\*\*

"I'm not ready to go back to town. I want to earn my full month's wages." Mary Grace pounded her fists on the new batch of bread dough as Luke stood near the counter, explaining that he needed to take her back to her pa's place.

"I am not happy about losing the best cook this camp has ever had. The men don't want to see you go either. Some of them are worried that you'll tell your pa about our gold strike. Would you do that if I asked you not to?"

"I heard you tell the men how you were going to divide the money with them. How come you can't divide with me, too? Heck, I work hard. I'm in this kitchen before the sun rises and after it sets every day. I cook and keep their bellies full three times a day." Mary Grace's voice rose louder, but she avoided eye contact with Luke. She flipped over the bread dough and pounded it harder. "Maybe I don't haul rocks, mud, or gravel, but I still work hard. Shoot fire! When the men's workday is over, they can go lay around, but not me. I have to prepare for the next day so they can have good food to eat."

Luke placed his palms up. "Settle down. I understand what you're saying, but I gotta think." He dragged his hands through his dark hair.

Mary Grace snapped before she could control herself. "Think about what, you bull-headed skunk? You hauled me out to this camp to slave over a hot stove for you and your bunch of men, and you think I don't deserve a bit more than what you been giving me? It won't be long, and all of you'll be filthy rich, and I'll still be a poor little gal from town." Mary Grace blinked hard to make a tear slip out of her eyes.

Luke smoothed down the front of his shirt and tugged down his rolled-up sleeves. "I agree that you should receive something extra, but I should talk it over with the men."

"Hellfire, man, I thought you were the boss man of this outfit." With her chest puffed out, she screamed, "Why do you have to go jawing with the men for? It's your decision if I'm thinking right."

Folding his arms across his chest, he explained. "This is my mine, and I am the boss. Get down off your high horse, missy, before you let your mouth get that sassy behind of yours in big trouble." Luke lowered his arms and pushed on the counter as he stared at her. "Now, I told the men I would divide my profits with them, but they won't like it one bit if I go giving part of their profits away. It will be better for all of us if they agree, and I feel that they will. You'll be one of them, and they'll be happy for you."

"So, when will you discuss my becoming one of them?" Mary

Grace asked, smirking.

"Later, when we have another meeting about how we're going to haul the gold into the land office. Be patient and keep your trap shut, please." He gave her a hard look that said she'd better do as he requested. "My main concern with you being here is that you might get hurt. This place is going to be very dangerous once word gets out about the gold strike. I should teach you to protect yourself. I know you can shoot a shotgun, but a rifle will be better. Shotguns are great for close-up shooting, but a rifle will hit a target at a greater distance."

"I've shot a rifle before. It was an old single-shot Pa used before he got himself a new shotgun. Sometimes he let me take it out back and shoot at rats that tried digging holes under the porch."

Luke grunted and stared at Mary Grace. "Well, at least you aren't afraid of guns, like some young ladies." Luke braced the gun up against his body and explained how it worked. "This gun is a Winchester 73, and it's a lot heavier and will do a lot of damage to a man. I have an old Henry rifle, but I'd like for you to have this gun for protection. It's heavy, but if you prop it against the windowsill or behind the counter while you're shooting, it will be a lot steadier. Just pull the lever down hard and bring it back up quickly. It will shoot about fifteen rounds before you have to reload."

"I need to go practice shooting this long thing—I mean gun."

"When you aren't busy today, carry it around with you. Get used to holding it up to your shoulder and pushing the lever down and back up. Tomorrow I'll take you outside to practice."

"If the men don't agree to share a portion of the gold strike with me, I won't need to learn how to shoot. I'll pack up and go back to Pa's stage depot and café."

"Don't start making threats. I don't like to feel like I'm over a barrel." Luke placed his fists on his hips as he turned to leave.

"Well, boss man, I'm not staying if I ain't appreciated." Mary Grace turned away from him, washed her hands, and placed the bread dough in the pans to rise.

***

Early the next morning, Luke rode into Crooked Creek to send a telegram to his banker friend, Mr. Anderson, in Denver. After sending it, he pushed on the bat-winged doors of Mary Grace's pa's saloon and café. Moon was singing an off-key country song about a gal leaving him. Luke smiled and sauntered over to the door that led into the kitchen. "Hey, old man, you've got a customer, and he sure could use some coffee."

"Well, if it ain't the man who stole my daughter, the best cook in these parts."

Suddenly, out of nowhere, a short, stout man rose from a table in the back of the room. He staggered across the room, waving his pistol high in the air.

"Now Wally, put that gun away before you hurt somebody. Get out of here and go sleep off that whiskey." Moon took a step closer to the man, but he yelled at him to back off. "I missed this fellow the other day, and now, I see I didn't blow him up in the mine a few days ago. What are you, a cat with nine lives?"

Luke stood tall, never blinking an eye and asked the drunk, "Why do you want me dead? What have I done to you to make you hate me enough to spend the rest of your life in prison, or swing from the end of a rope? Do I know you?"

"You cheated me out of all my money, and I lost my farm. My woman left me, and now you're going to pay." He raised his pistol, but before he could fire, Moon jumped the man and the gun exploded. Moon fell to the floor, and when the drunk realized what he'd done, he flopped down in a chair.

Luke hurried to Moon and immediately saw that he wasn't hurt badly. The bullet grazed his shoulder, but the shot could have done a lot more damage.

"Oh, Lord, forgive me. I killed my friend. I didn't mean it, I really didn't." Wally Moore looked at Luke and yelled, "I meant to kill you."

"Shut up, Wally. Luke won't file charges, but you gotta get this killing out of your system. Luke's a good man and he don't cheat at cards."

A man ran into the café and asked if he could help. "Please get the doc for Moon. He's hurt, but he'll live." The man hurried out of the door and yelled for the doctor.

"Listen, Wally. I didn't know you were gambling away everything you own. I don't remember exactly how much I won from you, but I will gladly give it back if it helps you get your home and family back."

"You would do that for me after I nearly shot a hole in you?"

"Thank the good Lord that didn't happen, but yes. How much money did you lose?"

I lost three hundred, not all to you, but most of it. It was money I needed to use for my mortgage payment. My woman was so mad she went home to her mama."

Luke pulled a flat wallet from his vest pocket and counted out three hundred dollars and laid it on the table. "When you're sober, Moon will give this to you. Are we even now? No more attempts at killing me?"

"No more. Promise. Thanks, man." Wally laid his head back on the table and sobbed.

Once the doctor arrived, Luke left the saloon without getting a cup of coffee and went home. He had come into the café to tell him that Mary Grace was doing fine, and just maybe, she'd come into town and see him soon.

\*\*\*

Over the next couple of days, strange riders passed the gold mine, but none of them stopped to chat. They craned their necks but continued on their way. Luke was sure they had noticed the lookout guards posted high on the ridge.

Luke had given strict orders that no one was to leave the camp and go into town. As far as he knew, the men had followed his orders. The fewer people that knew about his lucky strike the better for everyone. With all the traffic passing the mine, Luke's instincts were telling him that someone had leaked some information. At dinner that evening, he announced that there would be a meeting in an hour. He instructed Mary Grace to go to her room and stay there until he told her she could come out. "No eavesdropping, young lady," he commanded.

The men were none too happy when Luke discussed his feelings that someone had leaked information about the gold strike. "I know you all have noticed the traffic of strangers riding by the stream and looking at the mine. I want to know if any of you talked to someone about our activities here."

The men glanced around and murmured, giving each other curious looks.

Luke motioned for the men to quiet down. "Men, this is serious. I am not accusing anyone of doing anything wrong. Been too busy to stop and talk with anyone passing by the mine."

The men looked downhearted, and some were angry. Several voiced their opinions and wanted to know how soon they were going to start packing up the gold and heading into town.

"I'm waiting to hear from my banker friend in Denver. He'll tell me how to handle the gold. Be patient. I should be hearing back from him any time now."

"Where is Mary Grace with some coffee and something sweet? She is always serving us some of her treats when we have a meeting," Tom Butler said, a younger man who had hired on with Luke at the beginning.

"I'm glad you mentioned Mary Grace. All of you know how hard she works here cooking and cleaning. She's the best cook we've ever had. Well, fellows, it's like this. I feel that since we're sharing our gold with Harry and Jimbo, Mary Grace should also receive a portion."

"Damn, why don't we just give the whole town a bag full of money?" One mad man yelled.

"Well, I think we should give her something. Mary Grace has been a hard worker from early sunrise to late into the night. If we don't share with her, she's going back to her pa's place. That means we will be left with Harry cooking for us again. Beans and cornbread every day."

"Boss man, what do you want to do about giving Mary Grace some money?" Jeffrey asked.

"It is only right to share with her. Mary Grace is young and has worked hard all of her life. She certainly has worked for us without a complaint since she came here. Remember, she didn't want to come, but I won her in a gambling hand to cook for the camp. She was angry, but the gal has honored her position every day."

"I don't want her to leave as long as I am working here. We all work too hard every day to eat just beans," one man said.

"After your long day, you all can retire for the evening. Mary Grace stays in the kitchen, preparing treats for the next day for you. She does this so you'll have a good lunch and a full belly. I want you to think about this while you're pondering if she should have a share of the gold."

Luke strode into the kitchen and chose a platter of cookies that had been left on the stove. He was sure she had left them for the men to enjoy. He picked up the plate and set it down on the table. One by one, the men passed the platter around until everyone had a treat.

"Let's vote," Jeffrey said. "I'm ready to hit the sack."

"Do you want to do a secret ballot or just raise your hands to vote?" Luke peered at all the men.

"A show of hands will do," another man said.

"All in favor of Mary Grace receiving a share of the gold profits, please raise your hand." Luke looked around and smiled. Every man in the room had raised their hand.

"Thanks, fellows. After I tell her, I'll bet you'll be glad you voted yes." He smiled as the men filed out of the dining hall heading to the bunkhouse.

Luke tapped on Mary Grace's bedroom door and was greeted with the biggest smile he had ever seen. "You eavesdropped, didn't you?"

"Of course. I couldn't wait to know if I was going to have to leave or not." She couldn't stop smiling. "Oh, Luke, I have never been so happy. Thank you." Mary Grace leaped into his arms and laid a big kiss on his lips.

Luke was ready to scold her for eavesdropping, but the kiss caught him off guard. All he could think of was her firm, young body tight against his. He pressed the back of her head with one hand and kissed her again, deepening the kiss, never wanting it to end.

Mary Grace leaned into Luke's hard chest and melted into his firm hold. She finally slid her legs to the floor and pushed away from him. "I'm sorry," she said softly. "I got carried away."

Luke released the tight hold on her young body but continued to hold on to her arms. "I guess I did too, but I'm not sorry. I enjoyed it very much," he said with a cocky grin.

"Oh, you. Don't continue to embarrass me any more than I am."

## Chapter 9

Early the next morning, a young cowboy on his way to Denver rode near the Gypsy Lady gold mine, jumped down, and led his horse to the cold water that ran down the mountain in front of the tunnel. He bent down and cupped several handfuls of water and surveyed the area. A sentry of guards stood in front of the entrance and high on the mountain tops near the camp. He had thought to stop for a chat and some coffee with some of the men but decided he'd better mosey on toward town.

Later, after arriving in town, he bedded down his animal at the livery, checked into the boardinghouse, and rambled over to the stage depot and café.

"Welcome back, young man," Moon Winters yelled from the back of the café. "Where you been keeping yourself?"

"I've been ramrodding cattle, but I decided to head home. Hey, man, I'm starving. How about getting your gal to whip me up something good to eat? I could eat the hind end of a cow, hide and all."

Moon sighed. "Well, Joey, I got grub, but Mary Grace ain't cooking for me any longer."

"Don't tell me some young cowboy grabbed her up and rode off into the sunset with her?" Joey Green shook his head and grinned at the owner.

"Naw, she's working as a cook for the Gypsy Lady gold mine's owner and his men. Sure wish she was back here where she belongs."

"Has the gold miners struck it rich?" He asked, rubbing his belly.

Out of the corner of his eyes, Joey noticed several rough men sitting at a table playing cards and drinking beer. Their heads popped up and eyed him.

"Why'd you asked that?" Moon asked, a furrow forming between his brows.

"Not sure, but when I passed, I saw guards stationed in front of the entrance and all over the mountain top. I just had a thought that maybe they'd found something to be protecting. Thought I'd stop and chat, but I had an uneasy feeling and decided to move on."

"Well, I haven't heard of anything going on out there. Come to think about it, I haven't seen Luke or any of his men in town lately."

"Well, man, I'm still hungry. Whatever is on your menu today, give me a big helping. I wasn't kidding about being famished." Joe walked over to a table. The four men who had been playing cards stood, pushed their chairs under the table, and walked out the door.

***

Three men circled a man on the boardwalk. The leader of the group, Oscar Wise, a tall, bearded man with a deep scar running down the side of his face, spoke, "What you say we take a short ride up to that mine and see what the men are protecting? It sounds to me like they found gold and might be preparing to bring it into the land office."

Willie halted the men from getting on their horses. "Hey fellows, before we ride out there, why don't we go down to the land office and ask a few questions? They may have brought in some sign of a strike, and they're keeping it quiet."

The three men nodded and sauntered down the boardwalk to the land office. "Willie, tell anyone that tries to come inside the office that it's closed. We don't need to be seen in here." Oscar slammed the door in Willie's face.

One of the men pulled down the shade on the door and stood with his arms crossed over his chest while Oscar banged his fist down on the land officer's counter.

"Gentlemen, why did you close my door? If this is a robbery, you're out of luck. I don't keep money in the safe or anywhere in this office," Rex Smitherman, land office clerk, said.

"This ain't no robbery, but we want information." He glanced around the room at the two men with him. "We're interested in the Gypsy Lady Mining Camp. What's going on out there?"

"Sir, I am not obliged to tell you anything about another miner's business. If you want to know what's happening out there, why don't you go and visit with Mr. Tyler."

Oscar reached over and grabbed Mr. Smitherman's lapels and jerked him almost across the counter. "Don't give me no sass, man. I want to know what transactions have taken place between you and the mine owner."

Mr. Smitherman, a tall man and more muscular than he looked, grabbed Oscar's hands and shook them loose from his jacket. "You can act like a barbarian if you like, but this is my office, and I am not telling you anything about another miner's business." In a flash, Oscar and the man with him stared down the barrel of a Colt 38 pistol. "Now, I suggest if you want to know anything about the Gypsy Lady mining camp, you go somewhere else to get your information. Now, get out. Please know that I will be reporting this meeting to the sheriff."

Oscar backed away from the counter and walked to the door, waving at his partners to follow him. Once back together with Willie, all four climbed on their horses and rode out of town.

Once the men had reached within a few miles of the gold mine, one of the men noticed smoke coming from a cabin that was off the main trail. "Hey Oscar, let's stop over yonder and water our horses and fill our canteens."

The men rode to the shabby cabin where an older man sat on the porch steps. It was obvious the man was well into his moonshine jug.

"Hey, old man," Oscar yelled, "can we water our horses and get a cool drink for ourselves?"

"Shore, climb down. Come and join me for a snort. I make the best moonshine this side of Denver." The old drunk rolled off the porch steps and wobbled to a standing position. He waved the jug at the men who were walking their animals over to the water trough.

Oscar surveyed the area but didn't see any chickens, pigs, or even a cow. "The old man must make his living selling moonshine," he said to the other two men.

"Come on and join me, fellows. I don't get much company, and it's plenty lonely at times," the older man slurred.

"Sure. I'll be happy to wet my whistle." All three men took a swig and passed the jug back to the old man.

"How long have you been living out here all alone? This old place has been abandoned for years," Oscar said.

"I lived at the Gypsy Lady mine for years. Shoot fire, I practically dug that mine out with my bare hands until one day I fell and busted this here shoulder and arm. Couldn't work no more. A young fellow came along and helped me. He took me to the doctor, and later I sold my mine to him. He was a nice boy, too."

"So this fellow paid you for your claim?" Oscar quizzed the man.

"Yep. I took my money and built myself another kind of gold mine—my moonshine still," he said with a silly smile plastered to his face.

"Did you ever find gold in the mine before you sold it?"

"Shore did, but not much." He took another big gulp of the jug.

"I found gold nuggets that kept me in supplies at the store in town."

"Did the man know that you had discovered gold in the mine?"

Oscar glanced at his partners, hoping they couldn't read his mind. He was going to cook up some kind of scheme to get his hands on the Gypsy Lady mining camp.

# Chapter 10

After days of working around the clock to remove as much gold from the walls and stack it inside the cave, Luke declared it was time to send another telegram to his bank friend. He needed information, and he couldn't wait much longer.

"Luke, Mary Grace, and a few of his men who hadn't been to town in weeks, rode straight to the telegraph office. Several men called out to Luke and asked about the mine. Luke only smiled, shook his head, and continued onto the telegraph office. Crooked Creek wasn't the crowded town it had been the last time he'd been there, but the dusty road was full of riders and wagons. The boardwalk was filled with pedestrians as well. He was glad a bunch of rowdy cowhands weren't lining the streets.

Luke had just finished writing the note he wanted the telegraph clerk to send for him when Sheriff Dillin came into the office.

"Hello, Sheriff," Luke said. He noticed the angry expression on the sheriff's face and then glanced over the big man's shoulder. "Who do you have with you?" The men were strangers to Luke.

"One man is the old prospector who sold you the mine, Sam Wilson, and the other three are strangers to me. They're claiming that this old man sold them the mine, and they've come to claim it."

Surprised, Luke looked over at the older man whom he had helped to the doctor. "Did you see their claim paper?" Luke asked.

"Not yet, these fools insisted I come with them to see you and speak with Mr. Smitherman."

"Rex, has anyone besides Luke staked a claim on the Gypsy Lady gold mine?"

"Not to my knowledge, sir."

"Hello, Sam," Luke spoke to the old prospector.

"Howdy, young man," The thin, filthy old man slurred his words and stood on wobbly legs.

"So, Mr. Wilson, you have been in the cups this morning, have you?" The sheriff stated the obvious.

"Just a tad, sir."

"So, mister, you claim to have a bill of sale for the Gypsy Lady gold mine?" The sheriff turned to the rough-looking cowboy.

"I do. I have it right here." He took a piece of paper and waved it in the air.

"Well, Judge Wilson Thomas will be here tomorrow to preside over a murder trial that has been pending for several months. I'm sure he can stay a little longer and listen to you both while you make your case. He will decide who the rightful owner of the mine is."

As the sheriff started to leave the office, he stopped and suggested to the stranger that he'd better sober up the old prospector. "The judge hates drunks."

Mary Grace walked over to her old friend. "Oh. Mr. Sam, it is so good to see you. I've worried about you."

"Oh, my pretty girl," the old man uttered a guffaw upon seeing her. "I have missed your good cooking."

"Come on, buster. Let's go get you sober and cleaned up." The stranger grabbed the older man, jerked him off his feet, and shoved him out the door.

Luke watched the men stroll down the street away from the land office. "Mary Grace, how well do you know the old man, Sam?" he asked.

"He came into the café for meals whenever he came to town for supplies. I knew he had staked a claim, but he never said anything about it, and I never asked. I'd heard that he had gotten hurt, but no one said any more about him. I did miss the old man when he stopped coming in to eat. How did you meet him?" Mary Grace watched Mr. Smitherman wipe down his counter.

"I found the old man leaning up against the wall of his mine and his arm and shoulder were busted up pretty good. He said that he had been sitting there for several hours before I came upon him. I found his old mule grazing and hitched him to a flatbed wagon. I loaded him on the bed of the wagon and drove to the doc's office. I stayed until the doctor set his arm, then I drove him back to the mine. He asked if I wanted to buy his claim and become a mine owner. After we made our deal, I placed his things in his wagon and he drove away, and I haven't seen him since, until today."

"I don't guess anyone has seen much of him." Mary Grace headed for the door but stopped. "I can't understand why Sam would say that he sold those men his mine when he had already sold it to you. Something is not right."

"I have a sick feeling that those men have threatened the poor soul. Maybe we'll discover the truth tomorrow. Everything we've worked for is riding on the truth." Luke leaned up against the counter and gave Mary Grace a cocky grin.

"Well, I can't do anything tonight. I'll visit with Pa and stay the night in my old room. I'll see you in the morning."

"Have a good rest, and I'll see you at breakfast, maybe." He gave her a sweet smile and touched his hat.

## Chapter 11

Early the next morning, Moon's saloon was overflowing with men because the saloon had been converted into a courtroom. Judge Thompson banged his gavel on his makeshift desk and yelled for order in the court. "The next man who's out of order will be tossed in jail for a couple of days. This room will be quiet as I issue my sentence on the defendant."

The men in the room settled down as the judge glared over his wire-rim glasses. "We've heard all the witnesses and twelve men have come back in with a verdict of guilty. I appreciate the men who deliberated for the last ten minutes." The judge smirked and shook his head. "It is my opinion that this young man is the victim of fake evidence stacked against him. Each witness testified like they were reciting the same school poem that they learned in primary school."

Everyone in the courtroom laughed until the judge called the court back to order.

"The only witnesses I put any stock in are the doctor and Sheriff Dillin, who saw the gunfight take place. The other witnesses were in the saloon hugging up against the bar while Henry poured them hard whiskey, drink after drink. You see, men, I don't just come into town and flop my behind at this table and make a decision by listening to every man who wants to offer an opinion. I do some personal scouting and listen to folks talk. Because of this, it is my ruling today that Jason Bidwell is found not guilty of gunning Terrell Grimes down in cold blood. Mr.

Bidwell, you are free to go. This court is adjourned."

The men grumbled but parted ways to allow the young man to leave the courtroom. The judge stood, but the sheriff whispered a few words in his ear.

"All right, Sheriff, bring the men in, and I'll hear their case. I can't promise you I'll be able to decide as to who is right, but I'll try."

"Luke Tyler and Oscar Wise, please come forward," the sheriff called and waved to the two groups of men in the back of the saloon.

Luke and Jeffrey took their places on the right of the table while Oscar Wise and Sam Wilson stood on the left. Mr. Smitherman, the land officer, sat down in one of the chairs that lined the front.

Luke heard a racket at the front door of the saloon and knew who was causing the disturbance. The judge waited until the sheriff took care of it.

"Turn me loose, you dumb old polecat, before I hit you," Mary Grace screamed and clawed at a big farm boy who was trying to block her entrance into the room.

"Now Mary Grace," Sheriff Dillin said, calmly, "you can't come in here. A courtroom is for men only."

"But, Sheriff, I'm part owner of the gold mine that's on trial. Ask the boss, man, Mr. Tyler. I have every right to be here. Luke?" Mary Grace called loud enough to be heard over all the men's grumbling. "Tell this man to let me in."

"Judge, the young lady is correct. She owns a small part of the profits of the mine," Luke said with a frown in her direction.

"I will allow her in. Now let's get on with the opening statements. We start with you," the judge said to Mr. Wise.

***

Oscar Wise's face turned red, and he swallowed the saliva that had gathered in his throat from nerves. He had never stood in front of a judge before without handcuffs and irons around his ankles. He was determined to get his hands on the gold mine, so he straightened his shoulders and pointed at Sam Wilson, the old prospector. "That there fellow sold me his claim last week. I stopped by his cabin a few miles from the gold mine, and he needed food for himself and his mules. I gave him money, and he signed over his claim. I got a copy of it right here."

"Let me see your claim, sir," Judge Thompson demanded.

Oscar handed the folded piece of paper to him and grinned at his two companions.

Mary Grace bent down beside Sam Wilson and whispered to him, "What did those men do to you to make you sign that piece of paper?"

He hung his head and wiped at his red nose. "If I say anything, they may hurt me. I'm scared of them."

"Listen, you are safe here. The sheriff and Luke Tyler will not let those men near you. Please, trust me." Mary Grace took his hand and held it tight.

"The first thing they did was to bust up my moonshine still and said that they would do the same to me. I ain't got no way to make a living now. They didn't give me any money, either."

Before Mary Grace explained to Sam Wilson what she planned, she stood in front of the judge. "Excuse me, Judge. Before you continue with this trial, could you meet with Sam Wilson alone and talk with him? I heard that you are a fair and honest man, and I know you should hear what he has to say in private."

"Well, you're right, miss. If you think that will help settle this dispute, I'll be glad to speak with Mr. Wilson. For all of you that are here today, this is not a trial. It is a hearing to see if we can determine the owner of the Gypsy Lady gold mine. Moon, do you have a room that I can use to interview this witness?"

"Yes, sir. Come this way behind the bar into my supply room."

"Miss, please come with me, and all you other men take your seats. We will continue with the other side of this dispute when I return."

Judge Thompson, Mary Grace, and Sam Wilson marched behind the bar and entered a small room filled with boxes of liquor, glasses, and other supplies.

"Sorry, your honor, this is the best I can do on short notice," Moon said, as he pulled out a chair for Mary Grace to sit.

"This is fine. Please leave us and close the door. We want to be in here alone." Judge Thompson allowed Sam Wilson to tell his story about the three men coming to his place. Oscar Wise and his two companions eased toward the front door of the saloon.

*\*\*\**

Luke watched as the three men kept eyeing the exit, and finally the three eased through the batwing doors and left the courtroom. He caught a glimpse from the front window of the men jumping on the back of their horses and racing out of town.

When the judge reappeared with Sam Wilson and Mary Grace, the scowl on his face showed a sign of confusion. "Where is Mr. Wise?" When neither the sheriff nor Luke made a respond, a quivering, twitchy muscle in the side of his face became prominent. He crossed his arms across his chest and shouted at the two men. "When I asked a question in my courtroom, I demand an answer."

Luke shrugged. "Well, I saw them go out on the boardwalk, and then they rode out of town. I figured that they knew Mr. Wilson was going to tell you something that would prove they were lying."

The judge stormed around the makeshift desk and sat down. Deepening his tone, he glared at the old prospector. "Mr. Wilson, did you or did you not sell your claim to the Gypsy Lady gold mine to Mr. Tyler several months ago for the amount of one hundred dollars and two mules?"

With his eyes wide and Adam's apple bobbing, Mr. Wilson stuttered, "Yes, sir. Mr. Tyler carried me to the doctor and then took me home and helped me get settled." The older man crumpled under the scrutiny of the other people listening to his answers. "He's a good man and I'm sorry, Luke." He lowered his face down to his chin. "Those men were mean to me, and I'm afraid of them. I can't go back to my cabin alone now."

Judge Thompson leaned forward and sighed audibly. "This hearing is over with the court finding that Luke Tyler is the sole owner of the Gypsy Lady gold mine. Good day."

Mary Grace, Sam Wilson, and Luke walked out of the saloon. "Thank you, Mary Grace, for your help in there. You surprised me by getting the judge to interview Sam here." Luke patted Sam on the shoulder. "Listen, Sam, why don't you come with us out to the mine? You can sleep in the bunkhouse with my men and you'll get three meals a day. We'll talk about your future later. How does that sound?"

\*\*\*

As Luke stood on the boardwalk, a young boy wearing patched overalls and dirty unlaced boots ran up to him. "Mister, are you Mr. Tyler?"

"That's me, young man."

"Got this here telegram for you." He glanced at Mary Grace and turned a bright red.

"Here you go, sonny," Luke tossed the young man a shiny new quarter.

"Wow, mister, thanks." He smiled, then ran back toward the telegraph office.

Luke blew out a long breath, ripped open the telegram, and read it. A wide grin spread across his face. He folded the paper in two and placed it in his coat pocket.

"Telegrams are usually bad news, but you're smiling, boss man. Good news?" Jeffrey asked.

Luke's mind was on his upcoming visit from the banker, and all he could think about was planning every detail before their meeting tomorrow. "Luke, is everything alright?" Mary Grace questioned.

"Oh, I'm sorry. I had my mind on something else. Yes, everything is fine. My banker friend, Mr. William Anderson, and several of his experienced mining experts will be arriving tomorrow to check out the Gypsy Lady. Hopefully, we will have help getting the gold out of the mine, or Mr. Anderson may want to purchase the mine from me."

Mary Grace leaned her petite body toward Luke. "I guess I can stay another night with Pa. How about some lunch? I'm starving." Mary Grace looped her arm with Luke's.

\*\*\*

Moon stood behind the bar, drying clean glasses when he looked up to see his pretty daughter on the arm of Luke Tyler. "Well, if it isn't my daughter with her intended. I'm mighty pleased to see you both. People have been asking when your wedding will take place."

"Pa." Mary Grace flushed bright red. "What are you saying? Luke and I aren't a couple and I'm certainly not his intended, as you just suggested. Why would you say such a thing?"

"'Cause, gal, you've been living out at his place for weeks and people are a mind to talk. This is the first time you been back here in weeks, so naturally, people are talking about your up-and-coming wedding."

"Moon, you are jumping to a wrong conclusion. Your daughter has not been alone with me. Twelve people live at my camp and she has her private living quarters. I told you that before you allowed her to come and work for me. Your daughter is a nice young girl and has nothing to be ashamed of, let along be forced into a loveless marriage."

Mary Grace's eyes filled with tears and a painful lump lodged in her throat. "Luke is telling you the truth, Pa. How can you say those things about us? He's my boss and nothing more."

"Sorry if I jumped to the wrong conclusion, but I ain't going to have your reputation ruined because of him. He's to do right by you, or I'll shoot him."

"Moon, I'm standing right in front of you. If you got something in your craw, spit it out to me, not to Mary Grace." Luke stood straight as an arrow with clenched fists.

Sniffing back tears that threatened to fall, Mary Grace ran from the saloon up the staircase to her old bedroom. "Well, now see what you have done?" Moon said, tossing the drying rag over his shoulder. He glared at Luke.

# Chapter 12

Early the next morning, an old man knocked on Luke's door.

"Coming," Luke called, jumping from the bed and opening the door.

"It's seven o'clock, sir, and I have black coffee, just like you requested." Luke handed the older man a shiny quarter.

He returned a toothless smile and left. Luke grinned and closed the door.

In less than an hour, Luke was dressed and downstairs, shifting side to side on the stagecoach platform. The 9:30 a.m. stagecoach from Denver would arrive in a few minutes. Luke didn't want to be late meeting William Anderson, the banker from First Bank of Denver. He'd met Mr. Anderson years ago and was relishing the opportunity to spend time with him and talk over old times. William reminded him so much of his father, whom he missed terribly.

A few doors down, soft piano music flowed from the building. Luke eased down the boardwalk and pushed open the batwing doors to the saloon. He could smell freshly brewed coffee, so he sidled over to the bar. "How about a cup of hot coffee?" Luke asked the barkeeper. He placed a nickel on the bar, took his coffee, and sat at the table closest to the door so he could see and hear the activity taking place outside.

Jeffrey pushed open the door and glanced around the dimly lit room. His eyes opened wide when he saw Luke sitting alone.

"Hey, boss. I figured you'd be over at the stage depot or the café with Mary Grace." Jeffrey walked over to the barkeeper and ordered a cup of coffee.

"I was with her last night, but her crazy pa messed things up pretty good. He suggested that Mary Grace and I should be getting married. She was so embarrassed that she ran up to her bedroom. Moon said people were talking about us getting hitched."

"I'm not surprised," Jeffrey responded with a smirk. "People like to talk, and her being pretty and single and you, a handsome, rich gold miner. Well, it just seems like the right thing to happen." His grin widened at Luke. "You know it could be worst. She could be fat and ugly."

"You're so funny this morning." Luke lifted his hat and ran his fingers through his dark, straight hair. "I hate it that Mary Grace is going to be left here in Crooked Creek to bear such gossip. As soon as I get everything settled with the gold mine, I'll be heading home. I miss my folks, and I haven't heard a word from anyone in over a year. No idea what I am going to find when I get there either." He looked down at the old floor. "I hope to settle down near my home place."

"While you're settling down, why not take a wife? A woman can be a big help in more ways than one."

Luke's head snapped up, but before he could respond, Jeffrey continued.

"She can cook, clean, and wash your clothes, help with the farm animals, and work beside you in the fields. You'll never be alone again." Jeffrey chuckled.

"It's been a long time since I've been home." Luke's eyes brightened as he recalled memories. "I'm not sure if there are any ladies in the area where I want to settle. What you said is nice, but I'm not ready to get hitched. Besides, marriage is a serious business." Luke placed his hat back on his head and leaned back in his chair. "First, you got to find the right woman." Using a softer tone he said, "I want a woman that makes my heart beat fast, makes me smile for no reason, and a woman who will celebrate during good times and understand when times are bad. I want a special woman that will love me unconditionally. When I find that woman, I'll be ready to settle down."

"Do you think that a gal exists like that?" Jeffrey shook his head.

"Oh, I don't know, but I would hope so." Luke's thoughts went straight to Mary Grace while he drained his coffee cup and stood to leave the saloon. "The stage should be arriving soon." Wishing time would speed up, Luke paced in front of the depot. He needed his banker friend to help him decide the future of his gold mine. Luke glanced up to see Mary Grace race toward him. His eyes narrowed. *Might she be the woman in his future?*

"Hi, Luke," Mary Grace was out of breath, but she managed a shy smile.

Luke raised his eyebrows. "Mary Grace, I'm surprised to see you this morning. I figured you wouldn't be speaking to me ever again." When she didn't say anything, Luke continued. "I'm sorry your pa embarrassed you last night." Luke reached for Mary Grace's hands and pulled her body close to his.

Sobs trapped in her throat, and she looked toward the door to the café. "He embarrassed you, too. He just says whatever he thinks, whether it's true or not," she whispered. "I'm sorry, too."

Luke gazed down into the sweet girl's eyes but stepped away from her when he heard the stagecoach coming down Main Street.

"Whoa! You hard-headed big four-footed mules," Slim Peabody yelled as he pulled his team to a stop next to the boardwalk of the stage depot. "Hold your horses, folks," he bellowed to the stagecoach passengers as the carriage rocked back and forth. "Someone will help you out. They'll place a set of steps beside the door to help you step down without stumbling and breaking your citified necks."

A tall man, skinny enough to take a bath in a shotgun barrel, placed wooden steps in front of the door while a passenger inside pushed opened the red door. Two men jumped out of the carriage before William Anderson appeared in the doorway.

Luke rushed over and offered his hand to the older man.

"Thank you, my good man," he said and smiled at his friend, Luke.

"Welcome to Crooked Creek, Mr. Anderson. Maybe this time next year, the train line will have continued from Denver and come right into this small town," Luke offered as an apology for the old man's rough ride in the stagecoach.

"The ride wasn't too bad, but I have to admit the passenger

coaches in the new trains are a lot more comfortable. But, I'm here, and I am excited to test your mine. Lawrence and Samuel, come and meet Luke Tyler, the owner of the mine. These two men will be my right hand and will test your mine and the gold you've already discovered."

"Howdy, fellows and welcome. We want you to be comfortable while you're here. There are plenty of prepared bunks at the mine for your stay, but if you want to ride five miles back and forth to town, I will get you a room at the boardinghouse."

"We want to take care of this business as quickly as we can. There won't be any need for us to travel back and forth to town, but I have one question. Do you have a good cook?"

"Yes, sir." Mary Grace spoke up so quickly that Luke didn't have a chance to answer. "I'm the camp's cook. I came into town for supplies, and I will have a nice supper for you tonight. You'll be having lunch in town now, and I will see you later at the camp." Mary Grace hurried away and motioned for Jeffrey to come with her.

"Luke, I hope she can cook as good as she looks," Mr. Anderson said and watched Mary Grace and Jeffrey enter the dry goods store.

Luke was lost for words. He didn't want Mary Grace back out at the mine, but with Mr. Anderson expecting good food, he really didn't have much choice but to allow her to go. At least, she was willing to help. He'd have to have a good talk with her later—alone.

***

Mr. Anderson and his men had changed into work clothes while Luke ordered the removal of the boards from the entrance of the mine. Luke led the experts into the cave carrying a giant lantern, which he hung from the ceiling. He chose a small pick and pointed to the area on the wall where they had discovered small particles of gold.

Mr. Anderson moved in closer and removed a small chunk of dirt. He placed an eyeglass over his left eye and held the piece closer for a better inspection. Instantly he thrust out his chest and shouted, "Damn boy, this is gold, all right. Have you dug anymore from this area?"

"Yep." Luke's face beamed. He hurried over to the corner of

the room and pulled back a brown canvas. The mound of gold nuggets were unbelievable, the size of golf balls, set in the middle of a freight barrel. "I had the men stop digging until we were sure that it was gold. I wanted your advice as to what to do if it was gold."

"It looks like you made some repair in this part of the cave. Was the ceiling caving in on your men?"

"No, sir. Someone set off an explosion with a stick of dynamite and caused some damage, so I had my men repair the ceiling, sidewalls, and the floor. I kinda figured the explosion helped us discover the vein on this wall." Luke pointed at the sidewall where the two men had been digging.

"Well, sonny boy," Mr. Anderson said with a grin he could not contain, "you and your men discovered a rich vein, and it's a miracle. It's in the very front of the tunnel and not fifty feet under." He puffed out his chest and placed his eye glass back into his pocket. "I want to allow my two men to look this area over thoroughly. After they finish with their examination of the gold veins and the cost of digging, hauling it out, and transporting it to Denver, we'll be able to make a plan or possibly a deal."

\*\*\*

The fresh evening air felt good as the two men bumped shoulders as they walked side by side to the dining hall of the camp. Luke opened the door for Mr. Anderson to enter, when suddenly the older man halted.

"My gracious. What's that wonderful smell? My old belly is rumbling from that delicious aroma."

"It smells like pot roast and hot biscuits to me," Luke said, smiling.

"Lead me to it, young man. I'm starving, and I bet I could eat half a dozen of those biscuits."

"Mary Grace always makes plenty, so you can eat until you bust. She usually makes a delicious dessert, so you may want to leave some room for that." Luke waved at Mary Grace from across the room. He gave her a big smile and shook his head, laughing. Thank goodness she wanted to come and cook, he thought.

The next day, Mr. Anderson and his two mining experts worked from morning to night. After a cold dip in the stream, Mr. Anderson met with Luke in the dining hall after supper. He waited until all the men had departed for the bunkhouse, and Mary Grace had gone to her room. "Luke, my boy, I'm going to lay it out straight to you. You have a strong vein of gold in the front of the mine, but after searching hours, we didn't come up with much more. Now, this is a very wealthy, wide vein that you have discovered. I am willing to purchase your mine from you. I can offer you more money than you or your men dreamed of having without you having to do any more work."

Luke's heart raced, and he could feel it pounding in his chest. "A lot of money without having to do anything else to bring it out, you say?"

"You heard right. Now, you can continue to dig and search for more gold, but my men are the best. If there was more easy gold to find, they'd have discovered it."

"I have ten men and one gal to share my profits with. They know I will get extra because the mine belongs to me. Can you give me a figure, maybe off the top of your head that you are willing to offer?"

Mr. Anderson pressed his fingers to a smile on his lips. "I figure I should be able to offer you one million dollars. Mostly in green paper currency and maybe a little gold, but I will let my bank managers decide what's best." His old friend slapped a hand on Luke's shoulder and gave it a tight squeeze.

"Wow," was Luke's only comment. "This comes to approximately eighty grand a piece for my men and a hundred twenty-grand for me. Of course, I will have the expense of lawyers and other items to take care of." Luke's head was overwhelmed with figures. "And all this without having to do more hard work. Your offer is too good to believe, but as far as I'm concerned, you got yourself a deal." Luke was feeling a little lightheaded. His dream had come true because he never wanted to be a miner in the first place. Now he would have enough money to last him a lifetime, and he could take care of his folks.

"Give me a day, Mr. Anderson," Luke swallowed. He tipped his head back for a moment and closed his eyes. "I would like to talk this over with my men. Most of them have families and will be willing to take the offer and run, but a few might want to argue. But, this is my gold mine and I will make the final decision."

"You are a good boss man, Luke. I can understand you

wanting them to have a say in your decision." The old man grinned.

# Chapter 13

The men sat in the dining hall, mumbling among themselves as they waited for Luke to tell them the results of Mr. Anderson's and his men's finding in the mine. After a lengthy explanation about the mine and the offer from Mr. Anderson, the men were more than excited and pleased with Luke's acceptance of the banker's offer. They'd each receive more money than any of them ever dreamed.

"We'll be taking the gold nuggets to Denver and will receive a draft from First Bank of Denver. Guards will accompany us to Denver. Mr. Anderson has hired ten men to help guard the gold. Be ready to leave in the morning, and it should take us at least three days. Each one of you will be carry your rifle and handgun and will be taking turns standing guard at night. The men whom Mr. Anderson hired are riding along to help us, but we must pull our weight. Once news gets out that we're transporting gold to Denver, we may meet up with a lot of trouble on the way." Luke sighed and studied his men. "But, it's our gold, and I plan for us to arrive in Denver with it."

The men hooted and clapped. "No one is going to take our money away from us," one man shouted. Two men jumped up from the table and did a jig with each other. Luke laughed. "Now men, pack your belongings and prepare to stay a week or two in Denver. I'll pay for the hotel rooms, three meals a day, and boarding our animals, but I won't pay your bar bills or bailing you out of jail." Luke stared hard at each man. "Now on the trail, we'll be sleeping outside, so prepare for all types of weather. The nights will be cold."

Luke turned to Jeffrey and instructed him to place the two-man tent in the wagon for Mary Grace to have a place of privacy at night. All the men murmured to each other on their way to the bunkhouse.

Mary Grace stood and headed toward her bedroom, but Luke called after her. "Did you tell your pa that you're going to Denver with us? He's not going to like you traveling with this many men and be away from Crooked Creek for weeks."

"I don't need his permission to do anything. After he gambled my person away, he lost all ownership of me. Now that I'm no longer your cook, I don't belong to no man. I'm my own woman."

"Well, you have a right to feel that way, and I don't blame you. Since you'll be traveling with the men and me, I'd hoped that you wouldn't mind cooking for us on the trail. Harry and Jimbo will help you, like always."

She gave Luke a wicked smile before entering her room. "Guess I can do that one last time. I have to eat too." As she flipped the lock, she heard him laugh. Leaning on the door, she giggled. In a few weeks, she was going to be one rich, young woman, and no man would have control over her ever again. Sighing, she sat on her bed and thought of Luke. He had been so good to her, and goosebumps sprang up every time he was near her. She was going to miss him when this business was over.

***

Sun shone through Mary Grace's bedroom. She was already up and dressed. She rushed into the kitchen to make sure big pots of coffee were on the stove like she had instructed Jimbo to do. Harry had loaded the supply wagon with food to prepare tasty meals.

After the men were ready to travel, she hurried out and climbed on her pinto pony that she had raised. Her trousers, soft leather vest, and big floppy hat over her long, braided hair made it easier to travel. She kicked her horse in his sides and rode up beside Luke. "Good morning, boss man," Mary Grace said. "Jimbo, Harry, and I are going to drive the chuckwagon up the trail about ten miles and start breakfast. Does that meet with your plan?"

"Yep, go on ahead, but make sure to be on your guard at all times. We'll be along in a few hours."

Just as Luke had said, men came riding up with the gold wagon and parked next to the chuckwagon. "You guys made good time. I have the oats, ham, biscuits, and jam already. We just made two fresh pots of coffee." Harry hobbled over to the table and began setting out the plates.

"Good. I'm starving," Luke said, jumped down off his horse, and tossed the reins to one of his men.

The men filed into a straight line, and Mary Grace and Harry filled the men's plate with hot fluffy biscuits, plenty of oatmeal, and ham. As they sat around the campfire, Mary Grace poured refills of hot coffee.

\*\*\*

The men couldn't take their eyes off her posterior. Each man's smile widened whenever she bent over to serve the men.

James Thorp, the leader of the group, pulled Luke aside. "Mr. Tyler, I need to speak with you now." It was all the man could do to contain his anger.

"What can't wait until I finish eating?" Luke still held a cup of coffee.

"That woman has got to wear something a little more decent than those men's tight-ass pants. I hired on to guard your gold, not a little tart prancing around in front of my men."

"Now you hold on a minute. That young lady is no tart. She's a lovely girl who has worked at my mining camp as our cook and is a part-owner of the gold." Lowering his voice, Luke said, "Your men had better not touch a hair on her head."

"Well, you'd best hear me. I cannot watch my men every minute. I'll tell them to stay away from your woman, and I hope they'll heed my warning, but if she doesn't have a protector, well, there could be trouble."

"All right. Tell your men that Mary Grace is my woman. I will make sure she's well protected, but you make sure your men look but don't touch. Jimbo will serve the men coffee from here on out."

The big man strolled to the fire ring and loomed over his men. He spoke slowly but loud enough to emphasize his words. "Men, I am only going to say this once. Keep away from the young woman who is traveling with us. She is our cook and a darn good one at that, but she is Mr. Tyler's woman. Show her respect at all times, or you'll have to answer to her husband and me."

\*\*\*

Mary Grace couldn't believe what she had just heard. Luke told the hired guards that they were married? He'd never shown any interest in her except for her cooking skills. Sure he was kind and very generous to her in every way. He paid her good wages. He'd even given up his nice room for her to have privacy and purchased clothes for her to wear. Never had he stepped out of line and embarrassed her. What was he thinking? She eased from the circle of men, untied her pony to the back of the chuckwagon, and headed out to their last stop of the day.

\*\*\*

Luke's miners had overheard the guy's speech to his men, and they laughed and hooted at him as he walked past them. A few men jumped up and gave him a hard pat on his back. "We all knew you two should be together," Jeffrey laughed, and all the others smiled and agreed.

Luke wrapped his arms across his chest and watched Jimbo hitch up the horses and then drive the wagon away. He'd wanted to have a few minutes of privacy with Mary Grace before they left for the next stop, needing to explain that the man had misinterpreted what he meant. "Dammit, I was only trying to protect her virtue," he mumbled to himself.

\*\*\*

They repacked the chuckwagon and headed down the trail to their next stop. Mary Grace sniffed back tears for miles. Harry begged her to tell him what was wrong, but she turned her shoulder away from him and continued crying. Once they arrived at an area with a creek running nearby, the two men jumped down. There was plenty to do to prepare supper for the miners and guards.

Mary Grace jumped down and ambled over to the stream of water. She washed her face and tried to contain her emotions. When she returned to the chuckwagon, Harry was sitting on a block of wood peeling potatoes while Jimbo gathered firewood and started the cook fire. He hauled water from the creek, made several pots of coffee, and set them next to the fire to await the men.

Her job was to peel the carrots and onions and slice a piece of beef into thin slices for vegetable soup.

Jimbo placed a pot of fat grease over the fire for the cornpones Mary Grace would make to go with the soup. "You ain't never going to finish with those vegetables if you don't stop crying. Can't you at least tell Harry and me what's wrong? Maybe we can help." Jimbo stood in front of the makeshift table and watched Mary Grace slice the onions into small chunks.

"Ain't crying," she sniffed and jutted her chin out. "These onions are stinging my eyes." When she was finished with the vegetables, Mary Grace stood. Numbness overcame her body and mind. Hot tears began flowing down her red cheeks again as she sliced the beef into thin strips.

"Here now, Mary Grace," said Harry. "We ain't ever going to get this soup made if you don't let me take over here." Harry limped over, took the sharp blade out of her hand, and pushed her away from the table.

Jimbo wound a long arm around her shoulders, led her to a fallen tree log, and gave her a gentle tug to sit. "Now, miss, did someone hurt you in some way? If they did, I'd sure tell Luke, and man, oh man, he'll deal with them."

"No," she screamed, causing Jimbo to jump backward. Drawing her mouth into a straight line and biting her lips, she spoke with a shaky voice, "I don't want him to know that I cried." She took the tail of her long, white apron and rubbed it over her wet face. "I'm fine now." Mary Grace ran back to Harry, lifting her chin as to look confident, and carried his stool for him to sit on. She washed the prepared meat and tossed the pieces in the water. Jimbo grabbed the handle of the pot and hooked it on the tripod over the fire.

She retrieved a big bowl and poured cornmeal into it, carried a large bowl of fresh eggs from the back of the chuckwagon, and cracked six eggs into the cornmeal, adding a handful of sugar to the mixture. "Jimbo, please get me the milk bucket so I can pour some into this mixture. Harry sure chose a good milk cow to make this trip," she said, giving him a weak smile.

After he brought her the bucket, she poured several cups of it into the cornmeal. "The men will enjoy these corn pones with the soup. It'll help fill them up, too. We have about a dozen fresh apples left. Let's wash and slice them for dessert."

Harry and Jimbo glanced at each other with knowing eyes. She wasn't fooling anyone.

"You ain't gonna fry up some apple pies with them?" Harry asked.

"No, I don't feel like it tonight. I'm going to go to bed early."

With bulging eyes, Harry glanced toward Jimbo's surprised expression. Neither one of them could believe that she wasn't going to prepare the men something sweet to eat.

## Chapter 14

The weather was cold, dreary, and dark by the time the men arrived at their last stop for the day. Jimbo and Harry were waiting to feed them hot soup and corn pones. After the men had used big buckets of warm soapy water to wash up, they lined up with their bowls and coffee cups, then gathered around the fire ring, and ate in silence. The trail had been rough and the fierce, cold wind had flown in their faces for miles through today's trek with the wagon of gold.

Luke glanced around the chuckwagon and the surrounding campsite for Mary Grace. She was nowhere in sight. He signaled to get Harry's attention and mouthed, "Where's Mary Grace?"

Using his head, he motioned toward the tent. Luke ambled over, stooped down, and called her name.

When he received no answer, he tried again but still no response came from inside. He stood, speaking in a quiet voice, and said he would be back to check on her later. He joined Harry by the chuckwagon. "How were things with Mary Grace today after ya left earlier. I wanted to talk with her, but you drove away before I could." When Harry remained quiet, he asked another question. "Did she appear upset about what she overheard?"

"Do you mean, did she cry for ten miles in this nasty weather?" He stared hard into Luke's face. "You can bet your last dollar she did. That child cried for hours, but of course, she doesn't want you to know it. She was gloomy, just like the weather, and felt sick all day. As soon as we got settled here and the food was cooking, she went into her tent. That girl's heartsick. That's what wrong with her. You let that man think she needed protecting, but worse of all, you let all the men think you were married."

"After I said I would protect her, Thorp just assumed we were married. He was worried that one of his men might harm her in some way, and I'd never let that happen. You know that, old man." A slight muscle jumped in his cheek. Luke was madder than an old bulldog and upset that he had caused Mary Grace to cry.

"You gonna eat, or do you want me to save you a bowl of soup for later?" Harry asked.

"Later. I've got to straighten things out between Mary Grace and me." Luke turned and stormed toward Mary Grace's tent as rain pelted down over the fire, men, and horses. He quickly slid into the opening of the small green tent where Mary Grace was resting. Closing the flap, he could see the men scrambling to get out of the rainstorm.

"What are you doing in my tent? Get out before I scream my head off." Mary Grace raised upon her knees and was pointing toward the opening.

"Hush up this minute before I gag you. It's storming and I don't intend to get soaked. You know that I would never hurt you."

"Oh? What about hurting my reputation? You told all those men out there that I'm your wife when we haven't even kissed." She glanced away for a quick second and said, "Well, only that once, but I was excited, and you know it."

"Settle down and listen to me." A bolt of lightning hit the ground directly in front of the tent door. Mary Grace screamed and jumped into Luke's arms. "I'm sorry," she said, as she pushed herself out of his arms and sat back on her bedroll. "I've always been afraid of lightning and bad storms."

"That's alright. I'm not fond of them either. I just hope the men tied the horses tight to the picket lines." He pushed back one side of the tent flap and looked toward the animals. They all seemed to be intact. He tied the flaps of the tent.

"Look, Mary Grace, James Thorpe, the leader of the guards, told me that he was afraid that some of his men might do you some harm on this trip if they found you alone. He said that he wasn't paid to watch after you, so I told him not to worry. I would protect you." Another loud crash of lightning hit close, causing both of them to jump again. "He misinterpreted what I meant about protecting you. I never said that we were married. Please, you must believe me."

"I was embarrassed for sure. You have never even looked my way, and some of the miners were making remarks about us. I guess they just figured since we were together a lot in the dining hall and kitchen, that well, you know, we were messing around."

"Tell me who was saying nasty remarks about you, and I'll send them packing. They'll be sorry because they will not get any profits from the gold."

"No, I would never do that. The men were only talking among themselves, like men do." She glared at him. "Your men are nice and have been good to me, but most men always think the worst about a woman being alone with a man. I know we never did anything wrong, but they don't know that for sure."

"When we arrive in Denver, I'll make sure that your reputation is intact. You're a nice girl, and I would never let anyone smear your name. Your pa would kill me for sure." Luke gave her a cocky smile.

"Why were you cooped up in this tent when we arrived at the campsite? Harry said you were sick. Are you?"

"Yes, a little. I just needed to lie down and rest some. I'll be fine in the morning." Mary Grace was too embarrassed to tell him that it was her monthly, as most women called it. She always had terrible cramps and lying down helped.

***

Luke opened the tent flap once again. "It's coming down now. I hope you don't mind if I stay until the rain stops." Before she could answer, a flash of lightning hit close to the small tent, and she screamed. She grabbed her blanket, quickly laid down, and covered herself. "No, I'm glad you're in here with me. I'd be scared to death if I was alone."

Picking up another blanket, he clutched it across his chest and covered both arms. The weather had turned cold and the campsite was nearly dark outside except for a small lantern. The light shone from the chuckwagon where several men were most likely playing cards before turning in for the night.

"Mary Grace, go on to sleep, and I'll leave as soon as this storm is over." He glanced at her pale face, and she returned a weak smile.

"Thank you, boss man. I can hardly keep my eyes open..." she mumbled, then turned over, and pulled her knees up in a fetal position. She was asleep before she finished her reply.

After listening to the storm and Mary Grace's soft snoring, Luke could hardly keep his own eyes open. His shoulders curled forward, and he blinked rapidly to stay awake. It was still raining hard. He'd be soaking wet if he tried to run to the chuckwagon. Luke glanced at Mary Grace who was sleeping soundly. He turned his body sideways and stretched out close to the front of the tent and was asleep before he covered his tall frame. Late into the night, he heard a strange sound. He sat up and listened. It was Mary Grace weeping. He gently shook her shoulder, but she didn't respond.

"I'm cold," she mumbled.

What could he do for her? He shook out his blanket and covered her shaking body, then sat back on his knees and watched her. Her fragile body still shivered from the cold, so he lay beside her and wrapped her in his arms for the extra body heat. In a few minutes, she lay still and continued with her soft snoring. Luke felt warm for the first time all night, and he drifted into a deep slumber.

Luke had a wonderful dream. *He was cuddling a soft, sweet-smelling woman in his arms, and she was purring like a kitten. He lifted her long hair and was prepared to nuzzle her neck when—*

Something jerked his leg and dragged him out of the tent into the cold morning air onto the damp ground. He shook his head and looked up. Jeffrey stood over him.

"What the hell, Jeffrey? I just got to sleep. What's wrong?"

"Quiet, before all the men come rushing over here. You were in that tent, all snuggled up with Mary Grace. Man, are you out of your mind? Are you ready for a shotgun wedding?" Jeffrey bent over Luke's tall frame and helped him to stand.

"No. We haven't done anything wrong. I fell asleep while waiting out the storm, and Mary Grace was cold. I was just giving her some extra body heat."

"You'd better be glad that it was me that discovered your whereabouts. Several of the men have already been looking for you."

"Dammit, man, it's still the middle of the night. What do they want with me?"

"The night guards heard someone out in the bushes. They woke up the rest of the men, and they're all prepared for an ambush. Here's your gun." Jeffrey glared at Luke like he wanted to beat the living tar out of him.

"Are Harry and Jimbo making a fire and coffee like they usual? If those men think we don't realize they're out there, they'll make a move soon."

Luke turned to walk away when Jeffrey asked, "Where are you going?"

Luke shrugged. "Nature calls. Give me a minute, for goodness sakes."

"Be careful. We don't want them to nab you while you're busy."

Luke found a tree for some privacy. *One of these days I'm going to flatten that man and close his mouth. Talk, talk, talk is all he does.*

***

After speaking with Harry and Jimbo, Luke eased over to Mary Grace's tent and woke her up. He placed his finger over his lips and whispered, "Men are snooping around the camp. Please stay inside the tent until I come for you."

She nodded, reached for her rifle, and lay back on her bed.

With her hair tumbling down around her shoulders, she was a beauty. Luke smiled at her then scanned the area. The hired guards were nowhere to be seen, and only a few of his miners were milling around the fire. It wasn't but a minute when gunfire exploded, and everyone took cover near the wagon of gold. Several more rounds of gunfire were exchanged, and someone yelped.

Horses scattered from the area, and all the men came out of the bushes. They circled the ring of fire that had been built with the dry wood that Harry stored in the chuckwagon.

One of the guards emerged from the woods near the creek, dragging a scrubby-looking man who was wet and shivering. "Got one of the bushwhackers." The guard pushed the man onto the ground.

The wet man grabbed his arm. Blood flowed onto his hand.

"That man is hurt," Mary Grace yelled. "Jimbo, bring me the

medicine bag out of the chuckwagon and a few clean rags."

"You don't have to doctor him, Miss, because we're gonna' string him up right here. He won't try to steal anyone else's money," he said as he looped a heavy rope around his wrist.

As Mary Grace prepared to clean the hurt's man wound, she glared at the big-mouth man. "Ain't nobody going to hang nobody while I have breath in my body. Luke," she yelled and scanned the area. When she saw him, she demanded, "Tell them to behave themselves until you decide what to do with him." Mary Grace glared at Mr. Thorp, the leader of the guards, who was standing near the fire with his arms crossed.

"She's right. We'll tie him up and turn him over to the sheriff when we get to Denver." Luke circled the fire ring while glancing at the men.

"Why don't you just turn him loose?" Jeffrey suggested. "He won't be back, and I doubt any more of his friends will try to rob us now that they know how many men we have guarding our gold."

Mary Grace cut open the man's shirt and asked him his name. He whispered Paul White to her and stared at the ground. "I appreciate you taking care of my arm. I'm sorry to be so much trouble."

Once Mary Grace cleaned the man's wound, Jimbo gave him a cup of coffee. Jimbo sat the man down on a log near the fire. Mary Grace stood behind him with narrowed eyes at the nasty man who wanted to hang the poor fellow.

Luke wasn't surprised how protective Mary Grace was of the bushwhacker. She was a tenderhearted person. If they kept him tied up, someone would have to watch him, and he would be one more mouth to feed. More work for Mary Grace, Jimbo, and Harry. "I agree with Jeffrey. We don't need to be bothered with having to guard this man on the way to Denver. I've decided to let him ride out of here, but we'd better not ever see you again. Do I make myself clear?" Luke had turned and spoke directly to the man. "Tell your friends in Crooked Creek that we have a lot of men protecting our gold, and we should be in Denver in another day."

The man named Paul White strolled to his horse, turned, and looked at all the men who were watching his every step. He nodded at Luke, smiled at Mary Grace, then saddled up and rode quietly away from the campsite.

"You know what I think, Mr. Tyler," the loudmouthed guard who wanted to hang the bushwhacker said. "I think you're a yellow belly wimp. A real man would have hung that thief."

Before the man knew what hit him, Luke whipped around and slugged the man in the mouth with his right fist, causing him to lose his balance and fall into the fire. He screamed as two men pulled him out before any real body damaged was done.

*\*\*\**

"Terrell, get yourself back to your bedroll and let one of the men check your back for burns. Stay away from Mr. Tyler before you get more of the same from him." Mr. Thorp watched the girl rush to Mr. Tyler and began doctoring his right hand, bloody from hitting the man in the mouth. He smiled to himself. That young man sure was a lucky son-of-a-gun.

# Chapter 15

Mary Grace bounced down the stairs in Denver's most elegant hotel, The James, owned by J. W. James and his wife, Mildred. It was a lovely Victorian, five-story building. Luke settled himself and Mary Grace into this fine establishment after they arrived nearly three weeks earlier.

Mr. Anderson and the bank's associates worked long hours preparing a contract for his gold mine and the gold the men had discovered and brought into the Denver bank. Each man, along with Mary Grace, would be wealthy once the money was deposited in The First Bank of Denver. The men would receive whatever cash they wanted to have on hand. Mr. Anderson said that the men could transfer their money by a bank draft to whatever bank they wanted or just leave it where it was. Luke and Mary Grace had both decided to leave their funds in the Denver bank for now.

Crooked Creek bank was not secure, so Luke suggested that Mary Grace request money from The First Bank of Denver as she needed it. Luke planned to travel home to Pine Hill, Texas, and Mary Grace would be headed back to her pa's place.

During the three weeks, the couple enjoyed seeing the big city of Denver. During the day, they either rode their horses or Luke rented a buggy for their sightseeing trips. Sometimes they shared picnics near the lake that circled the town.

Luke soon discovered the city's night entertainment wasn't exactly a place for ladies. He did find one saloon, the Lady Gay, who presented traveling minstrel shows and performing troupes.

Across the street, a theater presented mostly burlesque skits and serious plays like *Uncle Tom's Cabin* and *Romeo and Juliet*. Mary Grace insisted on going to see the performances three times. Finally, Luke laughed and declared that enough was enough. The Opera House booked some top acts and musicals for Sunday evenings only, and Luke enjoyed taking her to see them.

Jeffrey and the rest of the men spent many hours in a saloon that hosted a variety theater from nine in the evening to two in the morning. The crowds were drunk and boisterous, and many fights broke out during the performances. Many mornings one or two of his men had black eyes or busted lips. He chuckled one morning and told his men that if they didn't get their money soon and leave Denver, they might be carried away on a stretcher.

Early one morning before the end of the third week, Luke received a note from Mr. Anderson. He wanted to meet with Luke the next day. Luke was sure what the meeting would be about, so he asked Mary Grace for dinner that evening. They had spent nearly the whole three weeks together, and the attraction between them grew. He had deep feelings for her and felt that she cared for him, too. But for now, he had to settle only for her friendship.

For their last evening together, he wanted to show her a good time. He took her to her favorite show and Annabelle's Restaurant. After dinner Luke pulled out a small black box and set it in front of Mary Grace.

***

"For me?" she asked sweetly, hoping to control her fluttery stomach. Instincts told her that Luke loved her.

"Yes, I wanted to give you something so you will always remember our time together." He nudged the box closer to her.

"It's a watch," she said, trying to hide the tears that threatened to fall. Small diamonds surrounding the circular face. It was hooked on a gold chain to wear around a lady's neck. "It's lovely, Luke. Thank you. I shall wear it all the time."

"Mary Grace,' Luke leaned forward and took her hand. "I'm sorry if I led you to believe that I was ready to settle down. If it were possible, you would be my choice for a bride. I have deep feelings for you."

"Please, Luke," Mary Grace interrupted him. "I'm too young to settle down and have a passel of young'uns. I want to travel, see the country, build a big restaurant, and have an income for the rest of my life. I love the watch, and I will always treasure it because you gave it to me." She shoved her chair back a few inches. "I'm tired. Do you mind if we call it an evening?"

"Of course not. I have an early meeting in the morning. Good news I hope." Luke took her arm and led her back to the hotel and stopped at the bottom of the staircase. "Mary Grace, I want us to stay friends, write to each other—"

"Thanks again for a lovely evening and the gift. I'm too tired to talk anymore tonight. Goodnight. I'll see you tomorrow."

\*\*\*

After Luke's meeting with Mr. Anderson, he met with his men and Mary Grace and told them that everyone's money was all set at the bank and for them to go and sign some papers. Everyone cheered, and a few danced around. Luke was pleased that the gold mine business was over. He announced to the men that he'd be pulling out the next day. He was taking the old prospector, Sam, with him to his home.

The men gathered around and patted him on the back, shook his hand, and said nice things about working for him. Most of the men were speechless, and a few had mist in their eyes. The men had worked hard, had a clean place to bunk down every night, and were fed great food. Now, their boss man had shared the profits of the gold mine with them. It was a miracle, and they were grateful now that it was a reality.

\*\*\*

Mary Grace hurried out of the meeting. Luke quickly followed her into the parlor of the hotel. "Wait, Mary Grace. We have to talk. I don't want to leave you like this."

"And how am I, Mr. Tyler? Angry, sad, disgusted, to describe a few of my feelings. There's nothing more we have to discuss. I'm staying here, and you're leaving. Goodbye, boss man, and thanks for the money."

"Hold your horses right there, Missy." Luke yelled at her backside as she attempted to run up the stairs. He whipped her around to face him. "Listen, you are not staying in this big city alone. You're getting on that stagecoach in the morning that will take you home to Crooked Creek."

"You're not my boss any longer, and I'm a grown woman. I can and will do whatever I want, and I choose to remain here in Denver. Jimbo and Harry are remaining here, too. So, I won't be alone."

Luke relaxed his hold on her wrist, and she wrenched it away, practically running up the staircase. He wasn't finished talking to the sassy mouth. "Now, you just wait," he yelled and chased after her up the stairs. Luke managed to grab her, but she whirled around, lifted her feet, and kicked at him. He snatched at her booted feet, and one boot slipped off into his hands. Surprised, he looked down at the boot and suddenly lost his balance and fell backward. Down the staircase, he tumbled and soon landed at the base of the stairs.

Mary Grace watched him land on the hard floor at the bottom of the stairs. She yelled for help and raced down to Luke. He lay as still as death. "Get a doctor," she cried to the desk clerk who had come out of the back room.

A man, who had been having dinner in the dining area of the hotel, heard Mary Grace's cry for help. "I'm a doctor," he said. He stooped down at Luke's side and told his companion to get his doctor's bag. The man lifted Luke eyelids and placed his ear down on his chest. "He's alive, but he has a bad bump on the back of his head. He could have a concussion."

Once the doctor's bag arrived, he listened closer to Luke's breathing and heart. He ran his hands up and down Luke's tall frame checking for broken bones. "I need a stretcher to carry him to his room. I don't feel any broken bones. Maybe a broken rib, but I'm not sure of that either. He will be fine once he wakes up."

A pair of men arrived with a stretcher, and Luke was lifted and carried up to his room. Mary Grace followed and turned back the bed covers, and the doctor and another man removed his clothes and boots. The doctor ordered a pan of ice and instructed Mary Grace to hold the ice pack on the back of Luke's head. The doctor turned Luke onto his side while he examined his ribs and checked his back. A significant red mark traveled down the center of his spine, but his legs and arms were not broken, and his neck seemed to be okay.

"This is one fortunate young man. He could have injured himself real bad tumbling down those stairs. A good thing the stairs were carpeted," he said matter-of-factly. "Is this young man married?"

"No," Mary Grace replied softly.

"Well, I will have to find a nurse to sit with him. He must not be alone, at least, until he wakes up." The doctor placed his instruments back into his bag and snapped it closed.

"I'll take care of him. He's my friend and was my boss for months. I'm the reason he fell, so it's my place to sit with him." She wiped tears from her eyes with the bed covers.

"Fine," The doctor said without looking at her. "I'll be back early in the morning to check on him. Good day."

Mary Grace raced to her room and grabbed up a few personal items—her gown and robe to wear in case she needed to spend the night in Luke's room. She wanted to be comfortable, and besides, he had seen her in her nightgown when he came to her room to talk while working for him at the mining camp.

Jimbo and Harry had heard about Luke's accident, so they came to his room to check on him. Mary Grace took the opportunity to do a few personal things and order herself some supper to be delivered to Luke's room.

"How do you think he's doing? Will he be able to travel home soon? I know he was wanting to get home soon because he wasn't sure his pa was still alive."Jimbo asked, without giving her time to answer.

"Hush up, Jimbo," Harry said, demanding that he stop talking. "Give Mary Grace a chance to answer one question at a time."

"Sorry, miss. I'm just so worried about Luke. He's been so good to me. I'd sure hate for him to be hurt badly."

"I know, Jimbo. The doctor thinks he'll be fine when he wakes up. He has a large bump on the back of his head, and I believe that is the reason he is unconscious. I placed a cold pack on the bump, which will help keep the swelling down."

"How did he fall on the staircase?" Harry asked.

Mary Grace shifted from one foot to another, feeling embarrassed that she was the reason Luke had fallen. "Luke and I argued. He said that I could not stay here in Denver alone, and I said I could, and I would. He said I had to go back to Crooked Creek on the stage in the morning." Her hands fidgeting to smooth the covers on Luke's bed. "I raced up the stairs and he followed.

He grabbed at me and well, I turned and kicked at him with my feet. He grabbed at my boots, and one of them came off in his hands. He lost his balance and tumbled down the staircase. Gosh, I was sure I had killed him."

"Surely that was an accident. Luke will understand when he wakes up," Jimbo said, but the expression on his face said otherwise.

"Does Luke think that he can make you leave Denver? We spoke about opening up a café together, and there's that empty restaurant on the corner of Main Street. A perfect place for a café," Harry said with hopeful eyes.

"I ain't going back home and have my pa use up all my hard-earned money on his so-called businesses. Oh, don't get me wrong. I'm going to set pa up better than he is already. I'm going to order better liquor for him to have in his saloon and pay for a decent cook. Even make some repairs to the stage depot and have a better stove placed in the room so the passengers won't freeze while waiting on the stage. Little things like that will improve the place, but I'm not giving him the money to do it. I plan to hire it all done from here."

Luke moaned and moved his legs into a different position. Mary Grace leaned over his face and spoke to him, but he gave no response. "At least he's moving some. That's a good sign." Mary Grace smiled for the first time since the two men came into the room.

"I can hardly wait to get started on our new café," Harry whispered and hobbled over to a comfortable bedroom chair.

"First thing, after Luke's leaves for his home, we'll go see Mr. Anderson and get him to help us bargain with the owner of the building. I want us to buy the building, not rent because I want it to be ours." Mary Grace was determined to be her own boss lady. "Can't wait to see what's upstairs. I heard there are rooms that we can use to live in above the café. Maybe there will be enough rooms for us all to have our own and if so, we can save money and be close to our business, too."

"We'll have to hire people to help us remodel the place," Jimbo whispered, not wanting to disturb Luke and have him overhear their plan.

"The first thing I want you to do is see the doctor here in

Denver. I'm going to go with you and see if he can fix you a better brace for your leg. I'm tired of seeing you hobble because your leg is rubbed raw."

Harry tipped his head back against the chair and looked skyward. "You're right, and I will go. I'm tired of hurting, too. It would be nice to help in front of the café and not have to hide out in the kitchen. I see how ladies look at me as I am hobbling past them."

"Oh, Harry," Mary Grace jumped down on the floor near him. "You are a special man, and everyone who knows you, leg or no leg, loves you. Please don't feel like you have to hide out."

Luke whimpered after he tried to turn over. He was trying to get up.

"Help me, Jimbo. Let's roll him over on his side."

Jimbo helped Mary Grace, and then told her to go outside while he helped Luke with his personal needs. She blushed and hurried down the hall to her room.

After the men left, Luke settled down and slept soundly. She pushed a comfortable chair over near the bed and cuddled up in it to rest while listening out for the man she loved.

# Chapter 16

After three days, Mary Grace was exhausted from lack of sleep. Luke would open his eyes and stare into space. She'd wave her palm in front of his eyes, but he didn't react. The doctor suggested that she get someone to help her bathe and shave him. It might make him feel better.

During the third evening after the doctor left, Mary Grace ordered some hot water, and she bathed Luke herself. She lathered up his shaving brush and gently dragged the razor over his face. As she placed a warm rag on his face, Luke looked at her. His eyes were clear, and he even managed a small grin.

"Well, hello," he said.

"Hello to you, too. How do you feel?" She removed the warm, damp cloth and placed it back in the pan of hot water. Mary Grace felt like jumping up and down, screaming with relief that Luke was back.

He nodded but said nothing, and his eyes followed her everywhere.

Mary Grace hurried over to the dresser and poured some soda water for Luke to rinse his mouth. "Here, swish this around in your mouth and spit. Your mouth will feel better."

Luke did as she asked, and she handed him a clean towel to wipe his mouth and chin. "Can I get you anything? You've been unconscious for nearly three days."

"Yes, I want something special. I want you to lie down on the bed beside me. I need to feel your sweetness, your warmth." He smiled at her, and she couldn't resist him.

Before Mary Grace knew what she was doing, she slipped off her slippers and crawled under the covers next to Luke's near-naked body. Her hair and face had to be a fright because she hadn't taken care of herself in three days.

He didn't seem to care as he kissed her forehead while kneading the back of her soft neck. Exhilaration flowed through her body, while feeling guilty for wanting him to do more. She wasn't sure what she wanted, but her heart beat swiftly, and she thought sure Luke could feel it through her clothes.

Luke moved slowly, moaning at the pain in his ribs. He winced and touched the bump on his head, but he kissed her lips tenderly.

His kisses surprised her. Passion awakened for the first time in her life. She had little experience with men, and she had never felt this warm sensation deep in her body.

He grasped her tighter, and she melted closer into his body. Her full breasts pressed up against his naked chest. He pushed her gently away. "Sweetheart, we have to stop or I'm going to do something we both regret. I'm only human." Beads of sweat popped out on his forehead. "Lord, have mercy on me. I want you so bad." He winced again as he moved away and rubbed his ribs. "Do you know what I am saying?"

"Yes, I want you, too. Please love me—like a woman?"

"Are you sure?" She nodded.

"Take off your clothes." She did what he asked without taking her eyes from his face.

He pulled her carefully onto his stomach until her face was under his chin and her breast brushed up against his hairy chest. He lifted her into position, grunting silently with pain from his ribs.

"Is this too much for you?" she asked.

"We'll go gently for both of us." He kissed her lips until he had fulfilled his passion. His breathing became heavy and her face was flooded with tears. Mary Grace wanted to scream to stop from the pain, but she soon relaxed. "Sorry," he said. "Are you okay?"

She nodded quickly, so he kissed her softly until their passion was spent.

"I feel like I've run a ten-mile race. How about you?"

"Like I've been split in half."

"I'm sorry."

"It was worth it," she whispered.

Afterward, the pain soon eased off, and words were unnecessary between them. Mary Grace started to sit up, but she saw the pleasure on his face. She settled down and laid her head beneath his jaw not wanting to leave him. This was how it should be between a husband and wife. She was thrilled that she was now Luke's woman.

\*\*\*

His chin rested on top of her head. She smelled so sweet and she felt so good in his arms. "My little bird, you were perfect. I know I hurt you, and I'm sorry." Luke held his side and sighed. "Ah, Mary Grace, you didn't disappoint me."

\*\*\*

Mary Grace was so thrilled to hear Luke's praise. She propped up on her elbow to peer into his eyes, but he had fallen back asleep.

The next morning, Mary Grace sat on the side of her bed and flexed muscles she hadn't used in a long time. She suppressed a groan, then tiptoed to the water closet to prepare herself for the day. Her face flushed at the thought of what they'd done. How would she look him in the eye again?

\*\*\*

Mary Grace's bedroom door was unlocked, so Luke knocked on the door and entered before she could invite him in. She was standing at the window looking down on the street. She turned to look at him.

"I managed to get my pants on, but I'll need help with these." He pointed at his boots and motioned for her to the chair. Afterward she stood and he took her in his arms. He began kissing her neck, but she pushed him away.

His hands slipped away, watching her circle the room, bending over and picking up the clothes that had been tossed on the floor.

Oh, how he enjoyed watching her. He'd hoped they could enjoy another little romp this morning, but he could tell that they had overdone their lovemaking last night. He slipped up behind her and kissed her on the neck.

"Please, Luke, I hurt too much to start something else."

"A hot soak in the tub will help," Luke said.

"I had a nice long bath this morning, and I'm not sorry one bit."

"I would feel terrible if you regretted our lovemaking last night."

"I'm very happy." She twisted around and kissed him firmly on the lips, catching him by surprise. "Should we wait until Pa arrives in Denver before we marry or, do you want to get married in Crooked Creek?"

\*\*\*

"What?" Luke smile quickly faded. He pushed her a little away from his chest. "I didn't plan at this time to get married. I'm sorry if you thought I'd changed my mind. I've got to go and check on my family; I'm not sure if pa is still alive, and I'm not sure my brother is living at home caring for my mama. I have no home of my own to take a wife to or anything to offer a woman except money. And to tell the truth, you don't need me for that." What an impossible situation, if not complicated, he found himself in.

Her expression changed from joy to disappointment. He reached for her, but she stood stiff, her eyes brimming with tears. She bit her lower lip but couldn't quell the quivering. She struggled the flow of tears that she fought to keep hidden. Her face said it all. She expected him to marry her.

Raising her hand to her face she said, "Luke, I can still feel your kisses on my lips, my body. You can't tell me you don't love me." She offered him a watery smile, waiting for his response.

"Oh, Sweetheart," Luke sighed, wishing he could change the situation. "I do have special feelings for you." He paced the room to regain his composure. "I'm sorry I made you cry. I can't believe that I misled you. Dammit, I'm a heel."

"Heel?" Mary Grace stared at the door. "That's the nicest name I could think to call you, but I'm a lady. Well, I was, until I lay down with you like a slut. If I didn't have money, I could work at any saloon since now I have experience."

"Hush that kind of talk about yourself." Luke glared at her. "You know I have strong feelings for you." Luke sighed. "But I have plans that I can't change at this time. The time for marriage is all wrong for me—now." Luke tried to take her hand, but she jerked away from him. "There's no way I can take a wife with me at this time." He rubbed his chest. "I don't know what lies ahead at my folks' place."

***

Mary Grace wanted to die, to bury the shame and disappointment. Instead, she raised her chin. "I'm a big girl and I can take care of myself. You go on your way and don't worry about me. I can see now that a future with you is impossible. I'm not a fool, even though I've acted like one."

"You didn't act the fool, but I did. I should have told you about my future plans before." Mary Grace scrubbed the tears from her face. "Listen, to me." He turned her softly around to make her face him. He placed both hands on her small shoulders. "Last night may not be over between us. You must promise to notify me if anything comes from our lovemaking. I will return, no matter what. I promise."

Quickly stepping away from Luke, she said louder than she intended, "Oh, that will be big of you." She shook her head and couldn't hold her temper any longer. "Get out of my life and stay out, boss man. If something happens because of *my mistake*, I'll take care of it."

Suddenly, Luke pulled Mary Grace into his arms and kissed her hard. When she tried to push him away, he shook her, while holding her tightly. "Mary Grace," Luke whispered in her ear. "We didn't make a mistake. We made love, and I'm sorry you misunderstood my intentions, but other than that, I am not sorry." He frowned. "Now pack your bags, and I'll help you get settled on the stagecoach so you can go home to your pa." He stormed out the door, and she heard the click of boots hurry down the stairs.

****

In less than an hour, Mary Grace sat on the stagecoach all ready to travel to Crooked Creek. Luke stood at the window of the coach and tried to talk to her, but she refused to make eye contact, and he felt ashamed of himself. He tried to talk to her again, but she gave him the silent treatment. With nothing to say, he climbed on his bay horse and took one of the reins of the two pack mules from Sam Wilson. They rode south out of town past the stagecoach.

***

Mary Grace leaned her head out the window, fighting to hold

her tears in check, and watched as Luke rode out of sight. She was so disgusted with herself. One thing for sure, she'd grown up fast when it came to men.

She yelled to Buck, a young driver, whom she'd known most of her life, to help her out of the coach and toss her two carpetbags down from the top.

"Aren't you traveling with us to Crooked Creek, Mary Grace?"

"No, not today. I changed my mind. Will you please see that my pa receives this small package? Please promise to give it to him personally. Here's a small tip for your trouble."

"Wow, Mary Grace, five dollars? I appreciate this. Let me know if I can do anything else for you." Buck rushed to the stagecoach and climbed back on the top. She watched him tuck her package under his seat for safety.

# Chapter 17

Mary Grace left her traveling bags in front of the stage depot. She asked a young boy to deliver them to the hotel. Hurrying upstairs to her room, she threw herself onto the bed and pounded her fist into a pillow. Luke had only been gone a few minutes out of her life, and she felt loneliness like she had never before. He was gone. How could she have grown so close to him, loved him, and given herself to him in such a short time? A few weeks' work, and then these last three weeks while waiting for their money. Three wonderful weeks. She rolled over on the bed and hugged the pillow, sniffing the scent of his bay rum shaving lotion and soap. She pressed her face into it while she cried herself to sleep.

Awakening the next morning, Mary Grace glanced around the room for Luke. She'd slept so hard she had forgotten for a few minutes that he'd left her. She rolled over on her back and studied the ceiling. As she watched two spiders on the rafters, she thought of her lovemaking with Luke. In spite of herself, she couldn't hold back a smile. She loved him so much. She said a prayer that he would return for her one day. But life goes on, and she had to get up and stop wallowing in self-pity.

After scrubbing the feel of Luke's arms from around her, she dressed and remembered that Jimbo and Harry wanted to open a café. A gold mine of a different kind, Harry had said.

After making sure her eyes were no longer red and puffy, Mary Grace met with Jimbo and Harry. Both men were surprised to learn that she was remaining in Denver and didn't leave with Luke. Mary Grace put on a pleasant face, and they discussed a plan to purchase the building on the corner of Main Street and turn it into a daily café for the working people of Denver.

After viewing the old diner with the previous owner and checking on the second floor of the building, they became more excited than ever. There were four large rooms upstairs. One had been converted into living quarters. Mary Grace and the two men bubbled over with excitement. They decided that Mary Grace would use the converted room, while Jimbo and Harry would each have a room to themselves. The corner room would be used for storage and supplies.

The three had an appointment with one of Mr. Anderson's assistant bankers, Josh Randall. A good-looking young man who looked like a model dressed in a dark suit. He invited the three customers into his office.

After much discussion, Mary Grace and her friends left to have lunch at one of the fancy restaurants in Denver. While enjoying the delicious food, Mary Grace took mental notes of the restaurant. She had no appetite, but she needed to celebrate her new future as an owner of a Denver café.

In less than three days, they stood in front of their new building, each with their own key. Laughter broke out among them as they carried their personal belongings into the empty, dirty building.

Mary Grace threw herself into making a new life for herself. She needed something to help her forget Luke. "We're going to have to have help in cleaning this place, then we can start making the needed repairs. Let's hire some of the local men off the street who don't have a regular job. It will help them out and we can get started right away," Mary Grace said, as she peered up and down the boardwalk at the men loitering on the street.

"I'll go to the dry goods store and get a bunch of brooms, mops, and buckets after I carry my things to my room. Which room do you want, Harry?" Jimbo asked.

"The one closest to the top of the stairs, if you don't mind," he replied.

Later that morning, Mary Grace hired five strong men and two youngsters who looked about fourteen. She hurried down to the

Marco Deli to purchase food to make sandwiches to feed her new workers. As she entered the deli, her eyes widened at the lovely artwork on the walls. There were many paintings of Italy. She took a deep breath and enjoyed the aroma of soup—onions, garlic, and other spices that she didn't recognize. The colorful deli's walls were painted a soft gold and the wood floors shone like glass.

She hurried over to the glass showcase and stared at all the choices, having no idea what the foods were.

***

The owner watched the pretty girl enter his shop. He had seen this lovely girl with the wealthy gold miner owner, Mr. Tyler. "Welcome to my deli, miss. My name is Marco, and this is my wife, Gianna. Are you the new owner of the café down the street?"

"Yes, my name is Mary Grace Winters, and I am one of the owners with two men. I am sure you'll meet them soon. This place smells wonderful."

"It's Mama's soup. She is cooking it very slowly. It is very good," he said and raised two fingers to his lips and kissed them.

"I will have to buy some for myself at another time, but today I want the makings for sandwiches. I have a bunch of hungry workers, and we are ready to start cooking in our kitchen."

"Yes, yes, we know. So, you need food to feed many. Let me suggest that you start with cheese." He held some yellow cheese up to show her and then offered pork roast, sliced turkey, and ham.

"Why don't you give me a little of all of that on the bottom tray. Add a lot of raisins to the basket because I have two boys helping me."

"Are the young boys your kin or the two boys who live at the orphanage?" Marco asked with a concerned look on his face as he sliced the meat.

Mary Grace thought for a moment. "I'm not sure where the boys live. Jimbo asked some men who were sitting around doing nothing if they would like to work. We're trying to clean the place so we can start making our repairs. Jimbo said the boys were young, but they were the first to volunteer to work." Mary Grace pondered Marco's question. "Do you think there will be a problem letting the boys work for us? They're eager to earn some money."

"The orphanage is a very bad place. The boys will have to

hide their money, or the man and woman who run the place will take it away from them."

"How do you know that, Mr. Marco?"

"Please, call me Marco. May I call you Mary Grace?" Marco smiled and wrapped more meat while Gianna gathered the items and placed them in a big basket.

"To answer your question, other boys have told me this. I told the authorities about how the children are treated, but they paid me no mind. So I told my wife we have to mind our own business, but that is a sad place for children to have to live." Marco totaled up her bill and she paid him.

"I'll return your basket tomorrow. I am sure I will be doing a lot of business with you." She gave the Italian couple a sweet smile and they nodded in return. Mary Grace's thoughts went to the two young boys and decided she'd better find out more about their background.

When she returned to the café, the front room was nearly unrecognizable. The men and boys had swept, scrubbed, and polished every inch of the room. One of the younger boys was wiping the glass windows dry.

"Oh my, I need to leave more often." Mary Grace whirled around and looked at the room and the smiling faces of the men. "I hope you're all hungry because I have a basketful of food to make sandwiches. After I put it all on the bar, please come and help yourselves." Mary Grace noticed that the men stood peering over her shoulder as she laid the sandwich items out. How long had it been since they'd eaten a good meal?

"I want to know how many of you are willing to work the rest of the week. I can pay you daily, or if you like, wait until the week is over. You just have to tell me what you want me to do."

The men prepared themselves a plate of food and ate in silence. Several ate like they'd not had food in days. This broke her heart, and she decided that once the café was open, she wouldn't turn anyone away hungry. Several of the men wanted their daily pay, but the boys didn't speak up about their money.

"Joe and Mike, how would you like your money, today or at the end of the week?" Mary Grace asked, mindful of what Mr. Marco had said about the man at the orphanage taking their money from them.

Neither one of the boys spoke. They stared at their threadbare shoes.

"Joe, is it true that the people who oversee the orphanage will take your money away from you and Mike if they know you have earned some?"

Joe jerked his head up and then glared at his friend, then at her. "How did you know that?"

"Mr. Marco, who owns the deli told me. If that is true, I will speak to that man about it. You earned your money, and you should be able to keep it and spend it on whatever you need."

"No," Both boys said in unison. The color drained from their dirty faces, and Mary Grace was sorry to have upset them.

"Fine." Mary Grace pondered the situation. "Why don't I keep the money for you in a safe place, and when you want some of it, I will give it to you. Tell the old man that you're only working for food. To prove it to him, you both can take a sandwich home." She smiled at them, and after shooting glances at each other, the boys finally smiled.

***

Early the next morning, Mr. Goodloe, the chief carpenter, and all of yesterday's workers showed up to work with a young handsome cowboy who had blond curls protruding from under his Stetson. He stood grinning behind Mr. Goodloe, while giving Mary Grace the once-over.

***

Tracy Taylor couldn't believe he was getting a chance to work for this beautiful girl. Clearing his throat to catch Mr. Goodloe's attention, he waited for an introduction.

"Oh, pardon me, Miss. I've hired a new man. This big strapping young man is Trace Taylor. As you can see he's tall and strong and he can swing a hammer. We need a man like him."

"Welcome, Mr. Taylor. Mr. Goodloe will have a paper for you to sign, so we can place you on our payroll. You will answer to him."

"Thank you, Miss?"

"You may call me Mary Grace. We don't stand on ceremony here."

"Please, call me Trace." He grinned, revealing his straight white teeth and deep dimples. His face was ruddy, like he'd spent many hours out in the sun.

Mary Grace couldn't stop herself from smiling at the handsome young man. "All right, Trace. Mr. Goodloe will get you started on a job this morning." She turned and walked into the clean kitchen.

Trace watched her hips sway side to side in the men's pants she wore until she disappeared out of the room.

Goodloe passed him a pair of leather gloves and a hammer. "Handsome young woman, Trace, but the way I hear it, she's already spoken for."

Later Mr. Goodloe and Mary Grace went over the layout of how they wanted the dining room to look while several men went to the lumberyard. Some of the others started breaking down walls and removing old appliances from the kitchen.

***

Mary Grace was down on her hands and knees scrubbing the front of the bar when she noticed a pair of shiny black boots standing near her head. She jumped up as fast as she could and looked into Mr. Anderson's assistant banker's handsome face. Flustered by being caught in a less than an ideal situation, Mary Grace felt her face flame with embarrassment. "Hello, again," Mary Grace commented, trying to adjust her hair with one hand while using the other to straighten her old brown shirt covered with a dirty long white apron.

"Hello to you, too." He said, offering her a bemused smile. "I'm sorry I didn't give you any warning that I was going to drop by. I was heading to the deli to get a sandwich for lunch and just thought—" He stared down at her apparel. "I just thought I would look inside to see how the remodeling was coming."

"Please, feel free to come by without an invitation anytime, Mr. Randall. Our repairs are coming along just fine. We are pleased with all of our workers. As you can see, we've made a lot of process. We hope to be open in a couple of weeks."

***

Josh Randall glanced around the room but made no comment. "I had another reason for dropping in." He smiled sweetly at her. "I was hoping to extend an invitation. I'd like it very much if you would dine with me tomorrow night." He stood with expectant eyes, waiting for Mary Grace to answer him. His father had insisted that he start his courtship with the little rich gal from the country as soon as possible. She was comely enough, and she seemed to be educated, but he really wasn't interested in any woman in this hick town. He had aspiration of traveling up north with one of his male school friends.

"Well," Mary Grace said after a long pause. "Yes, I will be happy to dine with you, Mr. Randall. Tomorrow night would be nice."

"Please call me Josh. I hope we will become friends, maybe very good friends," he said with a smile, but his heart wasn't in it.

\*\*\*

Trace Taylor watched the exchange and the whispering between his new boss lady and the dandy. He had met Mr. Fancy pants once before when he had business at the bank. For the life of him, he couldn't see what his new boss lady saw in that daisy.

# Chapter 18

Luke and Sam Wilson traveled for nearly two weeks and finally stopped at the fence that joined his folks' property. Many of the fence posts were leaning, and there were busted boards all along the fence row. Luke gave Sam a razor-thin smile. "We're almost home, Sam. This property line is where our north pasture begins. That is, if my folks still own the land."

"Hold up, boy.' Sam said, while trying to keep his hands from shaking. He'd given up drinking, but the shakes hadn't left him. "I see dust in the distance. A rider is coming our way." Sam lifted his old body into his stirrups and stared out over the horizon. "Keep your scattergun close."

Let's just see who it is."

A tall, thin man who wore a dark Stetson, leather vest, and heavy chaps over the front of his pants was cresting a small hillside. White foam flew from the horse's mouth, and on his chest and legs were signs that the man had rode his horse hard and fast. The man stopped within twenty feet of the men. Butch Tyler twisted his mouth into a sour expression. "Well, well, well. What brings you home after all this time?"

Before Luke could answer, his brother turned his horse around. "Come and see mama and then git. You aren't wanted here."

Luke placed his shotgun back in the scabbard. He didn't try to defend himself against his brother's verbal attack. Instead, he clasped his hands on his saddle horn and watched his brother head toward the sprawling white house that Luke remembered.

"That sure wasn't a warm welcome. Do you think the rest of your family will be happier to see you?" Sam moved his horse closer to Luke and gave him a sad frown.

"We'll see. I'm sure Butch will tell the others that I'm here." Luke looked at Sam with a deep, weighted sigh. "My mama will be happy to see me. Did you notice Butch didn't say for me to come see Mama and Pa? I pray that my pa's still here, alive. In the two letters that I received over the years from Mama, she had said that Pa wasn't well. But, Sam, I'm not going to be run off until I help them financially if no other way." Luke looked toward his home place and then turned toward Pine Hill. "I am going to give Mama time to digest that I've come home. I need to go to the bank in town, so let's go there first. Maybe I can find a nice gift to take to Mama."

Pine Hill wasn't the roaring town that he remembered when he was a young man. There were a few wagons and riders on the street, and ladies were strolling along the old, gray boardwalk. Most of the men stopped and stared at them and whispered to each other, probably wondering who the strangers were riding into their town.

It was past mid-morning before Luke finished his business with old Mr. Willard Jones, the owner of the bank. "Luke, sure glad you're home. Your family has had a real hard time. I'm told they're in deep debt with the businesses in town. They are behind with the taxes on their land. I have put off serving them foreclosure papers. You know, we have known each other for years, and with your pa sick and all . . . well, I will have to do it soon."

Luke was thrilled to hear that his pa was still alive. "Mr. Jones, how's my pa? I've only heard that he was sick." Luke asked softly.

"I haven't seen him in a long time, but I know he has recovered from the deathbed, if that is what you're asking."

Luke felt like he could breathe again. Swallowing and nodding at the old businessman, he said, "That's what I hoped to hear. Please pull up their tax records and I'll be back tomorrow to take care of them." Luke smiled as he reached out and shook Mr. Jones' hand.

"Fine boy, fine." Mr. Jones heaved up his baggy dress pants.

"I'll have the papers ready for you in the morning." He smiled and went back into his small office.

"Come on, Sam. We've got business to take care of. First, let's take our horses to the livery. We'll get them fed and watered and then I'll settle up with the owner. Afterwards, we'll go to the dry goods store."

"You think you brother is going to like you getting into his business? He acts like a bad hombre."

"He's only angry at me, but he'll have to get over it because I'm here to stay. I have already checked on the land that borders my folks' property. The deed should be ready for me to sign and pay for it. I'll take care of it tomorrow, too."

Luke stopped his horse in front of the double doors at the livery, and a handsome, barefooted lad wearing overalls that appeared too short raced out of the shadows of the barn into the sunlight. "Can I help you?" The youngster reached for Luke's reins.

"Is the owner here?" Luke looked around and didn't see anyone else.

"He's over at the café having lunch. I can help you, sir." The young boy adjusted his shoulder strap and pushed his dirty, floppy hat back out of his eyes.

"I bet you can. Our horses need feed and a good drink of water. How much do we owe you?"

"Oh, you'll pay my pa when he comes back."

"That's fine, son. Here's a little something for you for being so helpful." Luke flipped the young boy a shiny fifty-cent piece.

"Thanks. I ain't never had one of these for myself."

Sam laughed and caught up with Luke heading toward the dry good store.

\*\*\*

The bell over the door announced their entrance into Millers Dry Goods Store. The store smelled of fresh apples and straw brooms. Luke noticed a barrel of apples near the door and bundles of new brooms standing in the corner. A middle-aged woman who was fussing with the bun on the back of her head came rushing from behind the counter. "Well, if it isn't little Luke Tyler. How you doing, boy? Excuse me, I mean young man." She laughed and offered him a tight hug.

Sam couldn't hold back a grin. "Little Luke," said Sam under his breath."

Luke glared at Sam, daring him to repeat that remark. "Thanks, Mrs. Miller. It's good to be home."

"I bet your mama is thrilled to have her baby son home. I know she cried, bless her heart."

"I haven't been home yet. I had business at the bank, and I wanted to get mama a little something special," he said as he did a double-take around the store. "You sure have a lot of stuff, more than you had when I was younger."

"Oh, Luke, it's so good to have you back home. Now you listen to me for a minute. I know I should keep quiet, but I have to say what's on my mind." She leaned in close to him. "If you want to take your mama something special, you should get a wagon and take her what she needs and that's kitchen supplies. She hasn't been in here in several weeks. I know it, because my husband won't give your family any more credit."

"I am here to settle their account. Get it ready and I'll take you up on your suggestion. I'll take a barrel of flour, sugar, cornmeal, and anything else you know that will resupply her kitchen. I have money and I want her to have everything she needs. Give me a few hams, three dozen eggs, and a bag of potatoes, apples, and a bag of tobacco that my pa smokes."

"Mercy boy, did you rob a bank?"

"No madam, but I have done well and I have come home to help my folks." Clicking his fingers on the counter, he watched her mouth drop open. "I'll go rent a wagon to haul the supplies out to my folks. When do you think you'll have everything ready?"

She hugged him again. "God bless you, boy. I'll have everything ready for you in about thirty minutes." As she turned away, she suddenly stopped. "You know you said that you wanted to take your mama something special. She's been looking at some material in the back of my store. She needs a new dress for sure, but she couldn't afford anything."

"Do you have ready-made day dresses that might fit mama? Maybe bonnets to match."

"We sure do." Mrs. Miller beamed with joy.

"Throw in about five day dresses, ladies underthings—you know what I mean, and yards of that material, buttons, thread.

Everything she needs to make a nice Sunday dress."

"Lordy, you must have found a gold mine." Mrs. Miller laughed, walked behind the counter, and called Louis, her husband.

After renting a horse and wagon for the day and overnight, Luke and Sam stopped in the local café and had a satisfying lunch. "Boy, they can't cook like Mary Grace. She sure spoiled us with her good cooking," Sam commented and used his sleeve to wipe his mouth. Luke stared off into the distance, trying not to think about how much he missed her.

Once they were on the boardwalk, Luke removed his pocket watch and flipped it opened to check the time. It was time to walk over to the dry goods store and settle up his folks' account and pay for the supplies that he had purchased. He wanted to reach his folks' place before dark. "We'd best be on our way. We'll finish our tour of the town tomorrow."

Luke tied his horse to the back of the wagon and nodded at a few strangers as he headed home after many years. Sam climbed slowly onto his horse and rode beside Luke. The town people had plenty to talk about. They watched the young Luke Tyler, who had come home after many years, ride north out of town.

"Sam, this north pasture is the place where I first met Captain Johnson, a trail master of a large herd. It was because of him that I left home. I remembered he asked me how old I was.

"'I'm fifteen, sir,' I told him and sat taller in my saddle. After a few minutes he asked me if I would like to work for him as a ramrod. He needed more men to help him take his herd to Dallas, Texas." Luke continued with his story as they rode toward his home.

"'I have to ask my pa and if he says I can go with you, I would love it.' Well, later that afternoon, I kissed my mama's wet cheeks and told her I'd be home before she missed me."

Luke and Sam drove the wagon slowly down the long, fence-lined drive. Luke thought about his first days and nights on the trail. He missed his mama's good cooking and his soft bed, but he was being treated like a man. His older brother always treated him like a kid and ordered him around all the time. He made him do all the dirty jobs on the ranch and laughed at him when he got muddy or hurt himself.

Luke pulled up the reins, gazed into the blue sky, and spotted buzzards circling lazily overhead. Suddenly a bird dipped down low and then swooped up again. Several of the birds followed suit and repeated the maneuver. Whatever they were after must still be alive. Probably an animal, Luke thought, but it might not be. Sam nudged his horse into a trot and came upon a big boulder. He drove the wagon closer to Sam, who trained his shotgun at a red rag lying on the ground.

Suddenly a man shouted, "Come any closer and I'll blast you with my rifle."

"Hold on, fellow. We aren't going to hurt you," Luke explained. "We followed those buzzards overhead and found your hiding place."

"Come on around where I can see you. My leg is busted from the knee down to my foot. I need water badly, too. You got any you can spare?"

Luke jumped down from the wagon while Sam tied his horse and eased over to the boulders where the man sat leaning up against one. "You been out here long," Luke asked and passed the man his canteen.

He turned it up and drank thirstily, spilling water down his chin and neck. "That was good." Placing the canteen on his lap, he said, "thanks."

"Who are you?" Luke crouched forward to get a better look at the stranger. The man was in his mid-forties, had well-developed muscles, and a soft paunch around the middle.

"My name is Gerald Mitchell. I'm from Denver."

Sam stood back from the man and searched for the man's horse. "Where's your animal," Sam questioned.

"Those fools that jumped me took everything. My money, watch, hat, boots, and my fairly new horse and saddle. Last night, I won a big pot in the poker game, and they weren't happy. I rode out of town last night and camped about a mile from here. Left my campsite and headed this way. They were hiding behind these big rocks. They knew I wasn't dead, but they left me to die out here." He glanced at Luke and Sam. "Can you fellows take me to a doctor in town?"

"Today we're heading to my folks' place. It's about two miles from here. I'm sure my mama will help you and tomorrow we'll carry you back to town." Luke stood and looked down on the man.

"That's the best we can do."

"That's better than lying out here under this hot sun fighting off those buzzards." He lifted his arm for the men to help him off the ground.

The old cowboy's story had a ring of truth to it, so Luke and Sam loaded him onto the back of the supply wagon and headed home.

# Chapter 19

Luke stopped the horse and wagon several yards from the house as a little woman, dressed in a long, worn dress covered by a white apron, came running toward him. She waved her arms over her head with tears streaming down her wrinkled face. Luke placed the brake on the wagon, jumped down, and raced across the brown, dried grass in front of the house.

"Mama, oh my goodness. I have missed you so much." Luke whirled her small body around and around, while one of her boots slipped off her tiny foot. Sam moved over to the couple and picked up her boot. He held it while the mama and son reunited for the first time in years. Luke's eyes brimmed with tears, which made Sam smile.

Luke tipped his head back for a moment and closed his eyes as he held tightly to his mama's small frame. When he opened them, he saw his brother standing on the porch behind an old man in a wheelchair.

His mama had heard the front door close and she looked toward the porch. "Come, baby, and see your pa." She grabbed Luke's hand and led him over to stand in front of the porch.

"Hello, Pa." Luke noticed how old and fragile his pa appeared. The smile on his face brought joy into his heart, and he could tell he was happy to see him.

"Hi, boy. Glad you're finally home. Your mama missed you. Me, too."

Luke eased up to the porch, and before he could control

himself, he knelt down in front of the wheelchair and embraced his pa. He hugged and pulled him forward so he could wrap his arms around his fragile body. Tears slid down his face. "I'm so happy to be home."

Luke glanced back at his buddy. Sam stood watching the reunion between father and son from a safe distance. He took a red hanky out of his back pocket and wiped at his nose and eyes.

Luke's pa patted his son on the back and attempted to turn his wheels around and go back into the house. Butch stared down at Luke without any acknowledgement of his presence and took the handles of the old wooden wheelchair and reentered the house. Luke, Sam, and Mama watched the two enter the front door.

Luke cleared his throat and wiped his eyes with his clean white hanky. "Come, Mama. I want to introduce you to my friend, Sam Wilson. He came with me from Crooked Creek. While heading this way, Sam and I found a man out on the trail left for dead." Luke motioned to the cowboy lying in the back of their wagon. "His leg is hurt. Do you mind helping me care for his leg? I'll take him back into town tomorrow. I have to take this wagon and horse back to the livery anyway."

Mama glanced at the middle-aged cowboy who wore rumpled clothes with a musky smell. "Can you and your friend move him into the house, and I'll heat some water. He needs a good scrubbing and clean clothes before I can get too close to him."

"What about the bunkhouse? He will be fine out there."

"No, we haven't been using the bunkhouse. We have plenty of rooms in the house, so I don't want to hear any more about it. Move him into the room off from the kitchen, while I get him some of your pa's old trousers and a clean shirt."

\*\*\*

Once Gerald Mitchell was settled into a room, Mrs. Tyler instructed Sam to cut off his pants and scrub his hide with the bar of lye and hot water. When Sam had made the man presentable, she checked for broken bones and was happy that his leg had only been twisted but not broken. She wrapped the twisted leg from his knee to his ankle tight with white sheet rags. She gave him several large drinks of whiskey and told him to lie still and go to sleep. "I'll have some food for you after you rest." She didn't leave the room until she heard him snore.

\*\*\*

Luke stood near the room off from the kitchen observing Butch, who stood with his arms and ankles crossed, staring back at him. He'd not said a word to Luke.

"How is he, Mama?" Luke removed the sewing basket from her hands.

"His leg's not broken, thank goodness. He twisted it, but he should be fine in a couple weeks. I don't have any pain medicine, so I gave him a couple shots of whiskey to help him sleep. The doctor will help him better than I can."

"Thanks, Mama." He gave her a kiss on the cheek while Butch continued to glare at him. "Come outside the back door and see what I brought for the house. I need your help to tell me where you want everything to go."

She screamed when she saw what was in the wagon. "Oh Luke, how did you know that we were almost out of everything?"

Butch followed them out the back door and towered over her shoulder, then whipped around and stormed to the barn.

Sam carried a barrel of flour on his shoulder as Mrs. Tyler pointed for him to place it in the pantry. Luke carried the barrel of sugar and followed Sam. Soon the room was filled with the much-needed supplies to take care of the family for several weeks.

Luke took the three hams out to the smokehouse. It didn't resemble the building that he remembered. He opened the door to rats scurrying under his feet, causing him to almost drop the fresh meat. He laughed at himself and began to gather wood and pile it in the iron box.

Luke remembered back. As a young boy this was one of his daily jobs to keep a big wood supply so the fire would never go out. This room was to stay hot and help to cook the meat and protect it from wild animal. He hung the hams high on the hooks and closed the door.

Mama met him on the back porch with a big glass of cool water. "Luke, we owe the dry goods store so much that we can't have any more credit. How did you buy these supplies?"

"Mama, I was going to tell you and Pa later about how well I have done since I left home. I paid all of your debts in town. I will pay the back taxes tomorrow. I'm a rich man, and I came home to share my wealth with you. You and Pa can have anything you want. Oh, speaking of that, I have something just for you."

"For me? This food is everything I would pray for, son."

Luke headed to the wagon and returned with a paper package tied with brown cord.

"This is for me? My goodness." His mama looked into Luke's face with eyes brighter than the twinkling stars he had witnessed last night.

"Come, Mama, let's go back into the house. Do you think Pa is happy I'm home?" A wave of regret swept over him for staying away from home so long.

"Oh, son," his mama stopped and turned to look at him. "I'm sure he is. He's grieved for you, but whenever he mentioned your name, Butch got angry. Your brother has worked very hard to keep this place going. After your pa's health fell, well, it's been tough without being able to hire help."

"I'm here now and Sam is too. He's an old man, but believe me, he will be a great help. And company for Pa. He brought his old checker game with him." Luke grinned down at his mama and they both laughed.

"I'll get some scissors from my sewing basket." She hurried into the parlor, then returned, cut the cord, and unwrapped the paper from around the dresses and lovely material. "Oh, my, look, Luther," she cried, holding up two of her new dresses in her arms and rubbing the soft fabric against her cheek. "I've never had a store-bought dress before."

"They're lovely, and you deserve them," the old man said as he witnessed her smiles and tears. "You've worked your fingers to the bone, never complaining, and doing without to put food on the table." He rolled his chair toward Luke and patted his arm.

Luke quickly handed his pa a can of his favorite pipe tobacco. "You still smoke a pipe, Pa?"

"Sure do, boy, sure do. Thanks for the tobacco. I appreciate you remembering."

Luke ran his hand over his pa's shoulder and noticed his pa's head of cold black hair was thinning on top. He'd combed his hair over to the side to cover it. Would he lose his hair someday as well?

"Luther, there's five dresses and some unmentionables and lovely material. I'll make me a dress to wear to church. Luke, you'll take me to church soon?"

"Mama, 'I'll do whatever I can to make you happy. If you want to go to church, I'll even go with you."

\*\*\*

Butch stood in the doorway of the parlor and watched his folks gush over Luke's return with his wealthy gifts.

Luke motioned for Butch to come in and take a seat. He peered at his folks and then again at Butch. "Now that we are all together, I want to tell you about what I've done in town today and intend to do tomorrow."

His pa turned his chair, reached for his wife's hand, and motioned for Butch to sit down. Butch finally trailed into the parlor and flopped into an armchair.

"While I was away, I worked as a ramrod for years, gambled a lot, but this year I bought a gold mine from my new friend, Sam. The mine's near Crooked Creek, Colorado. I hired a crew of men to work the mine for me, and we were lucky and discovered a rich vein in the front of the cave.

"After working the mine for months, before we discovered gold, I notified a banker friend of mine in Denver. He brought two experts with him and they checked the mine over. After a few weeks, Mr. Anderson, my friend, and other stockholders of his bank, bought the mine from me. I received a sizeable amount of money that I divided with my ten men and my lady cook.

"Financially, we're all set for life. I left most of my money in the bank of Denver, but I can get my hands on it whenever I need some." He stared at his folks and Butch. They sat frozen, in disbelief for sure.

"I've come home to help with the ranch and I'm buying the property next door—150 acres. Butch and I can discuss how we'll handle the new herd of cattle that we'll buy."

"Listen, sonny boy," Butch leaped to his feet. "I ain't taking no orders from you. I don't care how much money you have. This place will be mine and mine alone after this old man—"

"Butch, sit down and shut up." It was all Luke could do not to hit his big brother in the mouth.

"Butch, please sit down and listen. Luke came home, his home, too. He wants to share with us his good fortune, not take over." Pa hung his head low, shaking his head.

Mama wiped tears from her eyes and stared at her husband whose body was winning the battle over his spirit, her eyes full of love and concern.

Hesitating before he continued, Luke gave her a reassuring grin. "As I was saying, today I cleared up our accounts at the livery and dry goods store. Tomorrow I'll pay the property taxes in arrears. Mr. Jones said he was going to have to foreclose on the property, but he was holding off because Pa is sick. He's been a good friend. I'll take care of them while I'm at the bank. I'll be signing the papers for my new home and property next door, too."

"So, you're going to move next door?" Butch scowled. "Have you even seen the house?" Before Luke could give him an answer, he laughed. "That place is run over with rats and every four-legged creatures that can get inside. It's been empty for two years."

"Thanks for the information, Butch. My plans are to help with whatever you feel needs to be done here first, and then I'll go over and repair my new place. Sam and I will help you, but I'd like to repair the bunkhouse and make it livable so we can hire two or three men to live here and help keep this place going. I'll open a bank account for you to draw money whenever you need it and have money here in the house for you to use for daily expenses."

"What are you doing? Just ride around giving your money away, like you're a big, rich man," Butch sneered.

"I don't feel like I am a bigwig, but I shared my gold mine money with my workers who were practically strangers to me. I believe I can share with my only brother and my folks. If you don't want to take any of the money for yourself, that's totally up to you. I want you to have whatever you need to run this place for Mama and Pa, but I don't want to oversee two ranches. I plan to settle down one day with a wife and children."

"Oh, baby, do you have a gal?" Mama stood quickly and rushed over to him.

"No, Mama, not right now but soon, I hope."

"Good luck, sonny boy. Slim pickings for gals in Pine Hill." Butch stood and walked upstairs to his room.

Mama watched the sad, angry man leave the room. "Oh, Luke, he'll come around. Butch has his pride. He's worked hard to keep this place going, but he'll be happy to have the load of bills off his back."

Sam came into the parlor and told Mrs. Tyler that old Mitchell was awake and hungry. "I'd be glad to prepare him something if I can use your kitchen."

"Mercy no, my good man. I'll finish with dinner in just a little while. You can take him milk and a biscuit with jam. That should hold him until I place supper on the table. With all the supplies you brought home, I want to bake a big peach cobbler. We all need a treat to help celebrate Luke's return."

# Chapter 20

The food and drink lacked flavor in Mary Grace's estimation. Or maybe it was the company. She sat across from Josh Randall. He'd stopped by the café and walked Mary Grace the few blocks to the fancy restaurant, Anna Belle's. Two heavy dark oak doors with oval glass opened into a room with lovely mirrors on every wall, which gave the room a spacious look.

The staff of men were dressed in penguin suits with stiff white shirts and black bow ties. The pretty servers, their hair pulled back in tight buns, were dressed in long black dresses covered with full white aprons. The ladies looked flushed and uncomfortable.

Mary Grace couldn't believe how under-dressed she felt sitting across from Josh. He wore a dark green suit jacket with a red silk scarf around his neck tucked into his vest. A gold pocket watch with a chain hung across the vest from one small pocket to another. He'd removed his top hat when they entered the restaurant.

Josh must have noticed that Mary Grace was only moving her food around her painted plate. "What's wrong with the meal, dear? Is it not to your taste?"

It wasn't the food. She wanted to tell him she held a big ache in her heart for someone else but didn't think he would appreciate the truth. Josh was trying to court her, but she didn't have any interest in getting mixed up with another man, not now anyway. "I'm sorry, Mr. Randall."

"Josh, Mary Grace, Josh." He swallowed and dabbed each

side of his mouth with his crisp white napkin. "I'm not my father. I'd hoped that you could call me by my given name. I already call you Mary Grace." He smiled and reached for her hand.

Mary Grace forced a laugh. "I will soon, but we haven't known each other very long. Please don't rush me."

\*\*\*

Josh really wanted to reach across the table and place his fingers around her scrawny neck and squeeze the breath out of her. He hated having to follow his father's order and court this little hillbilly. The sooner he got her in his clutches, the sooner he could get her money and leave this god-forsaken country. "How is your café coming along, sweetheart?" he asked, hoping to make her think he had a sincere interest in her new business.

"Oh, Mr. Randall, I hope to be able to have a grand opening in two weeks. We're going to do a small opening in a few days and hope to work out any problems. We'll be hiring waiters, cooks, hostesses, and a cleanup crew." Mary Grace's eyes sparkled with excitement. "Oh, listen to me. I sound like a silly goose going on and on, but I can't help it." She giggled a little as she looked around. "I can tell you now that the men and women who work for me will not be wearing clothes that make them miserable."

"You didn't eat very much. Would you care for some dessert? They have several to choose from." He prayed she would refuse, and his prayer was answered. Josh signaled the waiter over and signed the check. "I have an account here," he said and placed a small tip in the center of the tray. He stood and helped Mary Grace with her chair. "Come dear, let's get out of this warm restaurant and enjoy a cool walk back to your place." Josh walked Mary Grace to the door of her café but refused to come in and see what the workers had accomplished. He said he'd see her the next day, grabbed her right hand, and kissed the back of it.

\*\*\*

His cold, wet lips brushed her soft skin and when he walked away, she wiped it dry on the side of her skirt. That's one cold-hearted man and a cheapskate too, she thought as she remembered the tip he had left.

She entered the front of her new café. "Good evening, Jimbo and Harry. This place is looking wonderful."

Jimbo and Harry stopped drying water glasses that sat on the bar.

"I had dinner at Anna Belle's tonight. The food needs more spices, but the service was great. The people who work there have to be miserable in that steamy place with all the clothes they're forced to wear."

"Speaking of waiters, we need to begin hiring people and training them," Harry said.

"Jimbo, we need to make signs to place around Denver. I want a sign posted near Anna Belle's because we may get some of her trained workers to come and work for us. Also, please post signs near the edge of town. There are women who live down there who work hard for others. Maybe some of them will want to work for us. We need several good cooks. I don't want any lazy women or men."

A few days later, Mary Grace headed to the edge of town, looking for a dressmaker that she had been told could sew and make white aprons for her new waitresses at the café. She glanced at the slip of paper with the address, then noticed a young girl reading the advertisement that Jimbo had tacked on the wall. The girl was attractive, slim, but dressed in rags. Her hair was neatly pulled back into a bun, but her skirt had been patched in several places. Mary Grace approached her. "Hello," Mary Grace said.

The young girl jumped and spun around, then returned Mary Grace's smile. "Hello," she replied and sidestepped her.

"Wait," Mary Grace called to her. "Are you interested in a job?"

"I would love a job, madam, but no one will hire me." She bit down on her lower lip.

"Shoot, girl. You don't have to call me madam. I'm not much older than you. But why wouldn't anyone hire you?" Mary Grace asked. She stood silently waiting for the girl to give her an answer.

The young girl sighed. "I lived at the orphanage until today, but I've aged out. So, I need to find myself a new place to live, but I can't do that until I have a job and earn money."

"Wait a minute. You had to move out of the orphanage today?"

"Mr. Cotton said the orphanage is running out of money and can only afford to take care of the younger children, so the older ones have to leave and take care of themselves."

"You're telling me that young people like you who have no jobs or money have been tossed out into the street to struggle to survive on their own?"

"Yes, madam, sorry. Yes, that's what I mean."

"I can't believe this is happening." Mary Grace paced the boardwalk in front of the young girl. Suddenly, Mary Grace stopped walking and took the young girl's elbow. "What's your name?"

"Lucy, Lucy Smitten."

"Well, Lucy, I came down to this part of town looking for a seamstress. Do you know where her shop is located?"

"Yes, it's a few doors from here. Mrs. Gordon is her name. I have already asked her for a job, but she said she didn't have enough business to hire anyone."

"I need her to sew for me, but why don't you come and stay with me, and if you like, maybe you can work at my new café. We'll talk more about your situation over supper."

Lucy grabbed her cloth bag. "Oh, thank you, miss."

Back at the cafe, Mary Grace introduced Lucy to Jimbo and Harry and allowed her to tell them about her living situation.

"I have a big room, and Lucy can bunk in with me. We can't allow a young girl to live on the street."

"How many other children your age were put out of the orphanage?" Harry asked.

"Joe and Mike, the two boys who are working for Mr. Goodloe, will have to find a place to live. At least, they have a job." Lucy sighed. "There are about three girls and maybe three more young boys. Many of the boys my age walked away from the orphanage when they felt they were old enough to care for themselves rather than live under all the house rules. There are many younger children who need my help every day. It breaks my heart that I had to leave them this morning. The little ones were crying and begging me not to go away, but Mrs. Cotton practically pushed us all out the door like we were bags of trash."

"Do you know where Mike and Joe will spend the night?" Jimbo stood. "I had no idea when they finished work today that they had no place to sleep. I'm going to look for the boys before something happens to them."

"I thought the boys were only about fourteen, but I guess I was wrong," Mary Grace said. "Yes, please, Jimbo, go and search for them and bring them back here. We have to help some of these young people."

***

It was late into the night before Jimbo discovered the two young boys. They had climbed into the hayloft of the livery near the end of town. Once Jimbo told them they could come and stay at the café, they hurried after him. He bunked them on the floor in his room. Harry wouldn't care.

## Chapter 21

Early the next morning, Mary Grace sat in the First Bank of Denver across from the bank president. "I want to know about the problem the city's orphanage is having with money. Did you know that yesterday the people who oversee those children put about a dozen young people on the street without proper lodging, funds, or jobs?"

"I heard that they were having problems, but no one in authority has come to me for assistance. Why did they move the children out onto the street, as you say?"

"I was told that they couldn't afford to feed the older children, so they threw them out like trash. They need all the money they have to care for the younger children." Mary Grace stormed to her feet. "I won't have this. I tell you now there must be something done. I was raised by my father only, and I lived over a café and stage depot, but at least I had food and clothing. I never had to live on the street or go hungry, and by George, I am not going to allow this to happen to children when I know about it. Did you know that when the older boys make extra money, that overseer, Joseph, takes it away from them? That's wrong. He shouldn't be allowed to get away with doing that."

"Miss Winters, I can't do anything to help them unless someone from the mayor's office comes to me and requests a loan. I can't just give them my stockholders' money."

"Well, I have money, and I will see that those children will be cared for properly. I will go see the mayor right away. Thank you for hearing me out." Mary Grace strode out and marched across the busy street to the mayor of Denver's office.

\*\*\*

Mr. Randall watched as Mary Grace hurried across the street to the mayor's office. That young tart was going to squander her money on those orphan brats. Well, he would make sure Josh, his stupid son, hurried his courting and got wedded to Miss Winters.

\*\*\*

With clenched fists, Mary Grace confronted the receptionist at the first desk. "I want to see the mayor right this minute, please." She could see two men through a window in the mayor's office.

"I'm sorry, miss. He's not in today," The lady said, glancing at the office.

"Looks like he just arrived, but don't worry about introducing me. I'll do it myself." Mary Grace hurried to the office door and opened it before the girl could stop her.

"Good day, gentlemen. Mayor?" Mary Grace said, not sure which man was the mayor.

"Yes, may I ask what is so important that brought on this rude interruption of my meeting?"

"Yes, sir, you may. My name is Mary Grace Winters, and there is a very important matter I must discuss with you, now, as a matter-of-fact. It can't wait." She forced herself to look directly into the unsure mayor's eyes.

\*\*\*

The mayor couldn't believe that this young woman had come to his office. He had planned to go by her new café and welcome her to the city. It was rumored that she was a lovely young woman who was very rich because she had been part of the Gypsy Gold Mine.

"Mr. Mills," the mayor swallowed hard and smiled at the man in his office. "Would you mind coming back tomorrow, and we'll continue our discussion then? I'll use this afternoon to look over your account." He placed his hand across the back of the man and showed him the door. The mayor turned and gave Mary Grace a hard stare. "Well, now, Miss Winters, it's nice to finally meet you. I had planned to stop by your new business and welcome you to the city of Denver." Licking his lips he asked, "Now what is so important that you couldn't wait for an appointment?"

"Children, Mr. Mayor, children. Are you aware that the orphanage is turning young boys and girls out onto the street without money, jobs, or lodging?"

"Well, I heard that the orphanage was having difficulty with their finances. But, no one told me that the Cotton's, Mary and Joseph, were having that kind of urgent problems. When did they start putting the children out?"

"Yesterday. I happened to walk upon a young girl who was reading my advertisement for work. One of my friends went out last night and found two of the younger boys, only fourteen, hiding in a livery's hayloft. They had waited until the owner had closed up the place before they snuck inside. Children can't live like that, Mr. Mayor."

"Of course not. I agree with you, but what can I do?" He motioned for her to sit down, but she ignored his suggestion. He sat down and glanced at papers on his desk.

"You are the mayor, aren't you? Don't you have any say-so about what happens in your town?"

Tilting his head to the ceiling, he let out a heavy sigh. "Not really, Miss Winters. The orphanage funds come from charities. Times are hard now, even with the war being over for several years. Our churches have always helped, but a couple of the smaller churches have closed their doors and the preachers have moved on."

"So, you are saying that the children's home depends on charity of the people. Well, Mr. Mayor, I have money and I will make a donation to the city to help run the home, but I have a condition."

He wasn't surprised that this young girl would give some money, but he couldn't allow her to take over the place. Avoiding eye contact with her, he asked, "And what might that condition be?"

"I want a nice couple who loves children and who really cares about their futures. Mr. Cotton and his wife are not what I would call loving, caring people. I was told that he takes money away from the young boys who work for extra funds just to be able to buy shoes. This is wrong and you know it. If they are not replaced, I will do something else with my money."

"Like what?" His eyebrows furrowed, and he bit the inside of his mouth. "I don't have the authority to fire that couple."

"Who does?" Bright red spots popped out on her cheeks.

The mayor feigned interest in something else on his desk in order to gain control of this situation. "I'll have to speak with the priest at the Catholic church and let him know what's going on. I'm sure he'll be happy to talk to you soon."

"You do that. You tell him I can donate enough money to help with proper clothes, enough food, and wood for the fireplaces. I don't want to hear about young people who can help care for the younger children being tossed onto the streets."

"Thank you for coming and seeing me today, Miss Winters. I know where I can reach you. I will be in touch as soon as possible."

***

Mr. Randall was parading up and down in front of his son, Josh. "Now you listen to me, boy. That young woman wants to withdraw some of her money and help with the orphanage. I'm sure it will take several thousand to get the children's home supplied with food and clothes for those brats, and a new couple who will draw a salary and have a place to live. You need to get busy and marry that gal. We can't allow her to squander away all her money. People in Denver don't care about that orphanage. If they did, they would be donating the money that is needed to run a big place like that."

"Listen, father. I'm doing all I can to get her to like me. We take long walks, dine at the nicest restaurants, and I take her flowers. I can't ask her to marry me so soon. Mary Grace is a smart girl. She'd know that I am only after her money."

"I don't care what you do or how you do it. Make her feel obligated to you someway. Use your head, boy. Do something and make her realize that she must marry you." Mr. Randall chose a cigar out of a mahogany wood box that sat on his desk. "Now, get out of here and start romancing that little gal."

Josh Randall placed his hat on his head and stormed out of the bank. He went straight to the St. James Hotel and hurried up the staircase until he came to room eight. He didn't even bother to knock.

"What the hell, Josh. Can you even have the courtesy to knock before you come barging in my room like a drunken dock hand. I may not even be dressed."

"Forgive me, Mitch, but I'm furious." He threw himself on the bed and watched his friend standing in front of a mirror stroking his hair and then running a comb through it.

"You must have had a meeting with your old man. What does he want you to do now? Kill someone?" Mitch continued fussing with his appearance. He glanced in the mirror again and pushed out his lips like a fish.

"No, he wants me to hurry and marry Mary Grace. My old man is afraid she's going to fritter her money away before he can gets his hands on it – legally anyway."

"You told me that she's rich. Just how rich is she that she could spend all her money right here in Denver?"

"He mentions something near one hundred thousand dollars. Shoot fire, that enough money to last a lifetime. Mary Grace wants to make a donation to the orphanage to help the poor children. You would think she wanted to give them all of her money. She's about ready to open a gold mine with that new café on Main Street. Everyone will want to eat there because it's going to be for the working-class people, not the elite of Denver."

"I agree with you about the café. The local people don't have any place but the deli or the park. I'm sure even if she sells the café, she'll get all her investment back or more."

"Listen, Mitch. I want you and me to get out of this town. I want to escape from under my father's thumbnail. That old man makes me so angry. Sometimes I dream of choking the life out of him," he said, speaking through his teeth. He took a deep breath and slowly let it out as he rolled his shoulders.

"Oh, Josh, you shouldn't allow your father to get under your skin. We can leave whenever you decide. I'm ready anytime you say. I can't wait to get on the train and head to New York City." He walked over to Josh, rubbed his hand across his shoulders, and brushed a soft hanky across his sweaty forehead.

## Chapter 22

After several days of helping Butch repair the main fence and make the bunkhouse livable, Luke saddled his horse and told Sam that he was ready to go and have a look at his new house.

"Let's ride over and see how many repairs I need to make on the old place. It was a showplace the last time I saw it, but to hear Butch, it's fallen down." To Luke, it didn't matter what condition the place was in. He was thankful that he had money to make it look like it once did before he left home. "This is where my land starts," Luke said, pulling the reins of his horse to a stop. He pointed to the open fields covered in weeds. A few fields had been plowed under but left uncultivated.

The old prospector's eyes grew as they continued toward the structure. The sight of the house caused Luke's heart to jump a beat. As a young boy, he always thought that this must be what heaven looked like. But now, the big old white colonial house was covered with vines, dwarfed by a thicket of oak trees that lined the shaded lane leading up to it. "Wonder why the yanks didn't burn this house to the ground like they did so many others?" Sam asked, shifting in his saddle.

"The story I got from Mr. Jones at the bank was that Mrs. Wainwright had a brother who was a colonel in the Yankee Army, and when the Yankees rode up, she fell on her knees and pleaded with the men. Told them to take whatever that wanted, inside and out of the house, but pleaded with them not to burn her brother's home. They carried off the cattle, chickens, emptied the smokehouse and took all the quilts from the house, but they rode away without burning anything," Luke said, shaking his head.

"That's some story," Sam said.

Luke looked down the long driveway that had been beautifully maintained with pink and red flowered bushes between the shady oak trees, but today the bushes were covered in vines and briars, and dead limbs hung low to the ground. As they approached the mansion, Luke's heart dropped. The house still stood, but it was in grave condition. He always thought it to be a grand lady of a home. Mrs. Wainwright's lovely boxwoods were also overrun with choking vines. Luke was appalled at the place's disgraceful state. It showed years of neglect.

They stepped down from their horses and slowly climbed up the marble steps.

Luke ran his boot across the step and was pleased that the marble was intact. He looked at the graceful white columns with chips of white paint flaking off, tall and sturdy and reaching the second floor. He walked onto the porch and strolled over to a tall window, cupped his hand over his eyes, and tried to peer inside. The heavy dark drapes were pulled closed, so he tried the doorknob. It was locked, so he removed the key from his vest pocket.

\*\*\*

Sam had walked around the back of the house and found the door unlocked. He entered the kitchen and heard Luke coming in the front. The two men glanced at each other and smiled. They both stared at the big staircase that led to the second floor.

"Mercy, Luke," Sam said, "this is a beautiful old house. A place I have only heard about."

The two men walked through the large, dusty rooms. They headed through the large kitchen out to the backyard and surveyed the ice house, smoke house, livery, stables, bunkhouse, and barn. Standing off to the side about a hundred yards away was a fairly new structure. The two-story building had six windows across the first floor and across the top with two large wooden doors in the front.

"I don't remember that building being on the property before. Wonder what it was used for," Luke said.

"Reminds me of an old schoolhouse," Sam replied with a grin.

"I'll look it over after I check out the inside of the house more closely." Luke entered the parlor and looked at the hand-carved staircase. As a child, he dreamed of sliding down the lovely bannister. He caught a whiff of bee's wax that was used to make the pine floors shine like glass. Luke turned and walked over to the huge stone fireplace that stood in the middle of the room where two broken chairs lay in front of it. "This is still a lovely home. I need to hire some women to come and clean it for me. After I look at that big building out back, I'll ride into town and see if I can hire some people to start cleaning this place for me. Do you want to ride with me or go back to play checkers with Pa?"

"I'll go with you. I want to get a few more pairs of britches for myself, and you need to purchase Gerald some more clothes, too. I overheard him talking to Butch about staying on and working for him."

After the two traveled a few miles out of town, they came upon a wagon parked off the road. A young man in his early twenties and a middle-aged woman were standing near a campfire. Luke judged the woman to be the man's mother. He called out to them, "May we come into your camp area?"

The strangers didn't reply, but the young man waved his rifle toward them to get down. Sam and Luke slowly walked to the fire and noticed a small, skinned squirrel on a spit. Slim pickings for dinner.

"Where you folks headed?" Luke asked.

The woman glanced at her son and finally spoke, "We ain't got no place to go, mister. Our wagon wheel is broken, but after we change it, we got to decide which way to go. We've traveled from Denver, Colorado, after I lost my job as a cook there."

"Mama, hush. I'm going to take care of you." The young man glared at the strangers.

The older woman looked at her son and smiled. "I know, boy, but we must have help." She turned to Luke. "Can you help us with our wheel?"

"May I ask why you lost your job as a cook?"

"The owner and many of the customers got sick from some of the food, and the café had to close down."

Sam frowned and scratched his head. "What was wrong with the food that made people sick?"

"They think it might have been the beef, but since I didn't eat any of it, well, some people felt that I might have done something."

"Did everyone who worked at the place get ill?" Luke asked.

"No, not everyone. Jimbo didn't get sick."

"Jimbo? Did he work at the café?" Luke knew that there couldn't be many Jimbos who worked as a cook.

"He did, but he was one of the owners of the place. Nice man. He begged me not to leave, but I couldn't work there with people thinking I had done something to cause the beef to be tainted." She hung her head down and took the tail of her apron and wiped her eyes.

Luke was proud that Jimbo and Harry had bought a café, but he was sorry that something like feeding people bad beef had happened. He was going to have to write him a letter to get more details.

Sam mumbled to Luke, "Are you thinking the same thing I am? We sure could use a good cook."

"Yep, I was thinking the same thing. I hate cooking."

Sam nodded for Luke to say something to the woman and her son.

"My name is Luke Tyler, and this is my friend, Sam Wilson."

"My name is Mrs. Roberta Tiller and this is my son, Billy."

"Bill, Mama. My name is Bill."

"I was on my way to town to hire some women and strong men to help me get my new property and house back in shape. Would you both like to work for me? I need a cook and a strong back to help with the jobs around the house. Before you answer, you'll have a safe place to live and plenty of food to eat. I don't know how much I'm going to pay my new employees, but it will be a fair wage." Luke looked at the two people who stared at him with eyes widened. "If you aren't happy with my place, you can leave anytime with no hard feelings."

"Oh, son, God has heard my prayers." She covered her face with folded hands and cried. Then she looked up. "I'm a good cook. I never fed anyone food that I knew was bad."

"Mama, these men are strangers to us. I'm not sure we should just ride off with them."

"Son, these men aren't strangers—they're angels."

# THE GAMBLE

\*\*\*

After helping the young man change his wheel, Luke gave them directions to his new place. He told them to go out to the big white building and park their wagon behind it. He and Sam would be back before dark with some food and hopefully new hired hands to follow.

Luke's first stop was to meet and have a talk with the local doctor about his pa's condition. Something kept nagging at him because his pa would say that his legs pained him and he needed to get back in bed. Mama had mentioned that pa had no feelings in his legs. After a nice long consultation with Doctor Joseph Pike, he asked him to make a house call the next day to give his pa an examination. He was sure Pa would be angry, but he wanted to make sure that there wasn't something that may have been overlooked.

Luke's next stop was at the dry good store, and he asked if he had any mail. There was a wrinkled letter from Jimbo, and he could hardly wait to read it, but he shoved it in his pocket until later. He talked to Mrs. Miller about hiring some women to help him clean his house. Said that he was willing to pay them a good day's pay and feed them while they were working. If they wanted to camp out at his place, they were welcome to do that.

An attractive young woman who stood in the corner of the store was listening to Luke's offer to pay someone to clean his house. "Mr.," she said, pushing her little girl behind her back. "I need a job. I am willing to work hard and help as long as you need me. I can cook, wash, sew, scrub, whatever you need done." She was swaying from side to side.

"Now, Mrs. Miller, if you can find me about a half dozen young women like this one, I would be very happy." He turned to the young woman. "You're hired. When can you start?"

She smiled and her cheeks glowed a bright pink. "My name is Patricia Thompson, and this is my daughter, Nellie, who's eight. We might be late if you live very far from town because I don't have a horse or wagon."

"Oh, no, madam, you won't have to walk to my place. I'll hire a wagon to take you and anyone else who needs a ride to my place. It's a good five miles from town, and it's not safe for a woman and child to be walking alone on the isolated trail."

"Oh, thank you, mister. We'll run and get our belongings and meet you back in front of the store in just a few minutes." She took her daughter's hand and ran off before Luke could tell her to take her time.

Luke asked Mrs. Miller if she would ask around for him and post a note on the wall advertising for help. "I need men who are willing to do day work and a few men who would like to ramrod for me. My brother and I will be going to Dallas to purchase a herd this spring. I have a bunkhouse and another large building on my property. Have you ever been to the old Wainwright house? The reason I ask is I was wondering what the big building was used for."

"Before the war, Mr. Wainwright had a lot of children on his place. He and his wife were both teachers before they came here. But, once it wasn't safe for his children to travel into town to go to school, he built his own. We were told that he even taught his slaves' children, too."

"I'm going to use the building for something, but I'm not sure it will be a schoolhouse. Oh, I almost forgot. I have this long list of supplies. Can you fill that for me in about an hour's time? We're going to have something to eat and be back to do some clothes-shopping before we leave."

"Sure thing." Mrs. Miller called her husband as Luke and Sam walked out onto the boardwalk. Sam nearly stumbled over an old man who was rocking in an old wobbly chair.

"Hey, young man," the older man called in a hoarse voice. "I heard that you need workers. Well, I can work and I need a job." He pointed a shaky finger at Luke. "I'm old, but I can work, and I could sure use a place to get out of this cold weather."

Luke was surprised at the wiry man's grit. He smiled at the old man who looked like he had not had a good meal in weeks. His pants were covered with holes and one of his boots was held together by wire. The fellow had to have seen better days. "Where do you live now?"

"Nowhere, sonny. That old hag in the store will let me sit here for a while, but she'll come out with her broom and sweep me off her porch."

"When was the last time you have had a good meal?" Luke remembered the day he had come upon Sam at his gold mine. He'd had an injured arm and was not able to get up for several days

"Don't remember, but I don't take handouts."

"Get up and come with us. My name is Luk,e and this is Sam. Let's have a bite of lunch and talk about a job you might be able to do for me."

Sam jerked his head up and shook his head. "Luke, what are you doing?" he whispered "This old man can't really do much. Besides, who's going to cook for all these people?"

"The women will cook. They have to eat, too." Luke patted Sam on the back and headed toward the café. "Look. I cannot let people who are down on their luck go hungry when they are willing to work. Didn't you hear that old fellow? He isn't asking for a handout. These people want jobs."

As the trio walked to the café, they ran into the young woman, Patricia, and her daughter, Nellie. "Mrs. Thompson, Nellie, this old fellow is—" Luke suddenly remembered he'd forgotten to ask the man's name.

He limped up beside Mrs. Thompson and introduce himself. "Madam, my name is Arthur Turnbull," he said and attempted to bow from his waist.

Mrs. Thompson smiled and introduced her young daughter to the man. He smiled.

"Mrs. Thompson, we're going to have lunch. Please join us and then we'll get a wagon and our supplies and head to my home." Luke said, laughing at the expression on Sam's face.

Hours later, Luke took his newly hired employees to his new home. They were surprised to find that they would be working to repair a lovely colonial mansion.

The women quickly swept the place and organized the kitchen supplies in a corner until they could clean the room. The men went to the bunkhouse and settled their gear on the bunkbeds, then turned their horses out into the corral.

Luke asked the ladies to prepare sandwiches for supper. "Tomorrow will be soon enough to begin work," he said. He ambled to the front porch, sat on the marble steps, and removed the letter he'd received from Jimbo. He pulled his sheepskin-lined jacket up around his ears while taking the paper from his pocket. The envelope was wrinkled, and the pencil script was nearly wiped off. *The note must be weeks old.* His hands shook as he ripped open the envelope. He didn't realize how happy he was to hear from Jimbo, but sometimes letters weren't always good news. Once open, Luke took a breath and begin to read.

*Dear Mr. Luke,*

*Harry and me are doing okay. We have been working hard to open our new café. Mary Grace too. We want you to come back to Denver and see it. Mary Grace is helping the poor children of the city. She got two men sniffing after her, but Harry and me don't like neither one of them. Hope you will come see us.*

*Jimbo*

Luke couldn't believe what Jimbo had written. "Dammit," he said out loud. That little sneak didn't go back to Crooked Creek, he thought.

Sam had ridden up the drive and was sitting on his horse watching Luke as he read. "I hope you got good news, boy," Sam questioned.

Luke slapped the letter on his knee. "Sam, I would love to get my hands on that little sneak. Mary Grace planned all along to stay in Denver with Jimbo."

"Mary Grace stayed in Denver? We left her sitting in the stagecoach," Sam remarked. He removed his hat and scratched his head.

"Yep, I'm talking about that sassy-mouthed gal. Jimbo says that they have opened a café and she has two men trying to court her." He stormed back and forth in front of the mansion. "She doesn't realize that everyone in Denver knows that she's a very wealthy young woman. Jimbo and Harry don't like the men. He says so right here in this note."

"Mary Grace wouldn't like just any man, would she?"

"She was quite upset with me, especially when I told her I was leaving. I should have brought her with me, but I wasn't sure what I would find when I got here." Luke was hoping that Sam would understand his way of thinking when it came to him and Mary Grace.

"Mrs. Tiller said that she worked for Jimbo. Do you think Mary Grace and Harry might have gotten sick from the bad food?"

"Gosh, I forgot about that for a minute. You're right. She could have. I'll ask Mrs. Tiller if she remembers who may have gotten sick."

"If you really cared for her, you would have brought her with you," Sam mumbled under his breath.

"I do care for her and you're right. I should have asked her to come with me. I have to talk with Mrs. Tiller and soon. And I may have to go to Denver." Luke whirled around and walked to the corral through the wild blades of tall grass. He was going to have to make plans to return to Denver. He needed to check on Mary Grace's health and those fools that were sniffing after her.

Later Luke rode over to see his folks. He had purchased several new pairs of britches, shirts, long johns, and socks for Gerald Mitchell. At the supper table, he told his folks about the new people he had brought home with him from Pine Hill.

"What in the hell are you doing over there?" Butch said. "You're going to turn that place into an old folks' home or a place for the homeless. Those people are strangers, and you're turning them loose to roam all over the place. They sound like trash to me—lazy, no-good people who'll steal us blind. Before we know it, they'll be camping out on our doorsteps."

Luke stood and slapped his napkin down in his plate. "Butch, please come with me. You and I need to have a private discussion." Luke didn't wait to see if Butch was going to follow him or not.

Once outside in the cold wind, the two brothers stood a few feet from each other. Luke wrapped his arms across his chest before he spoke to Butch. "Listen, those are nice people who happen to be down on their luck but are willing to work hard to earn money to survive. They know that they don't have to remain here forever. But, putting aside the business of my hiring people, I want you to know that I'm not that snot-nose kid who grew up with you."

"Oh really, what happened to mama's teaty baby who hid under her skirts? I needed you to do a man's job, but all you did was whine."

"Maybe so, but I'm not that boy anymore. You and I are going to have to work together, and Ma and Pa don't need to be worrying about our relationship. But hear me and hear me good, Butch. I won't be pushed. I'm not afraid of you. Do we understand each other?"

Butch stalked a couple of feet away from his young brother.

"Why, Luke? Give me one good reason you feel you have to bring strangers to work on your place. There are people in town who will come here and help you."

"Good, I need more women and a lot more men to help with the outside of the house. But, I know what it is like to be at my wits' end. Over the years, I've been down on my luck and I was given a helping hand. At that time I made a pact with myself and the good Lord. Promised God if I ever had the chance to help someone, I would. Now, these are good people who just need a chance to get back on their feet." Luke looked away from Butch. "I hope you'll understand my reasons for hiring them, but if they offend you, stay away."

Butch headed up the porch steps to the house. He stopped on the top step and turned to Luke. "Come on, let's eat the good supper Mama cooked for us."

Luke's heart smiled. He and Butch had come to an understanding of sorts.

***

Someone was knocking on the door, a soft discreet rapping. "Wonder who could be visiting this time of the day? Must be a stranger." Mama mumbled all the way to the door. When she opened it, a tall, thin young man who wore wire-rim glasses held his hat in one hand and a leather black bag in the other.

"Morning. I have an appointment with Mr. Tyler. I hope this is a good time?" Before mama could answer, Luke raced into the front parlor and greeted the doctor. "Welcome, Doctor Pike. So glad that you could come this morning."

Mama looked from the doctor to Luke and back again. "May I take your hat and offer you some refreshment? It is becoming rather warm these days."

"Mama, I've asked the doctor to come and give Pa an examination. I want him to check Pa's back and legs. Pa's complained about pain in his legs, and I want to make sure that the feelings in his legs are a good thing. Please, let's take the doctor into Pa's bedroom."

"You'd better go first and prepare your pa for the doctor's visit. He's not going to be very happy, but you can handle him, I'm sure."

Mama was right. Pa was not happy, but he finally agreed to

allow the doctor to examine him all over.

"Mr. Tyler," the doctor said, "the feeling in your legs and lower pain is a sign that you aren't paralyzed, and with proper exercise to strengthen your legs, you may be able to walk again with the aid of a walking stick. Are you willing to do the exercises daily? Before you agree, I want you to know they can be painful, but in the end of a few months, you'll see some good results. I'll give you some medicine to help with the pain but also to relax you enough to rest well."

Pa glanced at the doctor with furrowed eyebrows. "Are you sure I am not paralyzed? I've been told that I'll never walk again."

"Mr. Tyler, believe me, if you had no feeling in your legs, I would agree with the other doctor, but you're in a lot of pain. That wouldn't be possible if you were completely paralyzed." The doctor snapped his black leather bag closed.

Pa's eyes were saucers. Then he grinned. There were no words to describe the joy he was feeling. He looked at mama and then back over at Luke. "Can my wife help me with the exercises or do I need a man?"

"Your wife can help you do most of them, but I would like a strong man with firm hands to massage your legs three times a week. The pressure will help build up your muscles. I also want you to have a strong bar built overhead, so you can stand and try to take a step or two daily. At first, your wife will help you move your foot, one step at a time, very slowly. But, all that will come in time. I will come back in two weeks and see how you are doing. Before I go, I'll instruct your wife on the exercises."

Mama and the doctor went into the kitchen while Luke helped his pa with his clothes. "Son, I want to thank you for having that young doctor come see me. I was afraid. Now I would never admit this to your mama, because I'm supposed to be a tough old bird. But I promise to work hard because I want to feel like a man again." He reached for Luke and hugged his tight. "You're a good man, son."

# Chapter 23

The grand opening of Grace's Café finally came with a whopping success. The minute the doors opened, the line of people that had formed around the corner of the building streamed in.

Mary Grace was thrilled she had trained all the young boys and girls from the orphanage to help in the kitchen, keep the tables cleaned, and set for the next customer. The youngsters worked steadily with genuine smiles on their faces.

Harry sat at the front and greeted everyone while Jimbo passed out mugs of coffee to the waiting customers. Lucy suggested that a few chairs be placed near the front for the elderly ladies to sit and wait.

"A fancy restaurant in Dallas did this to accommodate their customers," she laughed and said that she had read about it in a book.

After the last customer left for the evening, Jimbo, Harry and all the kids sat around a big table. "I can't thank all of you enough for helping to make this a very successful first day. Jimbo, will you help the boys bed down in your room, and the girls can sleep with me. We'll work hard tomorrow making more permanent room arrangements for everyone."

"Won't we be working tomorrow?" Mike asked.

"No, tomorrow is Sunday. We'll open every day from six in the morning until nine at night but we'll close on Sundays."

"People I know ain't going to like it one bit. They'll want you to be open," Lucy said.

"Well, my pa has a business and he never closes the doors, but I hated working on Sundays. Now that I have a business of my own, I will not be open on the Lord's Day. Sundays are a day of worship and rest."

"I'm happy to know I'll have a day off from work," Joe said with a big grin. Everyone looked at the young man and laughed.

\*\*\*

Mary Grace and Lucy dressed and walked four blocks to the Catholic Church for the early morning worship service. When the service was over, Mary Grace met the priest in the vestibule of the church. "Father, my name is Mary Grace Winters and I need to talk to you soon. I want to discuss the problems that the city's orphanage is having. I want to help, but the mayor said you need to approve my plans."

"Yes, child, I have heard your name from the mayor. Can you come to the church tomorrow? Let's say about 10:00 a.m. I'm disturbed with what is happening over there myself. I understand that some of the children who were forced to leave the orphanage are staying with you. Is that correct?"

"Yes. I couldn't let them roam all over the city begging for work or food. Since some of the older girls have been kicked out, the smaller children are left alone to fend for themselves. Something has to be done and soon. I'll see you tomorrow."

On the way back to the café, the two girls turned the corner and nearly ran head on into Mrs. Gordon, the seamstress. "Mercy, Miss Winters, what's your hurry?" she said laughing while adjusting her hat with a peacock feather.

"Oh, Mrs. Gordon, Lucy and I were talking about material and dresses. Would you have time to make some of the young orphan girls a few dresses? They're practically wearing rags."

"I was heading to my shop to work on a dress. Can they come today and let me measure them? I am going to work as much as I can this week, because I have to move out of my building." She looked right and then left, as if she didn't want others to hear her. "You see, I haven't had much work and am behind on my rent. The owner says he's going to charge me more each month. I've pleaded with him, but he says he doesn't care if I move because he can get more money from someone else with a better business."

"What does your husband do to help you?" Mary Grace had

never heard her speak about her husband.

"He's the janitor at the James Hotel, but they don't pay much. But, we are glad for whatever he earns each week," she said.

Lucy whispered something in Mary Grace's ear, and both of the girls hugged each other and smiled. "Mrs. Gordon, do you like children?"

"Lordy, I love them, but mine are all grown, married, and moved away. I see them about once a year and oh, I miss our little grandchildren." She looked at Mary Grace. "Why do you ask?"

"Well, I'll have to talk this over with the priest, but if he agrees, we need a couple to live at the orphanage and take care of the children. The home has a cook, a wash woman, and a housekeeper, but they don't have an overseer who will care for and love the children. We need a strong couple who will see that the money the home receives will be used for the children and the upkeep of the building."

"Oh my, Miss. I would love to care for the children. I could teach the girls to sew while my husband could teach the boys many things, like gardening, wood carving, building furniture, and caring for small animals. This would be a blessing and an answer to our prayers because our little house is too small for my sewing shop."

"You could still take in sewing for the community to make yourself extra money, but you and your husband will be paid a monthly salary."

"I'd better rush now, but bring the girls to the shop in a little while." Mrs. Gordon hurried inside her dress shop.

"God sure does work wonders, doesn't he?" Mary Grace said. Lucy wiped her eyes with a clean hankie.

***

Once Mr. and Mrs. Gordon were settled into the orphanage and all the older children returned safe and sound, Mary Grace felt she could concentrate on the café. She had hired Roberta Tiller, an older woman, to help make fresh bread daily and cut and clean vegetables. She cooked a variety of dried beans, homemade soups, and baked pans of cornbread. Harry took care of all the meat that came from the butcher's shop daily. The café had a special every day, but they served a variety of meats, vegetables, and desserts. She and Roberta spent many hours together every morning, working side by side, and got to know each very well. Mary Grace had never worked closely with another woman, and Roberta became a mother figure to her.

Every morning the two women worked side by side cooking and preparing delicious desserts. The men loved Mary Grace's sticky buns. She rolled the dough, allowed it to rise for the oven the next morning. The café smelled wonderful from all the sweet treats that were prepared each day. Pies and sweet rolls were everyone's favorites. She prepared bread pudding and peach cobblers for the evening meals.

"The café's running as smooth as butter," Harry said.

Mary Grace felt the same way, so she took off several afternoons and spent time with the smaller children at the orphanage. She loved reading to them and admired the boys' wood projects that Mr. Gordon was teaching them. The older girls enjoyed displaying the new dresses they had sewn with the help of Mrs. Gordon.

One of the younger boys came in the front parlor dangling a cage. Mary Grace asked the small fellow what he was going to use the cage for.

"One day, I'm going to capture me a song bird. They roost in a tree next to my window."

Mary Grace took the cage and examined how it was made. The complete cage was round with spindles except for the top and the bottom. An idea came into her head. "Did Mr. Gordon help you make this cage?"

"Yes, madam. He knows how to make everything," The boy replied and puffed out his chest.

"Will you take me to Mr. Gordon? I want to talk to him about a small project I'd like to have him make." Here was something that could make Harry's life so much easier. After leaving Mr. Gordon and the children, Mary Grace couldn't wait to talk with Harry. She'd asked Mr. Gordon to try to make a wooden leg that would strap onto Harry's stump and go all the way down into a boot. Wearing long pants over the whole thing, he could use his cane to limp around the room, and no one would be the wiser.

When she returned, she summoned Harry into the room. "I have a surprise for you. Mr. Gordon is going to try and make you a wooden leg. He's an excellent carpenter, and I know you'll love what he can do for you. Hurry and get ready. I want to take you over to the orphanage so he can measure your leg."

"Now, you just wait, missy. I might not want a contraption like that. Who told you to take on a mission like that without my consent?"

Jimbo was drinking a cup of coffee with a few of the older boys and overheard their conversation. "Come on, boys. We're going to have to hogtie this old man and carry him over to see Mr. Gordon. He ain't got sense enough to decide for himself, so we'll just have to show him."

"Oh, all right. Give me a minute and I'll go. You, big mouth, can hitch up the carriage and bring it around front," Harry said to Jimbo.

"Jimbo, the horse and carriage are already outside. I didn't take the time to take it to the stable." Mary Grace flashed him a smile.

# Chapter 24

A few days later, Mary Grace woke up and doubled over with cramps caused from her monthly time. She didn't realize how disappointed she was to see that nothing had come of the night she spent with Luke. She'd prayed about it, but now that she knew for sure, she felt a loss.

She loved and missed Luke so much. Sometimes she wanted to pack her bags, head to Pine Hill, Texas, and show up on his doorsteps. Mary Grace tried to forget him. She cried herself to sleep many nights, dreaming of him and the good times they shared and how wonderful he had been to her.

She was angry with her pa and Luke for gambling with her life, but Luke's winning hand had been the best thing in the world that could have happened to her. Living and cooking at the gold mine and then being offered part of the profits from the sale of the mine, how fortunate could a girl be? But their one night of lovemaking was like losing all awareness of her surroundings, the pleasure of his touch and closeness again.

Afterward, she'd shared hopes and dreams of marriage with him, but he denied feeling the same way. He claimed he cared deeply for her, but the time wasn't right for a wife.

Now, as she lay in her bed, gazing up at the rafters, she reflected on her future. Josh Randall practically asked her to marry him without really proposing, and Trace Taylor was in her sight every time she made a move. Neither one of them made her heart beat faster or gave her that tingling feeling when they touched her.

She was not interested in these men or any man for that matter. Her heart belonged to her boss man, a scoundrel of the worst kind.

\*\*\*

Christmas was coming in a few weeks, and the whole town was getting excited. Mary Grace had gone to the mercantile store and selected many toys to be given to the orphanage children. She ordered dolls, cribs, toy guns, cowboy hats, bows and arrows, baby clothes and other toys to be stored in the back of the store for needy parents with children. She imagined taking them to the storeroom to select what they needed at no cost. The children of Denver would have a wonderful Christmas this year, but she wanted her name to be kept silent.

As Christmas approached, the children who worked for the café delivered ham and turkey baskets to the poor families who lived in the city and the rural areas of town.

"Gosh, When I read them the note attached to the basket, the women cried," Lucy said.

Mike and Joe smiled at Mary Grace. "What did the note say?"

When Mary Grace didn't answer, Lucy pulled it out of her pocket and read:

*I hope you will take the time to celebrate the birth of our Savior, Jesus Christ. This is His day and we shall all rejoice.*

*Enjoy the food for your family and close friends.*

*Go to the mercantile and select whatever you need for your children at no expense to you. Santa has been busy.*

*Please use the money that is offered wisely. God bless you and your family.*

*Santa's Elves*


The older orphan children who were staying with Mary Grace, Harry and, Jimbo went to school each day. Even when the snow reached up to the windows, the children walked to the school. The boys rushed ahead to start a fire in the pot-belly stove. The older girls helped with the younger children's coats and boots. Each day, Lucy shared cookies with all the children. Before the weather turned cold, she'd taken all the children's sizes and Mary Grace had ordered them warm coats with scarfs and socks. The girls hoped that the items would arrive before the bad weather did.

Jimbo studied Mary Grace one day. "I noticed you don't spend any money on yourself."

"I have everything I need. My pa wasn't rich, so I wasn't used to much. Now that I have money, the important thing is those children."

***

The café was in trouble, and Jimbo had to deliver the bad news. He entered the backdoor of the kitchen where Mary Grace and Harry were enjoying a cup of hot coffee.

"Shut the door, boy," Harry yelled at him. "You wasn't raised in a barn."

"No, I wasn't and there ain't nothing else down at the barn." Jimbo unwrapped the long knitted scarf from around his neck, a Christmas gift from Lucy. He hung it on the hat rack and removed his heavy, fur-lined coat. Mary Grace had given him the coat, and it was the nicest thing he ever owned; he was so proud of the warm, grand-looking item.

"What you saying about the barn?" Harry asked.

"I went to the livery and the barnyard to purchase a beef to be dressed out by the butcher, like we've been doing since we opened. There ain't no beef cows. All the cows have been sold, and there won't be any more brought into town until spring. The ranchers sell all their beef in late fall, so they don't have to care for them during the bad snowstorms. A man said that we should have purchased our beef cows and kept them in a smaller corral during the winter and used them as needed."

"Why didn't someone tell us that? I never dreamed we wouldn't have meat during the winter months." Mary Grace stared at the two men who appeared as dumbfounded as she was. A trickle of dread for the café's future grew inside her.

"Mary Grace, this is not the end. We still have our chickens and pigs. Our mama sow just gave birth to eleven little piglets, and we have plenty of larger ones that are ready to be taken to the butcher. Men like chicken and pork," Roberta said.

"Sure they do, but most of them have been requesting steaks for dinner," Harry said, "One man told Lucy to bring her some real meat, and if she didn't, he was going to go somewhere else to eat." He rubbed a hand across his chest and coughed.

Mary Grace and Jimbo both noticed his reaction but neither

said anything to the older man about his health. She had already requested the doctor to drop by. But if she told Harry the doctor was going to examine him, he'd be madder than a hornet.

"Jimbo, do you think we could order a few cows from another area and have them shipped to us by train?"

"What part of the country are you hoping to get some beef shipped from before we have to close the doors because of lack of customers?"

"Well, shoot fire, I don't know." Mary Grace said, crossing her arms across her chest.

Harry raised his shriveled-looking hand and glanced from Mary Grace to Jimbo. "Hold on, you two. Let's ask around and see if we can find out how the other restaurants, cafés, and delis are faring without beef."

A knock sounded on the back door and Jimbo jumped up from his bar stool and opened the door to welcome the doctor. "Good morning, Doc," Jimbo said and helped the older man remove his hat, scarf, and coat. "I'll hang these things on the coat rack. Come in and have a nice cup of coffee."

Harry snorted and threw Mary Grace a hard glance. "You don't fool me, missy. I don't need a horse doctor looking at me."

"Good morning to you, too." Doc took the cup of coffee from Jimbo. "It is true that I am a horse doctor. In fact, I just helped Jed deliver a beautiful colt. Prettiest little filly I've ever seen. Now, you ornery old goat, I'm told you're having chest pains. Turn around and open your shirt and let me listening to that drum you've stored under all that fat."

"Fat? You dumb—" Harry started to stand, but Mary Grace placed her hand on his shoulder.

"Please, Harry. Be good and let the doctor listen to your heart. I want you, no, I need you here with me for a long time. Maybe he can help make the pain go away."

Harry settled down on the stool. He sighed and opened the front of his shirt, allowing the doc to place his cold instrument on his chest. "Dammit, man, you could have warmed that thing."

"Quiet." The doctor grumbled and moved the instrument across his hairy chest and down to his belly. After he finished, he told Harry to button his shirt, placed his instrument back in his black bag, and snapped it closed.

"What is it, doc? Is he going to be alright?"

"Mary Grace, I'm sitting right in front of you. I ain't no child."

"This old goat is going to outlive us all. His heart is as strong as a young man's."

The doctor crossed his arms and stood looking down at Harry. "I'm sure your pains are from indigestion. You probably eat late at night and too much." He peered over his wire-rim glasses at Harry. "A couple hours after you've eaten, the burning comes into your throat and then you start getting chest pains. Am I right?" the doctor quizzed Harry.

"Harry, I never see you eat while you're cooking. So, is the doctor right? Do you eat late at night?" Mary Grace asked, rubbing his shoulders.

"I don't have time to stop and eat, so I wait until the crew is cleaning the kitchen. I'll try to eat earlier if it will help stop these darn pains."

"Good, you do that and your health will improve." The doctor walked over to the coat rack and placed his scarf around his neck. Jimbo handed the doctor a few dollars, and the old man smiled. He put on his coat and hat and left.

# Chapter 25

Mary Grace was worried about the café. She had Roberta and Jimbo make hearty chicken stews and big pans of biscuits and cornbread along with many different delicious desserts that they offered for free. She was trying to keep her regular customers from going to other restaurants or cafés. She sat at a table in the corner, thinking of possible solutions. Trace came in carrying a bundle of hothouse flowers, five lovely yellow daisies tried with a soft white ribbon.

"Flowers for my fair lady," he said, bowed low at the waist, and gave her a wink.

"Oh my, Trace. These are lovely. Where in the world did you find flowers?"

He didn't wait for Mary Grace to ask him to sit. He slid into a chair and took her hand. "There's a shop with a hothouse in the back that raises flowers during the winter."

"I wish I had a hothouse for raising beef." She sighed and sniffed the daisies.

"Tell me what's wrong, my little dove, and I will make it right for you. There's nothing I won't do to bring my favorite girl's smile back to her face."

"You say the sweetest things. I don't like crying on anyone shoulder, but the café is in trouble. We can't find any cows for sale so we can sell steaks to our hungry customers."

"How long have you been out of beef?" He frowned and looked around the near empty dining room.

"A week or more now. Jimbo has visited all the ranchers near Denver, and most people who have a few beef cows are keeping them for their own personal use. One rancher told Jimbo that we should have purchased cows and kept them in our own corral for just this purpose. If we had known we couldn't buy beef from the butcher during the winter months, of course, we would have planned better."

"Maybe, I can help. I know some of the ranchers, and if I offer them enough money, they might just sell one or two. Would you like for me to try?"

"The weather is too bad for anyone to be riding around the prairie and driving cattle into town. Jimbo said yesterday that his horse stumbled twice, and he had to walk him for miles in the deep snow. He's still in bed trying to recover from that exhausting trip."

"Well, I'll ask around town and see if I can help. I care deeply for you. Hope you know that." He reached for her hand and brought her palm to his lips.

Mary Grace jerked her hand away. "Trace, I like you, but I'm not ready to get involved with anyone."

"What about that dandy who comes sniffing around you every day? Do you have an interest in him?" Trace shoved the table and bolted to his feet, his voice raising to an angry pitch.

"Josh Randall is a nice young man, but I am not interested in him. Please, don't call him names."

Hanging his head, he said low enough for her to hear. "Sorry, Sweetheart. I will get you some beef."

\*\*\*

Trace was desperate to do something that would assure Mary Grace that he was the better man in her life. Grace's Café was in trouble, and he planned to do everything he could do to help locate a rancher that would sell some beef cows. Whatever it took to win Mary Grace over.

Trace hurried to the livery, saddled his horse, and headed out of town towards some of the ranches. Mary Grace's rebuffs were taking their toll. He took a shortcut on a winding path toward town, then he heard a cow that sounded like it was in trouble. He stood tall in his stirrups and peered over a fence in the snowy pasture.

Within fifty feet, a mama cow was nosing a bank of fresh snow.

He leaped down from his horse and waded in the snow over to the cow who stood very still when he walked up to her. "What you got here, girl?" Trace stooped and smoothed snow off a small brown hide that belonged to a calf that lay dead and frozen. The mama cow butted Trace's shoulder, causing him to fall over in the wet snow.

"Mama, you can't do anything for your babe now, but your calf can be an answer to my problem," Trace said, trying to convince her to move away. Trace retrieved his horse and brought him close to the dead calf. He removed his bedroll, laid it open on the snow-covered ground, and wrapped it in his blanket. He tossed it over his saddle.

The animal had probably been attacked by wolves or coyotes. His horse was skittish and pulled away from him, not used to carrying a dead animal.

Holding tight to the reins, Trace climbed on his horse and walked him slowly out of the pasture. The calf wasn't large, but it would add some bulk to steaks and other good beef pieces.

After riding a mile along the wooded, winding path, Trace found a perfect tree limb to hang the calf and dress him out for the butcher. He tied a rope over the calf's two front legs and with the help of his horse, he pulled the animal up off the ground. Trace cut the head off and removed the dark hide. He gutted the animal and removed all his insides. Using his canteen of water, he sloshed the animal to clean off some of the blood. He lowered the carcass back onto his bedroll and placed it back on his horse, trying to contain his excitement. Now, Mary Grace would look at him with new eyes. Her café would be saved for a while, thanks to him.

Trace carried the calf to the butcher's back door. Once Mr. Spotswood viewed the meat wrapped in a blanket with wet dirt and snow, he said that he couldn't sell the meat in his shop. "It's too dirty," he said.

"You'll take this calf and prepare it to sell to Grace's Café. Only Mary Grace's business. Got that?" he demanded. "Mary Grace needs beef to help keep her business open."

Mr. Spotswood shook his head again, refusing to take the meat.

Trace was angry enough to kill someone. He was cold, wet, and tired, and he wasn't taking no for an answer. He grabbed the butcher by his apron and pulled him close to his angry face. "If you don't do as I tell you, I'll come back and burn this shop to the ground. Now, after you have it ready, send a note to her man, Jimbo, that you have beef for sale."

"Mr. Taylor, what am I to tell my other customers?" he said while glancing around uneasily.

Trace pulled back his lips, baring his teeth. "I don't care what you tell them, but you'd better do as I say. Just keep the meat in the back of your shop. Understand, butcher man?" He turned the small man loose, waiting to hear an answer from him.

"Yes, I understand. Grace's Cafe will be my only customer for this side of beef." The butcher backed away from the tall cowboy.

The next morning, Jimbo walked down to the butcher shop after receiving a note from him. "Hello, Mr. Spotswood. This note says you have some beef for our café?"

"Come in and stand over by the stove. It's freezing today." He motioned for Jimbo to come closer to where he stood drinking a cup of coffee.

"How did you get beef? Did a rancher decide to sell to you?"

"No, that cowboy, Trace Taylor, brought a calf in yesterday and he said I could only sell to Grace's Café. I know you need meat, so I dressed it out and wrapped it. How many steaks would like you today? It's a small calf, so there's not as much as a full grown cow."

"Trace Taylor? He worked for our carpenter when we were getting the café ready. He comes in to visit with Mary Grace. I think he's sweet on her." Jimbo grinned like a proud brother.

Mr. Spotswood glanced toward the door and back at Jimbo. "Please, Miss Winters is a nice girl." The butcher looked at his front door and then whispered, "That fellow is a bad man. Watch him around her. That's all I will say, but listen to my words."

"I will, and thanks for telling me. I care very much for her, and I wouldn't want her to get mixed up with someone bad." Jimbo studied the butcher, then took his leave.

Two hours later, Mr. Spotswood's young boy knocked on the café's back door with a wagon filled with wrapped steaks and a good portion of chopped beef, all ready for stews or soup.

Mary Grace clapped her hands at the sight of the meat while Harry limped around the wagon.

"Mercy, young man. You brought us just what we need. Thank you." Harry handed the young man a silver dollar and he stood looking down at it.

"Golly, I ain't never had a coin like this one. Is it a whole dollar?"

Harry laughed and held the back door open for the youngster.

Later that evening, the snow had let up and the dining room was filled like it had been two weeks before. Everyone ordered steaks and all the trimmings. The young servers were thrilled to have full pockets again with the tips they received.

Early the next morning, Mary Grace held her head over a bowl in the water closet. She felt that she was going to die. Lucy dabbed a damp cloth on the back of her neck and gave her water to rinse her mouth. "Don't swallow any of it."

Trace Taylor and Josh Randall were two more people who woke early in the morning sick to their stomachs. The doctor came by to see Mary Grace and announced that many of her customers were sick. Many of them were sure it was the meat because they could taste the smoky favor as it came up from their stomachs.

"Mary Grace, I spoke with the butcher, and he said that your cowboy friend—that Taylor fellow—came into his shop with a small calf. It was wrapped in a bedroll, the hide removed and gutted, but dirty. He said that he didn't want to fool with it, but the man threatened to burn down his shop if he didn't. He said that only your café had to have the meat. Mr. Spotswood washed and soaked it in salt water for an hour." The sheriff wiped his mouth with his clean hanky and stuffed it back in his back pocket. "I'm going to talk to that cowboy and find out where he found that young calf. I don't like men making threats to my people, either. He'll answer for that, for sure."

"I hope you get to the bottom of this, sheriff. I'm thankful that Mr. Spotswood did as the young man said, so the damage is contained. Harry said last night they served about fifteen steaks and that counted the one I ate."

The doctor snapped his bag close and glared at Mary Grace over his wire-rimmed glasses. "Stay in bed and after you feel that you aren't going to throw up, take the medicine that I am leaving Lucy. If you take it now, it will only come back up."

Mary Grace rested her left arm over her eyes and sighed. Lucy walked to the door of their bedroom with the doctor. "Do you think she'll be alright?"

"Keep her in bed, and if she's hungry, give her broth only. I'm worried about the fever she has. That meat had to be tainted with something bad to make several people so sick. You didn't eat any of the meat, did you?"

"No, I was too busy helping Harry cook and serve the meals. We have not had many customers this last week, but after hearing we had steaks, the place filled up after the snow stopped."

"That young cowboy had someone spread the word around," he said, tipping his hat to Lucy.

***

During the night, Mary Grace was delirious. She babbled and kept calling for someone. Lucy thought she was mumbling the name, Luke, but she wasn't positive. She continued to place cold, damp towels on her body to bring down the fever.

Early the next morning, Mary Grace was still sick, and the doctor was concerned about her. The other patients who had eaten the meat were getting better, but for some reason, Mary Grace was deathly ill. Lucy told Jimbo and Harry about Mary Grace calling out a name that sounded like Luke. Jimbo explained that they had all worked for Luke and that he and Mary Grace were very close friends.

Jimbo rushed to the telegraph office and sent Luke a telegram. He told him to come to Denver. Mary Grace was very ill, and she was calling for him.

## Chapter 26

Luke Tyler, Pine Hill, TX

Luke and the two ladies, Roberta Tiller and Patricia Thompson, worked hard to get his home in working order.

The two ladies had arranged to sleep on the first floor so they'd be up without waking the rest of the household. Sam Wilson, Arthur Turnbull, and Bill Tiller settled in the bunkhouse. Gerald Mitchell had been hired to work for Butch, and he would live over at his folks' place.

Everyone was soon settled in their home and knew what their job was, even Nellie, Mrs. Thompson's young daughter.

The ladies already had the furniture and the staircase shining with bee's wax, and Sam and Bill had helped them beat the heavy rugs over clotheslines they'd erected. Nellie helped her mama, Patricia, wash and dry the dishes that had been stored in the pantry. The Wainwrights had moved away from this beautiful home and left so many practical items that could be used. The ladies sorted through the boxes. choosing the things that were the most useful.

Luke visited his mama and brought her over to see his house and the process that his new employees had completed.

"Oh, my, Luke." His mama whirled around in the spacious front entrance of the house. She practically floated in the beautiful parlor. With the drapes removed from the windows panes, the sunshine's glow filled the room. "This place reminds me of a palace."

"Oh, mama. A palace, really?" Luke grinned and took his mama's hands.

"Oh, yes. This room is like one I read about. I'm so proud for you." Moving about, she was unable to stand still. "You know, your pa and I never were invited inside this house when Marie and Joe Wainwright lived here. They entertained a lot, but we were just plain folks."

"Oh, Mama. You and Pa are not just plain folks. You both are loving, kind, and generous people. The whole town respects you and Pa and would do anything for you. When I went into town to clear your accounts, everyone refused to take my money because they weren't worried about your debt to them. I had to make them take the money."

"Oh, baby, thank you for telling me that. This community has good families here who help each other, and after your pa got sick, the men and their sons came over and helped with the ranch."

"I know that I didn't come home like I promised Pa when I left as a kid, but I have always planned to return here and make my home. I've always loved this part of the country and planned to settle here. I'm so happy that I was able to purchase this home and the land that connects to you and Pa."

"Where are the ladies responsible for cleaning this beautiful home?" Mama asked.

Luke took her into the kitchen, opened the pantry door, and Nellie was inside filling a basket with potatoes. "Nellie, please come and meet my mama."

Nellie carried her basket in the kitchen and circled the counter. She held her skirt out by the sides and curtsied before his mother. "How do you do?" Nellie asked with a sweet smile.

Mama raised her eyebrows and gave Nellie a sweet laugh. "My goodness, child. You make me feel like royalty." Two chatting ladies opened the back door of the kitchen and suddenly stopped when they saw their employer and an older woman standing in the kitchen with Nellie.

"Ladies, I would like you to meet my mama, Mrs. Tyler."

"Please call me Maureen. I hope we will be friends."

"Please call me Patricia, and this is Roberta. It looks like you have met my daughter, Nellie."

"Yes, a very well-mannered young lady. I want to commend

you ladies on the job you've done to this house. Everything is so beautiful. I envy you for being able to live here." She said, laughing.

"Thank you. We are enjoying working on this lovely house. Your son is a nice man to work for, and he has made us feel at home here." Roberta reached out to take Mama's hand and give it an old-fashioned handshake.

"Patricia, will you and Nellie show Mama the rest of the house while I speak with Roberta? I have something to speak to her about."

The ladies went into the dining room and walked up the staircase.

"Roberta, when Sam and I met you on the road, you had been living in Denver. Is that right?"

"Yes, I worked as a cook, but the café closed. I couldn't get a job anywhere so we had to move on." Roberta lowered her head.

"What was the name of the café? Was one of your bosses a man named Jimbo?" Luke saw the surprised expression on her face.

"Yes, Jimbo, Harry, and Mary Grace. The three of them owned Grace's Cafe."

"Why did the place close?" Luke was so pleased to know that Roberta knew his dear friends.

"At first, the café didn't have any beef, and Jimbo couldn't find any to buy. With the bad snowstorms, ranchers weren't selling any cattle. Most of them had already sold their herds before the temperature dropped in Denver. Mary Grace said the butcher had told her that she should have bought some cows and kept them in a corral close by so when they needed beef they would have some. She didn't know to do that." Roberta sighed.

"How did you keep it going?"

"To keep the café open, we cooked thick vegetable soups, cornbread, and chicken and dumpling with biscuits. We made desserts and gave them away free with the meals, but customers stopped coming."

"Jimbo wrote that Mary Grace is sick. Was she sick when you and your son left Denver?" Luke asked.

"Yes, I'm afraid so. There was a young cowboy that hung around the café hoping to gain Mary Grace's affection. She liked

# THE GAMBLE

the handsome man, but she didn't lead him on. One day, he took a calf to the butcher and demanded that Mr. Spotswood sell the meat only to Jimbo. He wanted to save the café and win Mary Grace's hand, I guess. Well, anyway, the meat was tainted, and the next day, after we served steaks to our customers, people became very sick. Mary Grace was the only person who worked at the café that had eaten any of the meat. She was sick to death the next morning. Most of the people got over the sickness the next day, but Mary Grace remained ill. The doctor was called to her bedside several times. My son lost his job and was eager to move away from Denver. Lucy, a young lady that worked for the café, assured me that she would care for Mary Grace and that her pa, Mr. Winters, was coming from Crooked Creek to be with her."

"Thank you for telling me. I planned to ride over to Blount Town and catch the train to Denver. I want to check on my friends."

Before Roberta started back to work, Luke asked her if she would mind working at his folks' home. "Ma needs help with the cooking and cleaning even though she's never mentioned it to me. Now that Pa is going to be exercising every day, Ma will gladly welcome your presence and help. I will continue to pay your wage," Luke said.

"I'll be happy to help your folks. I can start tomorrow, or whenever you tell your mama that I'm coming."

## Chapter 27

Denver, Colorado

Mary Grace ambled around in her room while Lucy slept in a comfortable armchair. She had sat up on the side of her bed and felt she could walk to the water closet to take care of her personal needs. Holding on to the furniture, she felt much stronger than she had in days. She walked over to the window and pulled back the curtain. Cool air came under the windowsill, but it felt good. It was snowing, and all the rooftops looked white and clean with the moonlight shining off the top of them. A streetlight was swaying in the wind, and its light was casting shadows all around the area. A man was standing at the end of the boardwalk.

Snow swirled around him, and he pulled his sheepskin jacket close. He stood still for a moment before he glanced up toward her hotel room. With his hat pushed up, the man's face appeared. Luke. Her Luke was here. She quickly stepped back away from the window, but when she looked back down, she saw him step into the saloon next door.

She turned and walked slowly back to her bed. Lucy had awakened and was watching Mary Grace.

"Are you alright? You look like you've seen a ghost."

"I'm fine. I thought I saw someone I knew, but I was mistaken," Mary Grace said, giving Lucy a grin that couldn't be contained.

"Well, I must say you're looking better than I've seen you in days. Would you like a full-tub bath? I'll order some hot water to be brought up and will get a roaring fire going to warm the room. I'll wash your hair for you, too."

"Oh, Lucy, that would be heavenly. Please, I would love to have something to eat besides soft bread and soup. I am ravenous."
\*\*\*

Later that evening, after Luke had a shot of whiskey to warm up his insides, he went to Grace's Café. He banged on the door with the 'closed' sign.

Jimbo hurried down the stairs, yelling, "I'm coming. Keep your shirt on." He peeked through the glass door. "Who is it? We're closed for now."

"It's me, Luke. Let me in before I freeze my butt off," he said, rubbing his arms. He was happy he'd found Jimbo so quickly.

"Luke? Oh my goodness. You're here." Jimbo grabbed his old boss man, pulling him into the dining room.

A small lantern sat on the bar, casting light around the room. "Goodness, Jimbo," Luke said, glancing around the room. "This is a nice place."

"Yep, it is or was. We had to close down and will most likely sell it. There are rumors that people won't eat here again as long as we own the place. More than a few people got food poisoning, and they're blaming us."

"You wrote to me that Mary Grace was sick. Is she still sick?" Luke continued to look around in the dim light at the lovely room and floors.

"She's a lot better but still weak. I haven't seen her today. But, I bet she's going to be thrilled to see you."

"Has she missed me?" Luke hoped Jimbo would reassure him that coming was the right thing to do.

"Well, I can't say for sure because she hasn't even mentioned your name to me, but she isn't interested in those two bozos who are always hanging around." Jimbo smiled at Luke.

"I want to see her," Luke said, while toying with items on a table.

"She's at the hotel. The doctor has a room on the first floor. With her being so sick, he wanted her to be near him. Lucy, a young girl who worked for us, has been staying day and night with her in her room."

Luke couldn't wait until morning to see Mary Grace. He was sure she was the one in the window. As if she'd been expecting him.

He entered the hotel lobby. The desk clerk slept in a chair behind the desk. Luke peered at the pigeon holes that held the keys and saw Miss Winter's name on room five. He tiptoed to the staircase. Glancing at the floor, he remembered. This was where he'd landed when he tumbled down the stairs after Mary Grace had kicked him. What a vixen. He shook his head and continued up to her room. Softly he knocked and waited. In a few minutes, a pretty young girl opened the door a crack and peeped out at him.

"Yes?" the girl said.

"Sorry I'm visiting so late, but I need to see Miss Winters, Mary Grace."

\*\*\*

Mary Grace was sitting in front of the fire, drying her hair. She sucked in her breath. That voice. The voice of the man she loved. Forcing herself to sit still while taking in a few deep breaths, she called to Lucy, "Let him in."

Lucy stepped back and allowed Luke entrance to the room. "This is very improper, sir. Can't you wait in the lobby to visit with Mary Grace?"

Luke smiled at the young lady who acted so much older than her years.

"It's alright, Lucy. Please leave us. I'll come for you after my visitor leaves." Mary Grace gave her little friend a strained smile.

Lucy's eyes narrowed, but she didn't say anything. She took up her sewing basket and left the room.

\*\*\*

Luke walked further into the room and stopped near the rocking chair where Mary Grace was sitting. She was beautiful with half of her long blond hair tossed over her shoulder while she brushed it dry. "Hello, Mary Grace," Luke said. He stood still with his hat in his hands. The only sounds in the room were the crackling and falling of the logs in the fireplace.

\*\*\*

She had forgotten how big he was, wide and tall, so that she had to strain to look up at him. He removed his sheepskin jacket and tossed his Stetson on a chair. The muscles in his arm strained, and when he looked back at her, it appeared he hadn't shaved today. "What are you doing here?" Mary Grace asked. Her teeth began to chatter as if she were cold. "Did you find things at your home like you wanted?" It was like chatting with an old friend.

"Are you with child?" Luke asked. "So beautiful," he whispered

Her lips parted at the question, and her eyes stormed. Speechless, she sat as still as the stone figure in the park.

Luke frowned, his black brows pulled together as he continued to wait on her answer.

"Why, you despicable goat. How dare you ask me such a thing?" She jumped from the rocker and tried to move around him, but he sidestepped in front of her, blocking her from heading to the door.

"It's a simple question, one I need an answer to right this minute."

Mary Grace paused and returned to the rocker. Drained of energy, she began to shake. Tears filled her eyes. and she was too exhausted to hold them back. She was thrilled that Luke had come back to Denver, but not to find out if he was going to be a papa.

Luke stooped down beside her and placed his enormous, callused hands over hers. "I'm sorry, Sweetheart. I never meant to make you cry." The temper had disappeared from his voice

"Oh, Luke, I am happy to see you." She threw her arms around his neck and kissed him with all the desperation she had in her small frame. "But I think you had better go now."

"You haven't answered my question. I have dreamed of our night together, and I've been afraid that I left you with child."

"I'm not going to have a baby, Luke. Now if that is all you wanted, you have your answer. Please go." She wanted him to leave before she embarrassed herself by begging him to stay.

"Are you well enough to travel?" Luke hoped the doctor would release her and allow her to go to Texas with him.

"Travel? I'm not planning a trip." Mary Grace replied.

"Are you well enough? I have two tickets on the train tomorrow back to Pine Hill, and one of them is for you."

"What makes you think I want to go anywhere with you, especially to your home in Texas? You have a lot of nerve."

"Listen to me. You have lost your café and you nearly lost

your life. I'm going to take you with me, back to my home."

"How dare you. You think you can come into my room and tell me to pack my bags. You have lost your mind. I don't work for you, and you have no say over what I can or can't do."

"That's where you are wrong, missy. I own you. Your pa wrote me out a bill of sale." Luke flashed a sheet of paper under her nose and refolded it and placed it in his back pocket. "Now, let's be friends like we were before I left Denver. And besides, you were supposed to return to Crooked Creek and live with your pa. You lied to me. Jimbo wrote me about the café. If I could have gotten my hands on you, I would have blistered your backside. I would have never left you here in this big city alone, and you know that."

"You are a crude cad of the worst kind and a woman beater. Do you think I'll go willingly with you? You have lost your mind."

"Have you fallen in love with one of those men whom Jimbo says are sniffing after you?"

"You are an insufferable fool if you think I would or could fall in love with one of those two. Josh Randall is a nice young banker who only likes me because his father ordered him to. Of course, he doesn't know that I have figured that out. Trace is the cowboy who found the calf and brought it into the butcher. He wanted to save my café. He's very handsome, strong, and nice, but I know he's after my money, too. Isn't your money enough for you, Luke? Do you want mine too?"

"That question doesn't deserve an answer, and you know it. I'll be here in the morning to check you out of the hotel and have breakfast before we board the train."

\*\*\*

Mary Grace didn't respond to him one way or another. Luke took this as agreement. He circled behind Mary Grace and took his coat and hat from the bed. "See you in the morning, darling."

# Chapter 28

The train heading to Blount Town, Texas, would be leaving in one hour. Luke pulled out his pocket watch and realized he had just enough time to check Mary Grace out of the hotel and carry her trunks to the train. While in the lobby, he ran into the Mary Grace's doctor coming out of the dining room. "Hello, Doc," Luke said. "I want to know if you think Mary Grace is well enough to travel on the train to my home."

"Yes, I checked on her before I had breakfast, and she's recovered as far as I can tell. She's a little weak, but she's been in bed for nearly two weeks and has not being walking. With short walks, she will get her sea legs back and be just fine. The train ride won't harm her in any way. Have a good trip and come back to see us soon."

Luke smiled and watched the doc leave the hotel. Giving the hotel clerk a nod, he practically leaped up the staircase to Mary Grace's room. He knocked on the door, and like the last time, a young girl opened the door. "Good morning, young lady. May I come in? Mary Grace is expecting me." As he entered the room, the girl jumped in front of him.

"Sir, Miss Winters is too ill to have visitors, and she's sleeping. You must come back this afternoon when she is awake and feeling better."

Out of the corner of his eye, he saw Mary Grace quickly cover her face and pretend to be asleep. He placed his hands on girl's shoulders and moved her out of the way. In two steps, he stood looking down at her. Mary Grace lay so still with her lovely blond hair draped over her shoulders. She wore a pink gown trimmed with white lace and tiny pearl buttons down the front. A vision of beauty. "Mary Grace," Luke whispered. "Wake up, darling. You must get ready to catch the train."

The girl rushed over to Mary Grace's bed. With panic in her voice, she said, "She's too ill to go anywhere."

"What's your name?"

"Lucy, sir."

"Miss Lucy, I'm going to carry Mary Grace out of this room, dressed or in her nightclothes. It makes no difference to me."

"You will not take me anywhere, Mr. Tyler," Mary Grace sat straight up in bed and screamed at him.

"It's good to see you're awake. Now, like I told your little friend here, you are coming with me."

"I can't go anywhere and leave Lucy here in Denver alone. She's my responsibility." She smiled at Lucy.

"Fine. Lucy, hurry to your room and pack your carpetbags. You are going with us to Pine Hill, Texas, my home. Now hurry. You can leave a note with the clerk downstairs if you need to let anyone know where you are going and with whom."

Lucy glanced at Mary Grace as Luke pushed her out the door.

"Maybe Lucy might not want to leave Denver. You aren't her boss. You can't just snap your fingers and make her do your will."

"You just said that you are responsible for her; therefore, you are leaving, and she must go with us. I am only going to tell you one more time. Get out of that bed and get dressed."

"I can't." She slammed her palms down on the mattress. "The doctor said that I am too sick to get out of bed."

Luke shook his two fingers at her and made a clinking sound with his teeth. "You have a very short memory. I remember telling you before, as I took you to my gold mine, that I hate liars. You are lying, miss. I just spoke with the doctor before I came to your room." Luke sighed and glanced around the room one more time. "Don't make me mad."

The door opened and Lucy returned. "I packed and I left a note with the clerk." She glanced at Mary Grace who had covered her head with the blanket, her screams muted by the covers.

Luke shrugged at Lucy and winced at each nasty word Mary

Grace called him. "Such language, Miss Winters," Luke said and moved toward Mary Grace's bed. "Lucy, hold the door open for me and please pack a few things for Mary Grace. Meet us at the train." He passed her a few dollars and asked that she get a man to help her bring Mary Grace's trunk to the train depot.

"Lucy, don't you dare touch my things. I'm not leaving Denver with this crazy man."

Luke slipped his hands under the bedcovers and grabbed Mary Grace's shoulders and legs. The bedcovers covered Mary Grace's near naked body while it draped to the floor.

"Put me down! I'm going to scream my head off, and the sheriff will hear me and come and arrest you. He's a mean man and will have you shot."

"I haven't hurt you—yet. If you don't want me to stop and turn you over my knee on the boardwalk, so everyone in Denver can witness me blistering your butt, you'd better shut your mouth."

"You wouldn't dare touch a hair on my head. My pa will kill you when he hears how you have embarrassed me."

In just a few minutes, Luke passed the passenger cars and continued down the track until he arrived at the livestock cars. He struggled with one hand to get the sliding door open, but when he did, he dumped her inside on the floor. He pushed all of her bedcovers into the car and pulled the door closed, locking it on the outside.

The train's frustrated conductor hurried to Luke. "What's going on? Who did you put in that dirty livestock car?" He jumped to peer over Luke's tall shoulders.

"I have a wildcat in this car. Please don't open the door. I'll be back in about ten minutes to check on it. It's very dangerous." Luke winked at the older man and placed a couple of silver dollars in his palm.

The conductor raised his eyebrows at the money in his palm. "I'll personally watch this stock car until you return." The older man ignored the voice from within.

Mary Grace screamed Luke's name. "I'm going to kill you," she yelled and jerked on the sliding door.

Luke stood at the train ticket window and paid for another ticket for Lucy. If Mary Grace wanted this young woman to come with her, he had no objection. She appeared to be a nice girl, and if she had been an orphan, then she needed a nice home. His mother would be thrilled to have a girl around the place.

"Mr. Tyler, where is Mary Grace? What part of the train did you put her in?" Lucy asked, concerned over her new friend and boss.

Ignoring Lucy's question, Luke asked her, "Were you able to have her trunks delivered to the train?"

Lucy nodded. "Here's the rest of your money that I didn't have to use. I had a man put her trunk and my carpetbags in the luggage department."

"Good. Now, let's get one of the train's porters to find Mary Grace's trunk so you can get her something decent to wear. Right now, she's locked in one of the livestock cars in her nightclothes."

"Oh, my." Lucy passed her palm over her heart. "I bet she's mad at you."

"You could say that, but she'll get over it once she gets dressed and has some breakfast." Luke held onto Lucy's arm and led her through several passenger cars until they found a tall, smiling train porter. Luke explained the situation to him, and the good-humored man took them to the luggage car. Lucy retrieved a nice frock and everything else Mary Grace would need to get dressed properly.

"Give those things to me. I'll take them to her, and in a little while, we will come for you to eat with us. You sit over by the window and look at the scenery. I promise that no one will bother you."

Mary Grace was on her best behavior when Luke passed her a brown bag with a butter and cheese sandwich. "Is this the best you could do, Mr. Tyler?" She was starving and this pauper's lunch wasn't going to fill her empty stomach.

"Yes, my bag has two apples, and you may have one." Luke grinned as he took a juicy bite out of one of the apples and offered her the other one.

\*\*\*

She watched the juice run down Luke's chin as he grinned at her like a baboon. "Where did you get this feast?" Mary Grace frowned at the sandwich in her hands.

"Oh, there was a nice lady selling the lunch bags near the train. Quite a little enterprise, if I say so myself. She was selling them for fifty cents."

"My goodness. You expect us to eat this food that was made by a total stranger heaven knows when?" Mary Grace glanced at Lucy, who was taking another bite of her sandwich.

\*\*\*

"Eat up, darling. It will be tomorrow afternoon before we arrive in Blount Town." Luke finished his sandwich. "Would you ladies like to rest in a couple of the seats? I'm sorry this train doesn't have a dining car or sleeper departments." Luke frowned. He wished he could make this trip more comfortable for the girls. Luke stood and stretched. The train felt like it was slowing down. It was traveling up an incline which jerked the passenger cars side to side.

Lucy moved closer to Mary Grace and frowned.

Luke said he was going to head up to the engine car and talk with the conductor.

\*\*\*

After he left, Lucy sniffed. "Do you smell something bad, like a barnyard?"

"No, I don't smell anything," she replied.

"Listen, Mary Grace, I need to use the water closet. I know we are going to be stopping to take on water, but I can't wait. Mr. Tyler said for me to stay with you. Is it alright if I go?"

"You go and take care of your personal business. I'll sit right here and try to force the rest of this sandwich down my throat. Hurry while Luke is gone."

After Lucy left, she moved over to the window and suddenly caught a whiff of something that smelled like manure. She stood and looked around. She lifted one booted shoe, then the other. It was then she noticed a brown smear like mud on her pantaloons. "Oh, my Lord!" She lowered her head to get a better look. Dammit, the smell was awful. She must have rolled in manure in that blasted livestock prison. *I'm going to kill that man.*

Mary Grace gritted her teeth as she stepped out of her nasty white underwear, thankful that she was the only passenger in their car. She tossed the white pantaloons out of the window, and the white material went flying like a Civil War surrender flag and landed in some brushes directly beside the passenger's cars. Almost instantly, hoots and loud laughter came from the passenger car behind hers.

Lucy hurried back into their passenger car and took her seat beside Mary Grace. Her boss was as white as a sheet, but the bad smell had gone away.

"Are you alright, Lucy? Is the rocking of the train making you sick to your stomach, like people get when they sail on big ships?"

"Maybe, a little, but I'll be happy to reach where we're going. I feel like the train is going to flip over on its side because of the way it rocks back and forth. Why are the men in the other cars hanging their heads out the windows and laughing?"

Mary Grace looked out of the window. Sticking her head out, she met the eyes of the men who were still hollering and laughing. Then a flash of white. *Oh, my gracious.* Finally, the train had picked up speed and Luke returned from visiting the train conductor.

"We'll be stopping in a few minutes to take on water. Everyone can get off and stretch their legs and go to the outhouses set up for passengers." He peered at Mary Grace and Lucy, but neither of the ladies responded.

# Chapter 29

As the train prepared to stop, Luke stepped down and offered his hand to Mary Grace and Lucy. Both of the ladies hurried to the large platform that had been built for passengers to avoid the sun or sit on the few benches. A row of outhouses were positioned about fifty feet from the tracks.

Several of the men patted Luke on the back and laughed as they made crude remarks that couldn't be repeated in the presence of ladies. Luke didn't quite understand what the men were talking about until one said that someone in the front passenger car had tossed out a pair of white pantaloons that flew in the air before landing beside the train tracks for all the world to see. Luke shook his head but didn't make any comment. Since he and the girls were the only passengers in the front passenger car, it would be hard to deny that it wasn't one of them.

I'm going to strangle that little witch when I get her alone, thought Luke. She had really made a mess of things, because the majority of the men traveling on the train were going to Blount Town and Pine Hill to work for the railroad. Mary Grace's and Lucy's reputations would be ruined if he didn't offer a clever reason for the underwear to be tossed away.

A rowdy man passed a bottle of rye around to some of the other men. The man teased Luke about stripping away a lady's personal item on a moving train.

Luke had to come up with something that the men would understand. "Look, fellows, my wife is in the family way and the rocking of the train made her sick. She threw up her lunch, and we needed something to clean her and wipe up the mess. The young girl traveling with us tossed the wet, dirty clothes out the window. My wife is terribly embarrassed about the whole thing. Please, think of her delicate condition." Pinching the bridge of his nose, he held his head down with closed eyes.

"Oh, man, we're so sorry. Ain't we, men? We just thought you—well, you know what we were thinking." Swaying, he slapped and hugged a couple men standing beside him. "Shoot, we were all wishing we were you." He passed the bottle around to a few more men before they had to board the train again.

Luke took his seat next to Mary Grace in their passenger car. She shifted her body over and sat closer to Lucy. "Are you warm enough without your drawers on under that skirt?"

Sucking in her breath, she whirled around and stared into his angry face. "How did you know?" She tried to whisper so Lucy wouldn't hear, but her little friend stood and walked to the back of the car, allowing the couple to have a few minutes of privacy.

"Every man on this train witnessed your pantaloons flying in the breeze once you tossed them out the window. You and Lucy have become the laughingstock of Blount Town. They were sure that I had conquered one of you."

"What? I don't believe you. You're making all this up."

Angier than he had been in a long time, he turned to her and gave her shoulders a little shake. "I assured them that you, my lovely wife, are in the family way, and had soiled your clothes, so you tossed them out of the window."

"Me? Your wife? Going to have a baby? How dare you!" Disbelief flooded her face.

"Don't dare me, Mary Grace," Luke said through gritted teeth. "I had to say something to save my future's wife reputation. The men understood and stopped their laughing and ugly remarks."

Mary Grace turned to look at Lucy before she sat back against her seat. Luke meant what he said about marrying. What would she do with a bull-headed fool like him? She grunted and covered her face with her hands.

\*\*\*

He stood, glanced at Lucy, and winked. The young girl had overheard their conversation. Mary Grace didn't know how to whisper when she was upset. Luke glanced back over his shoulder and said softly, "Mary Grace, I really want you to be happy; therefore, we'll marry as soon as we can find the preacher in Blount Town. Everyone will think we have been married for a while, and this will put an end to any rumors that still might come from this situation with the underwear." He turned and walked out of the passenger car to stand between the cars and get a breath of fresh air.

\*\*\*

Mary Grace sighed and motioned for Lucy to come and sit with her. *Funny*, she thought. *Here I am a couple hours from being married, and I only have Lucy to share it with.* At least, she was a wonderful friend and the only one who knew that she loved the stubborn, gold miner, her boss man.

Before they left for the church, men were jabbing each other in the sides and grinning at them like they had never seen a couple eating dinner. Her stomach quivered when Luke touched her hand. Her cheeks blushed a bright pink. Instead of being upset with him, she felt a ticklish sensation coursing up her inner thighs between her legs. This caused her to lower her eyes and pretend not to be thinking of him.

\*\*\*

The cold February winds blew strong as he left Mary Grace and Lucy at the church. He went to the livery and hired a young man to drive a flatbed wagon to his home. Once he saw the new two-seater carriage parked out front of the livery, he knew he had to have it. He asked the young driver to go to the train depot and retrieve the ladies' trunk and carpetbags while he went into the dry goods store. He had seen the thin, coat that Lucy wore, so he purchased her a heavy cloak with a fur-lined hood. With the weather turning colder, he bought heavy blankets to have in the wagon and carriage to cover the girls' legs while traveling.

Once Luke had purchased other supplies, he and the young man drove to the church to pick up his new bride and Lucy. Before the ladies stepped out of the church, Luke offered Lucy the large box. "I wanted you to have this, young lady." Luke glanced at Mary Grace who seemed a little peaked.

Once Lucy opened the box, she covered her face. "Oh my, Mr. Tyler. It's too lovely for me."

Mary Grace grabbed up the cloak and wrapped it around her little friend. "What? You needed a new coat and I am thrilled Luke noticed."

"Thank you both." Lucy pulled her old coat off and slipped her arms into her new soft, dark purple and green cloak. "This is the nicest thing I have ever owned."

"Let's go, ladies. We have a young driver, Tim Boxer, who is going to drive the wagon for us. Lucy, you'll ride with this young man and keep him company. I've put blankets in the back for you both to cover up and stay as warm as you can."

He watched Lucy hurry outside and introduce herself to Tim, who helped her upon the bench of the wagon. With the wind blowing hard, she reached in the back and took a blanket to cover them.

"Mary Grace, I have a surprise for you, too. I hope you will like your wedding present from me. I told you that I want to make you happy."

"You didn't have to buy me a gift. I am not going to be your bride. You may own me, as you continue to say, but I refuse to be your lawful wife as the preacher kept saying."

"I'll give you time to get used to the idea of marriage. You belong to me in the eyes of God now. But, you and I are the only ones who know we aren't living together as a couple. Do I make myself clear about this?"

"Yes, master. I will be the perfect wife in front of your family and friends."

"If you call me master again, you'll be sorry, I can promise you that." Luke leaned his face so close to hers that she had to back up from him. "Now, I want you to have this carriage as your wedding gift along with these two black beauties that have been trained to pull it." Luke patted one of the horses. "Come, allow me to help you into the carriage. I thought you would like to drive the other ladies at my home to church or town."

"Oh, Luke, this is so nice, and the horses are grand. May I ride one of them around your place?"

"No, you will have a different horse with your own saddle to ride. You can take your pick of my quarter horses that have been broken already." Luke reached out for her hand to help her in the carriage. "Now use one of those blankets to cover up. This wind is cold and will get colder once we start moving."

The two horses' hindquarters swayed, just like they were keeping time with the rhythm of their hooves. Mary Grace's stomach felt like it was full of baby birds. As the team jogged alone, Luke spoke softly to her about his new house and his family.

Mary Grace had only remembered him saying that he missed his family, but he never made any other comments about them. He muttered about some of the people who lived on his ranch, but her eyes were glued to the majestic landscape and the rolling mountains in the distance. Below the mountains was an open range as far as the eye could see. She shivered from the chill, and Luke asked her if she was cold. She wished that he weren't alert to her every movement or feeling. It was like he could read her every thought.

Luke continued to talk about his family, and Mary Grace admired the bond he had with them. She wished she had been closer to her pa. After her mama died, her pa just shut down and threw himself into working and gambling.

Mary Grace sat stiff next to Luke, but after several hours and the cold wind blowing, she felt herself falling asleep. Luke pulled her closer to his side. She jerked awake and moved away from him.

"Be careful, little one, you might fall out of this moving carriage. I would hate to lose you on this rough trail." He tucked the blanket around her a little tighter.

In another hour, rain began pelting down on them. Lucy had a heavy cloak hood to help keep her dry, but Mary Grace didn't even have a bonnet. Luke must have read her mind again because he lifted his black Stetson off his head and flopped it down onto hers. She jerked awake and tried to give it back to him.

"You need it worse than I do," he said and began removing his black coat.

"No, I don't need it as bad as you do." She pushed the hat back into his hands.

"For gosh sakes, put the hat on," Luke bellowed.

"And if I don't, are you going to hit me?"

"Hit you? Lord Almighty." Luke wiped his hand over his face as if to hide his frustration. "Put the blasted thing on your head." He took it and placed it back in her hands. She finally placed the waterlogged hat over her long, soaked hair.

He must have felt her shiver because he removed his coat and told her to put it on. She refused, so he pulled on the reins. "We're not moving until you put on that coat." He could be as stubborn as she was. Giving up, she slipped her arms into the coat and snugged it like a blanket.

Luke tried to adjust the top of the carriage over them, but the wind had blown it out of position. The rain poured down over his face, as Mary Grace fell back into a deep slumber. She tried to get warm by snuggling up against him. Finally, after she nearly tumbled off the side of the carriage, he grabbed her by his coat and lifted her onto his lap. Water poured down from his hat and caused her to shiver while pulling his coat tighter over her small frame. In a few minutes, soft snoring came out of her rosy puckered lips which gave him comfort and warmed him, too.

As the sun went down, one of the horses stepped in a deep hole causing the carriage to tilt to one side, making Luke jerk the reins to get the animals back on the trail.

Mary Grace woke up from the rough movement. She glanced around and realized she was sitting in Luke's lap.

"Hold still, sweetheart, before I drop you over the side of this carriage." Luke helped her to move off his lap and get adjusted back in the seat next to him.

"I'm sorry. I guess I fell asleep." He was soaking wet. "Goodness, I have your hat and coat. You must be freezing," she said and unbuttoned his coat.

"No, please leave my coat and hat on. We're only about thirty minutes from my home. Just sit still and try to stay dry. I don't want you getting sick again.

# Chapter 30

The sprawling two-story house looked inviting with its lights shining from the windows. "Is this your house?" Mary Grace stared at Luke with wide eyes. "It's lovely, even in the dark."

"Wait until you see it in daylight. It is your home now, too. You can make any changes you like. I want it to have your touch."

Mary Grace didn't say anything but turned around to view Lucy in the flatbed wagon coming up beside them.

"Follow me, Tim," Luke said. "We'll drive to the livery and get out of the rain. I'm sure a couple of men will come out of the bunkhouse and help with the animals."

Sam Wilson was thrilled to see Luke. He called for help, and Bill Tiller came charging out of the bunkhouse, carrying a big lantern.

"Welcome home, Mr. Tyler," Bill Tiller said. He took hold of one of the black horses' reins and led him inside the livery stable.

"Unhitch the animals, feed them, and give them a good rubdown. We'll take our belongings out of the carriage and wagon tomorrow morning," Luke instructed the young man.

Luke helped Mary Grace down from the wagon, but she nearly stumbled.

"I sat so long that my legs feel like rubber, she said, shivering.

Luke grabbed her elbow. "Take it slow, Sweetheart. You need to get your land legs and then go inside and get out of those wet things," he said.

Tim helped Lucy down from the wagon, and she hurried over

to Mary Grace. "Oh, this is a lovely place. I never dreamed Mr. Tyler's home would be so grand."

"I didn't either," Mary Grace said. "I guess we'll meet his folks in the morning. Luke said they live on the next ranch."

"Come on, ladies. Let's get you inside out of the cold. There's a blazing fire in the front room." Luke rested his hand on Mary Grace's back and ushered her inside the back door. A young lady stood at the wet sink filling a coffeepot with water.

"Welcome home, Mr. Tyler." The woman's seemed surprised at the two drenched women standing at the door. She wiped her hands on her crisp apron and offered a smile.

"Patricia, I want to introduce my new bride, Mary Grace, and her young friend, Lucy. I need to take them into the parlor where they can get warm. Will you please bring them both a towel?"

"It's so nice to meet you both. Yes, I'll bring you clean towels and soft blankets so you can remove your wet things." She hurried out of the kitchen.

Luke led the girls into the parlor and told them to sit down in the two rockers. "Oh, no," Mary Grace said. "I'm too wet to sit in that nice chair."

Patricia rushed back into the parlor with towels and blankets. "If you don't need my help getting undressed, I'll prepare a light supper for all of you. Will breakfast food be acceptable?"

"Anything will be appreciated, Patricia. I'm sorry that we're keeping you from your bedtime." Luke took his coat from Mary Grace.

"Please, I am happy to help, and it's wonderful that you have taken a bride. Your mama will be thrilled."

"Thank you. I'll take them over tomorrow morning to meet everyone. How is Nellie adjusting?"

"She loves it here, and she's enjoying playing checkers with your pa and Mr. Turnbull. They're filling her with all kinds of war stories." Patricia laughed and hurried back into the kitchen.

Mary Grace watched the interaction between the woman and Luke. "Who is this Nellie you asked about?"

"Patricia is a young lady whom I met in Pine Hill who needed a job, and Nellie is her eight-year-old daughter. You will meet everyone tomorrow." Luke took Lucy's soaked new coat and walked out of the parlor, pulling the double doors closed.

Mary Grace and Lucy helped each other with the removal of their wet things. The girls placed their shoes in front of the fire to dry but rolled up their other things in a towel. They wrapped themselves in the soft blankets and sat in the two rocking chairs in front of the fire.

"Oh, Mary Grace, do you think I will be able to find a job in town? I already love this house, but I can't live with you and Mr. Tyler."

"Why not live with us? This house has many rooms, I'm sure."

"It probably does, but it looks like Mr. Tyler already has a servant to do everything for him." Lucy rested her head against the rocker. "I could easily go sound asleep."

With a gentle knock on the door, Patricia stepped inside the room. "Would you like for me to take you to your rooms now? I can serve you a tray of food there. You both look ready to drop."

"Yes, that would be wonderful."

Patricia led the girls upstairs. She stopped at a lovely room near the stairs. "This will be your room for the night. Mr. Tyler might want to rearrange the rooms later." Patricia stepped back and allowed Lucy to enter. A fire had been built in the fireplace. A large bed dominated the room, and there was a private water closet.

"Oh, this is so nice. I never dreamed of having a room like this. Thank you, Miss." Lucy glided into the room.

Patricia walked to the end of the hall and opened a double door. She stepped back and allowed Mary Grace to enter. The first thing she saw was a four-poster bed with a large canopy. A thin white screening was pushed back against each post. A lovely wedding-ring quilt with pillows to match draped over the bed.

"I had Bill come in and lay a fire to warm the room. You have a nice water closet with your own private tub. For now, Mr. Tyler doesn't have running water in the house, except for the kitchen. He does have plans to have it installed later. I feel you and Mr. Tyler will be very comfortable in here. Please let me know if you need anything. I'll bring you a tray of food. Oh, here comes Bill with your trunk."

Patricia and Bill left her standing in the middle of the beautiful bedroom. A cold chill ran up her back. She wasn't sure if it was from being so cold before or new nerves. Hurrying over to her trunk, she opened it and saw that Lucy had put in one of her matching gowns and robes. It looked like a gown a bride would wear. "Oh, mercy."

Mary Grace ambled over to the fireplace and dropped the blanket that she had used to cover her body down in the parlor. She slipped on the soft blue gown trimmed with small yellow flowers embroidered around the neckline.

Suddenly an angry thought flashed into her mind. *Luke is not going to share my room. He can sleep anywhere but not in here with me.*

She hurried over to the door and hunted for the key but couldn't find a keyhole. Would her husband build a bedroom door that a person couldn't lock? She searched for a chair to place under the doorknob, but there wasn't a straight chair in the room. She squeezed behind a four-foot chest and shoved it, but it wouldn't budge.

The blasted thing was heavy, even with the empty drawers. She turned her back to the piece of furniture for leverage, pushed with all of her might, and moved it in front of the door. "There," she said to herself. She brushed her hands together and felt sure she had locked him out.

"I hope you aren't attempting to lock me out of my bedroom, my dear bride."

"How did you get in here?" She hurried around him and peered out the doorway where he stood.

"I came in the nursery door that leads out into the hallway. It will be quite convenient for the nanny who will care for the babies during the night."

"What babies? Now you listen to me. You are not staying in my room. Get out. I'm exhausted, and I want to go to bed."

There was a knock on the door. "That must be Patricia with our supper trays." Luke pushed the dresser back, opened the door, and motioned for Patricia and Bill to bring in the two trays of steaming food. "Put the food down on the little table in front of the fire. Thank you both for your help. Good night." He motioned for her to sit. "Come, Sweetheart, and eat some of this hot food. I know you're hungry and it will help you sleep." He stood by one of the rockers and waited for her to join him.

She stood frozen to the spot, not even blinking.

"Mary Grace, I don't want to start our marriage off by me being the bad guy, but I will if you don't behave yourself and come over here—now."

Realizing she wasn't getting anywhere with Luke, she slowly walked to the rocker and sat down. He poured her a cup of hot tea and a cup of dark coffee for himself.

"All this food smells so good. Patricia is a good cook, but her food is not nearly as good as yours. I've missed your cooking."

"So, I am going to be your cook." When Luke didn't reply, she asked another question. "As your wife, what other jobs will I have?"

A tick moved in his jaw, but he didn't respond right away. Then, "Mary Grace, I realize you weren't ready to be my wife, but since we had to marry sooner than I planned, you are my wife. I expect you to 'act' like my wife in every way. In time, when you are ready to be my real wife, then you'll let me know. But know that I will never force myself upon your body."

"So, if I am to act the part of your wife, you will also be a proper husband to me. Is that correct? No visiting the upstairs in the saloons or staying out all night playing poker?"

Luke avoided giving an answer but when he did, he surprised Mary Grace. "Yes, Madam." He shifted and locked eyes with hers. "I will be an ideal husband."

Mary Grace looked at her new husband. She was deeply in love with him, but there was no way she was going to allow him to know it. "Well, you can't stay in my room. It won't be proper."

"It is proper for a man and woman who are married to share the same room, and we will share this room. I will grant you the bed, and I will sleep on the divan."

Mary Grace turned and looked at the pretty, floral sofa placed under the two wide windows in the room. "That thing isn't made for a six-foot tall cowboy to sleep on."

"If you object to my sleeping there, I guess I'll have to sleep in your bed with you. I don't have any objections to doing that." He gave her a grin and a wink.

"I don't want you in here, especially in my bed, you big bully."

"Now, Sweetheart, let's not start calling each other names.

Come and eat so we can go to bed. I'm exhausted." He reached for a biscuit and ham."

# Chapter 31

Mary Grace had a sleepless night until early morning. Soft snoring came from Luke. His long legs draped over the end of the divan and his head was nearly off the edge of the cushion.

She smiled to herself, turned over, and fell into a deep sleep.

Fresh air was flowing across the room with bright sunshine bouncing off the wall. Mary Grace slid out of the bed, tiptoed across the room, and lowered the window. A mama bird chirped on the window ledge.

She hurried over to the fireplace and stirred the coals while tossing in a few smaller sticks to flame the fire. The floor was so cold. One of the first things she'd do was ask Luke to order a nice rug to go in front of the fireplace. After hurrying out of the water closet, she wrapped herself in a warm robe. She sat close to the fire and held her hands out in front of her. A knock came at the door.

"Come in," Mary Grace called.

Lucy entered the room, glowing with the biggest smile. "Oh, Miss, this is the most beautiful house. I am so glad that Mr. Tyler asked me to come with you."

"I told him I was responsible for you, but that's not exactly the truth. You will be eighteen soon, which makes you a grown woman. You won't have to answer to anyone then."

"Oh, Miss, but I do. I have to work and earn money, so I will have to get a job to support myself."

"I guess that is true. You can work for me if you like, maybe be my maid or help me in the kitchen. I'll be cooking like before."

"Can't I do both? I'll enjoy taking care of your clothes, drawing your bath, and you know I love to cook, too."

Mary Grace laughed and hugged Lucy. "Girl, you can do whatever you want to do. I'll meet with Luke and ask him how much he's going to pay you. Never agree to work for a man without knowing what he's going to pay you first." Mary Grace shook her finger in Lucy's face. Both of the girls laughed.

"Good morning to two of the prettiest girls on this ranch. What's so funny?" Luke asked.

"Lucy is curious about what her responsibility will be in the house and how much she's going to be paid."

Quirking an eyebrow, Luke glanced at Lucy and back at Mary Grace. "I believe I will let you decide what her duties will be and how much she is entitled to each month. Room and board, and clothes should be included as part of her payment."

"Oh, no, Mr. Tyler, that is too much. I ain't worth all that," Lucy replied, her eyes pensive.

"I'm sure Mary Grace feels different." He glanced at his new wife, and she smiled at him for the first time in days.

"Oh, my," Lucy said.

Luke stared at Mary Grace, seeming to enjoy her lovely blue robe. "You slept in this morning. You seemed to have had a restless night. Were you having bad dreams?"

Mary Grace whirled around. Just the sight of her handsome husband caused fluttering in her stomach when she was close to him. "I never slept better, Mr. Smarty Pants. I was just tired from the long trip in the cold and rain. I'm ready to get started with my duties."

"As my wife, Miss Know-it-all, you don't have any duties. You can do whatever you choose to do or sit on your sassy backside all day. The choice is yours," Luke said and strode out of the room, whistling as he walked downstairs.

"Oh, Miss, you are so lucky to have such a wonderful man love you. I pray God will send me someone just like him," Lucy said, and she started straightening up the quilt on the divan.

"Be very careful what you pray for, Lucy. Very careful.'

\*\*\*

In less than an hour, Mary Grace and Lucy went downstairs to the kitchen. Nellie had helped her mama, Patricia, prepare a buffet of breakfast food. Mary Grace insisted that Lucy sit and have breakfast with her and Luke.

"I will this morning, but from now on, I will be working in the kitchen. I'm a servant here," Lucy said and took a seat at the table.

"Now wait just a minute," Mary Grace said. "There aren't any servants in this house." She gave Luke a hard look, and he nodded for her to continue. "I will be helping with the meals, cleaning the house, and working in the kitchen garden come this spring. Everyone who lives here will work and eat together like family. That means you, Patricia and Nellie. I want Sam and Bill to eat with us, too. We will not be cooking and serving meals all day. Meals will be at the same times each day, so everyone will know that it's time to stop and join around the table."

Patricia and Lucy stared with their mouths open. Luke laughed and held a chair for his wife.

"My wife has spoken, and I agree with her. I want everyone to enjoy living and working here—together, as a family."

"Mercy, I never thought you would be working in the kitchen with me. Of course, I will be happy for the help." Patricia said.

"This is my house and I intend for it to be a welcoming one. I have to make it a home, along with others who live here. I won't have anyone living here who is not willing to work as hard as I do."

Luke smiled and held out a chair for Mary Grace to sit at the table. He turned to the others and said. "Today, my new bride may not be able to get started in the kitchen because after breakfast, I'm taking her to meet my family. We'll be there for a while. Mama may never want Mary Grace to leave once she meets her."

Mary Grace got more acquainted with Patricia and Nellie while enjoying the delicious breakfast. Lucy and Nellie chatted like they had known each other for years.

Luke stood and asked Mary Grace if she was ready to go to meet his mama and pa. She allowed him to take her hand in front of the ladies, as a loving couple.

"Luke, please tell me who I'm going to meet this morning. You have spoken so little about your folks while at the mining camp."

"My mama will be so excited to learn of my marriage and she'll love you. She can't wait for grandbabies, so please don't get embarrassed if she mentions something about them. My mama is a good countrywoman who says whatever she's thinking. You have to love her for it." Luke laughed at Mary Grace's surprised expression.

When she didn't say anything, he went on to describe his pa. "Pa is not in good health. He sits most all day in a wheelchair. My pa is a quiet man and doesn't often speak unless someone asks him a question. Mama says that little Nellie has made him laugh a few times while playing checkers." Luke smiled at her and continued.

"My brother, Butch, lives with Mama and Pa. He's kept their ranch above water all these years that I've been away. Since I returned, I was able to get the ranch out of debt and pay the back taxes. At first, he would have liked to kill me, but he's softened since I moved into my place next door. There was one time before I came to check on you we almost came to blows. He would have beat me to a pulp. Thank goodness, that didn't happen."

"Are things better between you two?"

"Yes, we're getting along so much better. This spring we'll be going on a trip to purchase a herd of cattle and drive them back here. We'll share the herd and the range, since my land adjoins my folks. In the future, Butch will inherit their ranch."

"Why won't you get a share of it?"

"I don't need it and besides, he's worked his behind off for years without my help or money. I wouldn't enjoy having any part of it."

"You know, Luke, even though you and I have our differences, there is one thing I like about you. You're a caring man. You help people who are down on their luck. You share the shirt off your back if someone needs it. And you were so generous with your men who worked at the gold mine—even me."

"I was down-and-out after I left home and I was always offered a helping hand. I promised God if I could help someone, I would, no matter how small or large." Luke looked down at the ground and shook his head. "Speaking of the miners, those men actually did ninety-nine percent of the work. If not for them, the gold wouldn't have been discovered. It felt good to share the money with them and you, too."

"Sometimes, I feel like I forced you to give me my share." She cringed at the thought. He should understand how she was feeling at the time. "I know the men voted to allow me in on their share, but I made you feel sorry for me, and I threatened to leave the camp if I didn't get a cut of the gold, but in my heart, I wouldn't have left. You were very good to me and well, you deserved better than for me to have a fit of anger and leave you, Jimbo, and Harry."

"Well, that is good to know. But, remember this. You earned a share, and the men knew that you did, so let's forget it," Luke said with a grin.

"Here we are. We are close, and most of the time I walk over to see mama. She enjoys sitting with me in her kitchen and chatting over a cup of coffee. Maybe you will begin doing that too. She'll enjoy your company." Luke rounded the carriage and helped Mary Grace to the ground.

A man hurried out of the barn to take Luke's horse and tie it to the hitching rail. "Morning, Luke, Madam." He removed his hat. "Gerald, this is Mary Grace. My wife."

"My goodness. It sure is nice to meet you, ma'am."

Luke and Mary Grace went to the front porch and watched as Arthur Turnbull attempted to stand.

"Howdy, young fellow," he called. "Who's that pretty little gal you're holding on to there?"

"Mr. Turnbull, this is Mary Grace, my wife."

"Shut my mouth. When did you get her?" Before Luke could answer, Butch came out of the door pushing Pa in his wheelchair onto the porch.

"Morning, son," his pa called to him. "Come on and bring your guest with you. Butch, go get your mama and tell her we have company."

Butch stood staring at the couple but said nothing, then entered the house. "Ma, Luke has come over and brought a gal with him. You'd better come outside and meet them. Roberta, you may as well come along too."

Butch turned and held the front door open for his ma and Roberta. As soon as Roberta saw Mary Grace, she clapped her hands and rushed down the few steps into Mary Grace's arms.

"Oh, Roberta, I'm so happy to see you. The boys hunted Denver over for you and Billy. How did you ever come to be here?"

"We'll speak about that later, but you'd better meet Luke's folks first," Roberta said. She looked thrilled to see Mary Grace.

Luke took an audible breath and expelled it. "Mama and Pa, I want to introduce you to my wife, Mary Grace Winters, now Mrs. Luke Tyler. We were wed in Blount Town."

"Your wife? Why, son, you've been home for weeks and never said anything about getting married," Mama said, never taking her eyes off Mary Grace. "But no matter. I am most pleased to meet you, Mary Grace. Welcome to our home."

"Well, mama, when I went back to Denver, I found that I couldn't live another day without making this wonderful girl my wife. It took some persuading, but I finally convinced her to be my wife."

"Come closer, child, and let me get a better look at you. These old eyes aren't what they used to be," Pa said and held out his hand.

Mary Grace walked slowly to the front porch and took his hand in hers. She felt instantly connected to the older man.

"My, you are a beauty."

"Thank you, sir. That's sweet of you to say." Mary Grace reached for Luke's mama's hand, but instead, she walked into her open arms. These wonderful parents of Luke's accepted her immediately. A sense of calm came over her. She was home.

Swallowing laughter, Mama suggested that they return to the kitchen and have some coffee and a sweet roll. "You have to tell us all about yourself, Mary Grace. Do you have family, brothers, or sisters?"

"Mama, give the poor girl a chance to get inside." Pa said, smiling at his wife.

Roberta hurried to the door. "I have just taken a pan of pastries out of the oven, and I'll make a pot of fresh coffee."

Mary Grace had a desire to move closer to Roberta and give her another big hug, but she would wait and speak with her privately. She had missed the older woman so much after she and Billy had disappeared from the café. There were several answers she wanted to get from Roberta because she never dreamed she would abandon her and the café. They had been like mother and daughter, or so Mary Grace thought.

*\*\*\**

Butch shook hands with Mary Grace and said welcome to the family but left to go to help Gerald in the barn. He couldn't believe Luke's good luck. He thought for sure Luke would hitch up with Patricia. Maybe, just maybe, he would have a chance with her now. He had been hankering to walk out with her ever since she arrived.

## Chapter 32

Early the next morning, Mary Grace and Patricia were cooking when Mary Grace asked about Butch, Luke's brother.

"What do you want to know about him? He's a silent man and appears angry all the time." Patricia frowned.

"Why do you think he's angry all the time?" Before she could answer, Mary Grace said, "He's quite handsome. Does he have a lady friend?"

"I have never heard his ma speak about a lady friend of his. He hardly ever leaves the ranch to go to town. Since we've been here, Luke does most of the shopping."

"Why do you think he's angry all the time?' Mary Grace questioned.

"I'm not sure. I've tried to spend a few minutes with him, but he looks at me like I am a traitor or a murderer."

Mary Grace laughed. "Maybe he's jealous. Are you and some other man friendly in his presence?"

"How do you know so much about men? You're too young to have been around many."

"Maybe so, but I worked in my pa's café and bar since I was knee-high, and I heard it all from men about women when they didn't know I was listening."

"Well, Luke and Billy are the only men I come in contact with daily. Billy, who wants to be called Bill, is too young. Luke and I have been cleaning this house with the help of a few ladies from town."

# THE GAMBLE

"I bet Butch thinks you have an itch for Luke." Mary Grace giggled.

"You think?" Patricia laughed and covered her face with her hands. "I wish he were jealous and would call on me. I like him, maybe too much."

"What would you think about working for Luke's mama and Roberta coming over here and working for me? I haven't talked with Roberta, but back in Denver, we were as close as mother and daughter. I miss her something terrible. She'd like to work for me and be close to her son every day. What do you think?"

"So, you're thinking if I was in the house with Butch, and Luke wasn't around, he might feel comfortable talking with me?"

"Yes, and I understand from Luke's mama that Nellie loves Mr. Tyler and that other man, Mr. Turnbull. She says Nellie has become their playmate." Mary Grace laughed, and Patricia's expression brightened.

"Do you think we could change positions without anyone being the wiser? I'd hate it if Butch thought for one minute I wanted to be near him."

"I'll talk with Luke's mama and tell her I miss Roberta so much and would like for her to live with me. She'll understand, and besides she thinks the world of you and Nellie already. She told me so yesterday."

"Oh, my goodness. I can tell that you and I are going to be the best of friends. When do you think you will talk with her?"

"Let me talk to Roberta today, and then I'll speak to Luke about it. Men like to think that certain things are their ideas." Mary Grace gave a little laugh and finished her coffee.

\*\*\*

Later that night, Mary Grace lay propped up in the four-poster bed when Luke came strolling into the bedroom. She'd hoped to speak with Luke about Roberta coming here to live, but he was gone all day and into the night. "You were missed at supper, darling. Where were you?"

"It's nice to know that I was missed, dear," He answered her back with the same amount of sarcasm.

"It just so happened that I invited your mama, your pa, and Butch to have dinner with us. You were sorely missed, Mister, and do you think that I could tell them where my husband was? No. I couldn't even begin to make an excuse for your sorry self."

"This should teach you not to have a dinner party unless you ask me first."

"This is my home. I don't have to ask your permission to do anything, if I remember correctly."

"Mary Grace, I went to town to have some money transferred from Denver to our bank in Pine Hill. I also posted a letter to Jimbo and Harry. I am hoping that they will come and help Butch and me when we go get our new herd. I'm going to need a chuckwagon cook and helper."

"Did that little business take you all day and into the night? Or, were you busy playing poker, hoping to win yourself another little gal?"

Luke unbuttoned his shirt, pulled his shirt tail out of his pants, and stood staring at her. "You'd better take this warning to heart, wife. You're going to make me jerk you out of that bed, and when I do, you'll be sorry. Don't you dare talk like that to me again."

"Oh, I see clearly now. I have married a woman beater!" She pulled the bedcovers up to her shoulders.

He stopped and looked down at the divan with disgust. "For your information, smarty-pants, Mr. Booth's barn caught fire and I stopped to help his hired hands put it out. We worked for hours to keep the fire from burning the house down." He sat to remove his boots, then sighed and leaned his head back on the soft cushion. "I took a bath in the bunkhouse before I came into the house."

***

Mary Grace felt like a skunk, talking so ugly to Luke when he didn't deserve it. She slipped off the bed, wriggled into her robe, and hurried over to the bottles of sherry and brandy on a table in the corner of the room. She poured him a half glass of brandy and carried it to him. As she reached out to give him the glass, she heard a soft snore. He was asleep? Just when she was ready to apologize for laying into him for missing dinner, he sat straight up sound asleep. Mercy sakes, the man was dead tired.

Quickly, she removed his socks and loosened his belt buckle. She took his shoulders, twisted him around, and then picked up his legs and laid them up on the divan. After she had him straightened out, she placed a quilt over his long body. Some smut dirtied his forehead. Using a soft cloth, she wiped it off.

He opened his eyes and caught her wrist. She stumbled across his chest. "Thanks for tucking me in, sweetheart," he said with a husky voice. "How about a goodnight kiss?"

"Oh, you." She pulled away from him and pushed to stand. He closed his eyes and was fast asleep immediately, a silly grin stretched across his face.

Mary Grace lowered the light on the lantern and climbed back into her bed. Glancing at the ceiling she prayed, "Lord, help me be a good wife to that ornery, wonderful man."

\*\*\*

Later the next afternoon, after Mary Grace spoke with Luke about the exchange of living arrangements, Mary Grace and Patricia entered the back door of Luke's parents' home. "Good morning, Mrs. Tyler, Roberta," she said. Mary Grace glanced around the kitchen and asked if they had time to sit down for a small discussion.

"Anything for my favorite girls." Mrs. Tyler smiled. "I do wish you girls would call me Maureen."

"Roberta, you know how I feel about you—like the mother I never had. Patricia knows I like her, too, but we were hoping you two could change places. You will come and live with me and Patricia and Nellie will live and work here."

Mrs. Tyler's eyes widened.

"It has nothing to do with you, Mrs. Tyler, or anyone here, but Roberta is like family to me, and her son, Bill, already lives in my home."

"Girls, It's a wonderful idea." She leaned closer and whispered, "Butch is always making up excuses to ride over and see Luke. I'm not dumb or blind. Having you, Patricia, here all the time will be good for both of you." She winked, and the girls laughed.

"What's so funny," Butch asked as he barged in the back door.

"Oh, Butch, Patricia and Nellie are going to live here and work for us. Little Nellie will be here all the time, and I know those two old men on the porch will enjoy having her around. They're always sad when she has to go to Luke's."

"Do you dislike working here, Roberta? I thought you were happy being with us," Butch said, a frown replacing his smile.

"I enjoyed working for all of you, but now that Mary Grace is here, I want to be with her all the time. We were very close in Denver," Roberta said, her face warming.

"Listen, you big bully. Nellie and I can go somewhere else if you don't want us here. Just say what you're thinking."

"Butch, shame on you. You apologize to these girls. They just want everyone to be happy here, and Patricia is a hard worker. She and Roberta have made Luke's place a showplace." Maureen stepped to her towering son and pushed her finger into his chest.

Blushing as red as a beet, Butch swallowed and stared at the floor. "I'm sorry. I hope you'll be happy here." He grabbed his hat off the wall rack and rushed out the backdoor.

Once he was out of earshot, the girls laughed, then sat at the table enjoying being together.

Patricia stared at the door. "Butch might be one hard man to live with. I pray he'll accept my presence here on a daily basis."

"Oh, he will," Mary Grace said.

"Good, because I sure enjoy his."

\*\*\*

Two weeks passed and Mary Grace had gained her strength back, and the color had returned to her cheeks. She was so thankful that Luke had come to Denver and brought her to his home as his bride. One night, soon, she was going to become his wife in every way, and she looked forward to it with all of her heart. Mary Grace pulled the curtains back and looked down at her new home—a home she never even dreamed of having. She dressed and went downstairs to help Roberta with breakfast.

"It sure smells wonderful in here. Reminds me of the mining camp," Sam said and took his plate and walked over to the buffet to fill it with ham, scrambled eggs, and sticky honey buns.

"Where's Luke?" Mary Grace asked Sam.

"He's in the barn getting ready to ride into Pine Hill to pick up the lumber that was ordered for Mr. Booth to rebuild his barn. Tomorrow the men will gather at his home for a barn raising."

"Oh, Mary Grace, we'll need to cook food and take it over to the Booths' house to help feed the men." Roberta's eyes sparkled like a young girl's.

"Of course. I wish Luke had told us about this earlier. I still have time to make a few dozen sticky buns for an early treat for the men."

"They will love that," Luke said, removed his hat, and picked up a plate to help himself to some breakfast. "A big pot of beans and cornbread will go a long ways too, if you don't mind cooking up four or five big pots."

"Goodness, Luke. We can prepare something better than old beans," Roberta said with a laugh.

"Beans will fill a hungry gut while working from sun up to sun down, "Luke commented.

"How many wagons are you taking to Pine Hill to get the lumber? Do you need me to drive a wagon?" Mary Grace asked with expectant eyes. She wanted to get out of the house and enjoy the nice weather.

"I have two. Sam and I will drive one each and Mr. Booth has three large flatbed wagons. Five should bring all the lumber we need to his place." Luke frowned at her expression. "And…I'll be happy to have you ride along with me if you like. While we're loading the wagons, you can pick up some needed supplies."

"Great, I would love to tag along. Let me get my coat and hat. I'll make a list with Roberta, and we can stop at your folks' home and see if they would like a few things from town."

Luke beamed when Mary Grace mentioned his mama and the others who lived next door.

# Chapter 33

"Morning, sugar," Lulu Bridges said to Trace Taylor.

He glanced up to see one of the doves who worked at the Lily White Saloon sashay toward him. Lulu rubbed up against him. "Morning to you. I'm surprised you're up and dressed this early. I thought you gals slept until noon."

Glaring at him, Lulu said, "What do you mean, you gals? Are you lumping me in the same category as the other ladies who work here?"

"Now, Lulu, that wasn't my intention at all. I came in here to get a cup of coffee before I go help raise a barn with some of the other townspeople. Some man by the name of Tyler is paying a good day's wage, and I could use the money."

"You mean Luke Tyler? The rich miner who came back home and bought the property next to his folks? They say he's stinking rich. He's come in here a couple of times and had a beer. The men tried to get him to play poker, but he never did while I was here."

"You didn't make a play for him? I'm sure he would have swept you up," he said, tapping her on the nose.

"One of the girls said he brought a gal back from Denver to Pine Hill, and they are married. Her name is Grace or something."

"Mary Grace Winters? He's married to her?" Trace was shocked to learn that the wealthiest gal in Denver was here in the same little town where he was hiding out. He'd have to be careful and not let her see him. By now, she had surely heard that he was a wanted man for stealing cattle and robbing a few poor farmers.

"Yes, I heard something about her being sick, and that rich man caught the train to Denver to check on her. When he returned, they were married. Some of the other girls tried to get him to notice them," she said laughing. "Just their luck. Handsome, rich, and now married."

"Listen, I have to go. If I ask, will you help me with something without asking questions? I'll pay you good if I can count on you to keep your mouth shut."

"I guess. If there's money involved, I'll help." Lulu placed her hand on her slim hip and gave him a wicked smile.

Trace hurried out and joined the men riding to Booth's ranch. He lowered his hat when they reached the farm and broke up into smaller groups to build the rafters and the sides of the barn.

Several men had been there earlier laying out the foundation for the walls. The barn floor was going to remain dirt, but big logs were lined in the trenches so the walls and roof would be sturdy.

When women arrived with lunch, the men hurried to set up makeshift tables. Big pots of homemade beef soup, cornbread, beans, and sausages, hot tamales, sliced tomatoes, whole dill pickles, and Mary Grace's fried apple pies were ready to serve. The men ate until they were about to burst, and many stretched out on piles of unused lumber.

Trace waited until Mary Grace went into the house before he fixed himself a plate of food. He lowered his hat over his eyes and sat as far away as he could from the men without appearing unfriendly. Mary Grace chatted with her new husband. He recognized the older woman who had worked at the café. She and Mary Grace carried a few pots to their wagon.

"See you around supper time," the older woman called, then Mary Grace led the horses out of the yard, away from the building site. A few of the men waved and rubbed their stomachs.

The routine was the same for the next two days. Once the barn was built, all the men patted each other on the back. Mr. Booth's family was so proud of their new barn, and tears flowed down Mrs. Booth's cheeks as she thanked all the ladies for helping her feed the men. Mary Grace and other woman were the last to leave, along with her husband and the old man who had lived near the mine.

***

Early the next morning, Mary Grace read the note Luke had left her, informing her he had to take care of some business at the bank. He would be home to have lunch with her. They needed to discuss what he should do with the old white school building on their property.

During breakfast, Mary Grace asked Roberta, Bill, and Sam if they had any ideas what they could do with the building. She told them that Luke was looking for suggestions.

"What about a schoolhouse?" Roberta said. "They use an old barn now for the school."

"We could divide up the children by age, but we'd need more teachers, and the school board hardly pays a decent wage to the teacher we have." Mary Grace sighed and glanced at Bill and Sam. "You got any ideas?" she asked the two men.

Sam sighed. "What about an orphanage? I peeked into the windows, and it has a lot of separate rooms. So many kids don't have a place to live. Think of all those boys living on Denver's streets, camping out in the woods near Crooked Creek."

Mary Grace nodded. "You know, Lucy was kicked out of the orphanage in Denver the day I met her. She was looking for a job when I walked up to her. The staff there made the older children leave because they didn't have enough money to feed them. I hired a new couple to run it before I had to leave Denver. There are a couple of boys now living with my friends, Jimbo and Harry, in Denver."

"An orphanage sounds like a big responsibility to take on," Bill said, glancing at his mother. "Mr. Tyler is going to turn this place into a working ranch, once he buys several hundred head of beef. There'll be fields to plant with hay and oats. He's told me he wants to plant fields of corn and other vegetables to share with his neighbors who live in town."

"Gosh, you're right. Small children would be running all around the ranch, and that could be a problem. Maybe Luke will have another idea for the white building." Mary Grace removed plates from the table as the men left the kitchen to go to work.

Mary Grace and Roberta put on a pot of cut-up beef to boil and a large pot of dried black-eyed peas to soak for supper. They strolled outside and looked over the ground near the kitchen.

"This would be a good place for a nice kitchen garden. What

do you think, Roberta?" Mary Grace strolled around the smooth ground. "We could place a tight fence around it to keep the rabbits and raccoons out."

"We can also place some grass and lettuce in a small trough close by the garden. A full trough will keep the smaller animals fat and sassy and out of our garden."

"You are so smart. I love that idea." Mary Grace laughed.

"So, what do you want to plant? Small red potatoes, green onions, carrots, running green beans on poles, butter beans, and anything else?' Roberta asked.

"Let's go in the house and write down all the items we need. Luke can hire a man to come and plow up the ground for us. The next time we go to town, we can buy seeds and some small plants. Let's plant strawberries and let them run up the fence." Mary Grace couldn't wait to talk to Luke. Mercy, it seemed she wanted to discuss everything with the man whom she riled up quicker than a man with a mess of cockleburs in his socks.

After a long day, Mary Grace sat in the parlor waiting for Luke to return. She'd taken a leisurely bath and dressed in one of her nicest day dresses. Her hair shone from a good brushing, and she'd tied it back with a blue ribbon that matched her dress. "Roberta, y'all go ahead and eat supper. I want to wait for Luke. I'll eat with him." Sam had a funny expression on his face. "What's wrong? Are you worried about Luke?"

"Well, he told me that he was going to the bank early so he could get back and do some things with you today. I'm surprised he's so late. I expected him home before lunch." He shuffled his boots over the pattern on the rug.

"I'm sure he will be home soon. Please have your supper." Mary Grace collapsed into the rocking chair in front of the fireplace. Hours later, she blew out the lantern in the parlor and left the light on in the kitchen. Luke would come in the back door. She stared at the kitchen counter and picked up a cookie under a glass bowl that Roberta had used as a cover to keep the cookies fresh.

Mary Grace strolled up the staircase and entered their bedroom. She loosened her collar and unfastened all the buttons down the front of her dress. Dropping it to the floor, she pulled on her flannel nightgown, climbed into bed, and sobbed into her pillow. *Luke's in town with another woman.*

## Chapter 34

Luke thanked Mr. Jones, Pine Hill Bank's president, and exited the bank. He nodded at some young girls who giggled and hurried by him.

"Gosh, he's so handsome," one of the girls said.

He took out his pocket watch and checked the time. His plan was to hurry home and have a nice lunch with his new bride. He wanted to take Mary Grace for a ride over to the old schoolhouse. Maybe she'd help him decide what to do with it, if anything. After he donned his Stetson, he untied his horse.

A voice behind him made him gasp.

***

"Just keep doing what you are doing. Get on your horse. You will ride beside me out of town. If you do anything funny, I'll shoot you, and you'll never see that lovely bride of yours again." Trace Taylor's leg brushed up against Luke's as they walked their horses away from the bank and then kicked them into a trot out of town.

About two miles out, Trace pointed to a big grove of oak trees off the road. "The name's Trace. Stop here and I'll tell you what I need from you."

Luke pulled his horse to a stop and sat waiting for his kidnapper to explain what he wanted. Trace pointed the gun at Luke's chest. "I'm already a wanted man, so killing you won't matter. They can only hang me once."

Luke didn't react. He sat on his horse, his eyes narrowed.

"Mr. Tyler, I know you're a rich man, and I also know that Mary Grace has plenty of money. Now that you two are married, you have twice the amount of money, and I want some of it. I tried to persuade Mary Grace to be my girl in Denver, but she got sick and I got run out of town. Instead of saving her café, I nearly killed several people and her business was shut down. Did she tell you about her little nightmare?"

Luke shook his head. "Jimbo wrote me that she was sick, and two men were sniffing around her. So, you must be one of the men who claimed to be in love with her."

"Ha. I never loved a woman, especially a hard-headed gal like her. Oh, she's beautiful enough, but man, you have your hands full with that smart-ass. If we'd ever hooked up, I would have had to beat some obedience into her. That gal wanted everything her way. She might have wrapped that young banker around her little finger because he was willing to do whatever she wanted. He already had a sweet friend, a handsome daisy, hidden away from his pa, if you get my meaning."

***

"So, you want money. How much will satisfy you?" Luke had heard enough about his wife. He cut straight to the point.

"I want twenty-five thousand dollars and I want it tomorrow. I'm going to send my friend to the bank with a note from you, requesting the money. After she brings it to me, I'll let you go."

Luke knew it was a lie. This man wasn't going to allow him to go on his way, especially since he'd said his name. He wondered who this friend was that was going to help him collect the money. "Your friend might have a hard time obtaining that amount of money from Pine Hill Bank. They don't carry a large amount of money any time. They have to request it from the First Bank of Denver."

"You're lying. All banks have plenty of money," Trace said.

"Why would I lie? I want to be turned loose. So, I want you to get the money as soon as possible," Luke said, trying hard to keep the sneer from his voice.

"We'll see tomorrow." Trace reached for Luke's horse's reins and led him off the road. Luke tried to determine how far away he was from town.

Trace stopped the horses in front of an old shabby cabin

hidden in a thicket of trees. He pointed his pistol into Luke's back and pushed him into the dark cabin. With the light of a struck match, he lit a lantern sitting in the middle of a small table. Spiderwebs hung from the ceiling, and rats scurried back into their holes.

"Your maid service wasn't notified of your visit," Luke said sarcastically.

"Don't worry about the service here, buddy. My woman will be here in the morning. Until then, move over to the cot by the fireplace. I don't want my guest to freeze before he writes a note to the banker."

Luke walked over to the dusty cot. On the end lay a wool blanket.

"Sit," demanded Trace. "Put your hands behind your back." He tied his wrists together and then bent down and tied his ankles tight.

Luke felt like a hog-tied calf. "When will supper be served? I missed lunch and now dinner," Luke asked, hoping the fool had remembered to bring food at least for himself.

"I'll make some coffee, but sorry to say, I only have one cup." He laughed at his own joke, but Luke didn't comment.

After Trace finished his coffee, he started for the door. Luke called to him to stop. "I need to go outside before I retire for the night."

"All right, I'm going to untie your hands while you hop outside and relieve yourself. If you try anything, I'll shoot you in the leg. I need you alive for a while."

Luke watched him untie his hands. Trace seemed to be a little shaky. The man was probably wishing he had a strong drink of whiskey. After completing his personal needs, Trace held the door open while he hopped back to the cot.

"You might as well sleep, Money Bags. My friend won't be here until daylight. Hopefully, she'll remember to bring something to eat," Trace said and tied Luke's wrists to the rickety cot.

"Now, if you try to get up, I will hear you. I'm a light sleeper." Tracy laughed. "Man, I sure wish I'd brought a deck of cards. We could have played a game or two. Is it true you won Mary Grace in a poker game in Crooked Creek?"

Luke just stared at the tall, shabby-haired man who needed a bath and a shave.

"Fine, don't answer me, but I heard that rumor in Denver." He tossed another log into the fire before he stretched out on the other dirty cot. The lantern, with its dirty glass globe, flickered and sputtered and then it went out. The cabin was in total darkness except for the fire dancing blue and red lights on the logs. It was only a few minutes until Tracy was snoring.

Luke watched the shadows of the fire flashing off the ceiling. The rats were returning, probably in hopes of finding crumbs on the floor. He pulled on his wrists, but he was tied tight. He pushed on the rope twisted around his ankles. He was hog-tied for sure. He couldn't help but think about Mary Grace waiting for him to return for lunch.

She'd be furious that he stood her up. Sam would be worried for sure because he knew Luke had gone into the bank to get money to pay the men. Surely the men would be upset that he didn't meet with them to give them their wages.

It was funny that the cowboy hadn't searched him once they reached the cabin. Five hundred dollars sat in his coat pocket. Bill and Roberta would be concerned about him, too. Surely, in the morning, Sam would talk to his brother, Butch. Maybe, they'd form a search party starting at the bank in Pine Hill. Sam was old, but he was a smart old coot. He'd know something was definitely wrong. Sam had been his sidekick for months, and he knew that if Luke said something, he'd keep his word or else tell someone if he changed his mind. Hopefully, the men would find him soon.

\*\*\*

"Sam, did Luke come home last night?" Mary Grace asked the moment she saw him. "He didn't come to our room, and I'm worried about him."

Sam was standing in the kitchen drinking a cup of hot coffee. He was waiting for Bill to come in and ride over to Luke's brother's ranch. They wanted to get Butch and Gerald to help form a search party. "No, he didn't, but we're going into town. If we find the boy, I will personally bring him back to you."

\*\*\*

After telling Butch and Gerald about Luke not returning from the bank, Butch asked, "Do you think he drew out some money and someone saw him? Maybe he was robbed."

"Luke was going to withdraw money from the bank to pay the men who didn't volunteer to help with the barn raising. He'd offered a wage to the men who needed a job and told the men to meet him in front of the bank around ten o'clock."

"That's where we need to start. Let me tell Pa what we're doing. He can't help, but he needs to know. I'll tell him to keep quiet about Luke's disappearance. Mama doesn't need to worry unnecessarily."

The men searched for tracks and any other clues for Luke as they rode slowly into town. They passed a black carriage on the road.

"That Lulu just gave me a nod," Gerald said. The others laughed. The pretty girl had drinks with him in the Lily White Saloon. He turned back in his saddle and watched her carriage. "Wonder who she's going to visit outside of town?"

\*\*\*

Lulu stopped her borrowed horse and turned around in the carriage seat, watching the dust form from the four horsemen who rode hell-bent past her. Were they looking for Trace? She took up her whip and tapped the horse's back. Once she arrived at the path that would take her to the cabin, she drove the carriage as far as she could. Lulu tied her horse to a tree limb, took a large basket off the seat, and headed down the well-worn path to the cabin.

Just as she reached the cabin, Trace hurried out and retrieved the basket from her hands. "Here, give me that. Gosh, I hope you brought something good to eat. I'm starved."

Well, damn, she stiffened. *This man doesn't have any manners. He doesn't even know how to appreciate a lady.* She followed him into the dirty cabin and ignored him as she glanced at the cot. That rich man, Luke Tyler, struggled to sit up. He wasn't the neat well-kept man she'd seen many times in town. How long had he been tied to that nasty cot?

Terror flooded over her for the first time. What had she agreed to do for the cowboy she'd only met a few days ago? She needed to tell Trace soon she wasn't going to be involved with a robbery or a murder.

"Get over here and put out this food. I'm going to take Mr. Money Bags outside for a minute. Fix him something to eat. I don't want him passing out from hunger before you get back from the bank."

A false smile plastered her face. She had an awful feeling in the pit of her stomach. From the basket Lulu took a biscuit with ham and laid it on a white cloth napkin.

Trace pushed Luke down on the cot, walked over, picked up the food, and handed it to him.

"Thanks, miss," Luke said, glancing past the tall, lanky cowboy.

"Did you bring paper and a pencil?" he said as he dug down into the basket. "Here it is." Trace snatched Luke's biscuit out of his hand and tossed it on the floor. "Here, write a note to the banker that you want to withdraw twenty-five thousand dollars in small bills."

"I already told you that the bank won't have that kind of money. You need to take me to Denver to withdraw money like that."

"I am not taking you anywhere. You got that? If Lulu comes back without money, I'll kill you. Understand?"

Finding her nerve, she quickly said, "Trace, I've changed my mind. I'm not going to help you. You scare me. I never dreamed that you would kill someone." Her voice quivered.

With a cry of fury, Trace sent her flying across the room to land at Luke's feet. Husky laughter came from Trace's throat. "Girl, you will do as I say or I will shoot him right between the eyes now." He trained his gun on Luke and cocked the hammer back.

"All right, I'll help, like I said before, but please don't kill anyone." Lulu tried to stand. Trace reached down and jerked her up against him.

"You're beautiful, and a very appealing woman, but I will carve your pretty face until no one will recognize you ever again. Do you understand me?"

"Yes." She remained still but trembled all over.

"Now, write a note and make it look neat. Sign your name and fold it. Give it to Lulu." Trace demanded, then watched his every move.

"Aren't you going to read it?" Luke asked.

"No, I know you want to return to your new bride. And if Lulu returns with money, I'll set you free." Lulu and Luke glanced at each other. Both of them knew he was a liar.

"Be on your way to town now, Lulu. Remember to act natural and ask for the bank president. He'll be the one to open the safe and get that much money."

"But, Trace, won't he wonder how come Mr. Tyler's not coming for that large amount of money himself?" Lulu couldn't imagine the bank president handing her that amount of money. She'd end up in prison for sure or hang from a noose.

"You just use that wonderful personality and others parts of your body to get his attention off what he's doing. I've seen you woo men out of their pay at the Lily White Saloon. Now git, girl, and come back with money for both of us. I'll make sure you're paid well, and none will be the wiser." Grabbing Lulu by the arm, he walked her to her carriage. He acted the gentleman and helped her into the seat and untied her horse. "I'll be waiting," he said.

***

Luke recalled meeting the girl, Lulu, in the Lily White Saloon. She'd come up to him while he was alone enjoying a drink to warm his inside before starting home. He wasn't a man to hang out in the bar. There was always trouble brewing in one of those places, and over the years he'd been in enough bar fights to last him a lifetime. What had Trace offered the young girl to help kidnap and rob him? She'd tried to get out of the deal, but he said he would hurt her bad, and she believed him.

## Chapter 35

Lulu frowned as she sat looking at the black horse that was hitched to her carriage. "Trace, please promise me you won't harm Mr. Tyler. I'm afraid."

"You'd better be scared, gal. If you don't bring back the money, I'll make your life miserable. Now remember that. Git going and come back with a bag of greenbacks."

Lulu drove to the front of the bank and hitched her horse to the hitching post. She should have parked the carriage around the side of the bank, but she wanted to make a quick getaway. She straightened her hat and smoothed her dress once she was on the ground. Using her hanky, she wiped the road dust off her forehead and cheeks. Slowly, she entered the bank and looked around. There was only one clerk behind the window cage.

"Good morning, young lady. How may I help you?"

"I need to see the president of the bank, please," she stuttered and dabbed at the sweat on her top lip.

"I'm sorry, miss. Mr. Jones left for Denver this morning." He looked at the clock over his shoulder on the wood-grain wall. "He left this morning on business. He'll be back in four days, but I'll help you, if I can," the friendly clerk remarked.

"No, thank you. I'll come back." She placed the note back in her drawstring bag and hurried out the door. Just as she was going out, she bumped into Gerald Mitchell, whom she knew from the saloon.

"Pardon me, Miss," he said. "Are you alright? I nearly plowed over you."

"I'm fine. Please, let me pass. I must go." Lulu hoped he wouldn't remember seeing her in the bank. She hurried out to her carriage and drove out of town. A glance back showed Gerald standing in the doorway of the bank watching her drive away. He tipped his hat.

\*\*\*

Sam questioned the clerk about Luke. "Yes sir, he came in this yesterday morning and withdrew cash. He said he needed the money to pay the men who worked on the barn raising at Booth's place. I gave him the money he requested, and he left." Sam peered at Butch, but before he could say anything, the clerk broke in, "There was something funny. Several of the men have come in here looking for Mr. Tyler. They want their pay."

"You're saying that Luke never met with the men out front of the bank yesterday? He told me the men were going to gather out front, and he was going to pay them. Did he withdraw several hundred dollars from you?"

"Now, Mr. Wilson, I can't tell you that. Customers' business is private. I don't know anything about a meeting in front of the bank."

"You don't have to tell me anything. I know that's what he planned to do." Sam rubbed his chin and looked at the other men. "Something is terribly wrong."

The men headed to the sheriff's office to report foul play.

The sheriff listened to Sam, then asked, "Do you know anyone who would want to harm him?"

"No, but I think this was a robbery. He came into town to withdraw about five hundred dollars. He was to meet the men who worked at Booth's ranch. He didn't tell Mr. Booth that he was paying all those men. Mr. Booth thinks they're all volunteers, and it should stay that way."

"I won't say anything, but you think someone may have watched him go in the bank and then robbed him after he came out?" The sheriff rubbed the back of his neck.

"I think someone took Luke out of town somewhere. We need to go see if we can pick up a trail." Sam hurried out of the door with Butch, Bill, and Gerald on his heels.

\*\*\*

Lulu was terrified as she walked to the cabin. Trace jerked open the door and stepped in front of her.

"Where's the money?" He glanced down at her empty hands.

"Listen to me, Trace. The bank president was not there. He left for Denver this morning, but he'll be back in four days. You told me only to talk to the president, so I hurried back here." She blew out a series of short breaths to gain control. Lord, she wished she was somewhere else. She knew better than to leave. Trace was a crazy madman, and he would surely kill her and that Tyler fellow.

*\*\*\**

Trace was in a dark mood as he stormed into the cabin. He glanced at Luke. "I should shoot you right now," Trace said and pointed his revolver at Luke's head. His nerves were strained to their limits.

"Trace, he didn't know the bank president was gone, but he told you that the bank might not have that much money." Lulu touched his arm. "C'mon back here. Do you have any cards. We can play a game or two."

Luke stared at the gun. "Listen to me, Trace. Why don't you take me to Denver, and I'll withdraw all the money you want. I left the bulk of my money there. I can walk into the bank and get anything I want. It's a big city, and you won't even be recognized. You and Lulu can escape easily in that crowd of people."

"You might be a rich gold miner, but you're as dumb as dirt. It takes money to ride a train. If I had money, I wouldn't have you hog-tied on that cot." He sneered.

*\*\*\**

Luke said a silent prayer and continued with his deal. "Come over here and reach in my jacket pocket. I have money, and you can use it to purchase tickets. You can go first class with the money I have."

Trace practically leaped across the room and pushed Luke's head back as he rammed his hand into Luke's jacket's pocket. He pulled out five hundred dollars in small bills that were folded.

"What are you doing with this much cash?" Trace waved the money around, and then fanned it in Lulu's face.

"I was planning on paying some men for their work at Booth's farm. Many of them helped build the new barn."

"Well, some of this money is mine." He was almost giddy while counting the money. "I worked two long days helping with that barn raising."

"I don't remember seeing you there. Where were you?" Luke asked. "I was there the whole time."

"I didn't know who you were until Mary Grace showed up with the old woman, who cooked at the café in Denver. I put two and three together and realized you were the rich gold miner that she married. I stayed away and waited until Mary Grace went into the house before I fixed myself a plate of food. One thing I do remember about your gal— she's a great cook."

As he headed across the room, he noticed Luke's pocket watch in his vest. He grabbed it and flipped it open. "If we hurry, we can catch the three o'clock train to Denver." He took out a pocketknife and sliced the ropes on Luke's wrists and his ankles. "All right, let's go. It's about twenty minutes to Pine Hill and another hour to Blount Town. Let's hurry. Maybe we can catch the afternoon train to Denver. We can be there in two days. A man with as much money as you have will be able to get the bank open even if it's closed. Let's go." Trace pushed Luke out the door.

Luke glanced backward to see Lulu staring down at her feet. Softly she said, "Trace, you don't need me. Mr. Tyler can go in the bank and get his own money. I'll stay in town and forget any of this took place."

"Sorry, sweetheart. I'm not leaving you here to run to the sheriff and turn me in. I don't trust you." He grabbed her around the neck, his hands shaking.

"Well," she yelled, "you trusted me to go into town and get you twenty-five thousand dollars. How did you know I wouldn't take the money and keep going where you couldn't find me?"

"Honey, you were afraid that I might harm this handsome gold miner, right?" He twisted her head an inch from his. "I will still harm him if you don't behave yourself and come along on my arm like a loving wife." He pushed her away.

\*\*\*

Looking at Luke, she almost cried, "Of course. I'll go with you." She dragged her feet and followed him to the carriage. "But, Trace, I don't want any of the money. I want you to go your way, and I will go mine. Do you agree?" Lulu prayed he would agree to her terms. She was scared to death of this man whose hands were shaking from lack of whiskey. Working in the saloon, she knew all the signs of an alcoholic. She and Luke had to be very careful in his presence.

"Don't start making demands, gal. I give the orders and decide what will take place." He whipped her around, took her cheeks in his hand, and squeezed. "I'm in control of your lives, you and Money Bags."

She turned her head away from his foul breath. How she ever got involved with this man was a mystery.

## Chapter 36

The men rode back to Butch's ranch, tied their horses to the hitching rail, and went inside the backdoor. "Where in the blazes have you men been?" Patricia practically screamed at the men like a bad-tempered fishwife.

Sam, Gerald, and Bill bypassed the furious woman and continued into the parlor where Luke's pa was waiting. Butch stopped in front of Patricia. "Who do you think you are screaming at? Listen Lady, you only work here. We don't have to report to you about anything."

"Oh really, so I'm only a servant here?" She took deep breaths to calm her nerves. "I may only work here, but I've cooked two full meals today for men who didn't show up to eat or even have the manners to let the cook know they weren't going to be here to eat."

"I will not have you yelling at us. I will not tolerate a foul-tempered, big-mouth woman. Got that?"

Pointing her finger into his heaving chest. "Well, mister, you can get another cook to help your mama. I will not live where I'm not respected. I slaved over that hot stove, waiting and wondering if you were hurt or shot." Patricia was fighting with all her might to keep the tears from falling from behind her eyelids.

Something finally registered to Butch. "You overheard what I told pa this morning, didn't you?" Butch demanded. "You scream and now eavesdrop on my conversations?"

"You big barbarian. I was in the dining room putting dishes on the table when you hurried inside and told him about Luke. You weren't whispering. I couldn't help but hear you." Patricia couldn't remember ever being so angry.

Before Patricia knew what happened, the angry barbarian pulled her into his arms and kissed her hard on the lips. She hardly had time to shut her mouth. Her knees grew weak as her arms flew up and down on her sides. When he deepened the kiss, her breath mingled in a heated flurry, and her blood pounded in her ears. She heard a low moan and realized that it came from her. Finally, she grabbed hold of the front of his shirt. Her stomach whirled and the anger that had made her scream at him melted away. "Gracious," Patricia whispered. "What took you so long?"

"So, you've been waiting for me to make the first move. You'd better be glad I didn't beat you."

"I'm not afraid of your bark." She laid her head on his chest. "What's happening? Have you found Luke?"

"No, I'm afraid not. We think someone robbed him and took him somewhere. We're going back out. Just came to get some supplies in case we have to camp out." He looked over her shoulder at the stove. "Do you think you could rustle up some food for us now? We're starving." As she turned to walk away, he grabbed her again and whispered, "Lady, I'm starved for something else."

"Wait," she said, holding her hand out in front of herself. "Are you proposing marriage?" An expression of devilment played on her face.

He frowned and surveyed every inch of her lovely face. "Lord help me, woman. You get right to the point." He snickered and shook his head. "I guess I am. Will you?"

"Will I what?" she questioned him on purpose, hoping for a proper marriage proposal.

"Will you, Patricia Thompson, mean-spirited, high-tempered woman, be my wife?" He asked while placing both hands on her rosy cheeks. "Dammit, gal, you're going to be the death of me."

"How romantic," Patricia said, trying to hold back a grin. "You know I have Nellie. She'll have to approve."

"Nellie and I are this close." Butch held up two fingers crossed. "She'll approve."

"Then, Mr. Tyler, hard-headed bully, I would love to be your wife."

Sam, Gerald, and Bill came back in the kitchen with Pa rolling his chair behind them. "Get out of here, Romeo, and find your brother. We'll have time for a big celebration when you return safe."

Sam and Bill started out of the backdoor when Mama came in. "What's happening? Lucy said Mary Grace is beside herself with worry about Luke."

"Mrs. Tyler, your husband will tell you all about it. We must hurry." Sam, Bill, and Gerald hurried out of the house and were climbing on their horses when Butch called, "Wait, I'm going too."

"Well, Romeo, we thought you had other business to take care of," Gerald said, laughing.

"My brother comes first, and then I'll take care of my personal affairs." He climbed on his horse, and they rode down the road to track Luke and his kidnapper's trail.

A short way down the road, Gerald called a halt to the men. "Look, there's wagon tracks or maybe a carriage heading off the road here. Looks like it went a good ways into the woods."

"You know, there's an old cabin in this part of the woods. Maybe someone is hiding out there." Butch climbed down off his horse and hurried into the thicket of trees. When they reached the shack, the other men got off their horses and tied them to tree limbs. They didn't see any animals or hear anyone inside.

Butch kicked the door open, barging inside with his pistol drawn. A lantern sat on the mantel of the fireplace. He attempted to light it, but it was out of oil. He stuck another match and held it up high, but there was no one inside.

Gerald came in with a branch on fire to give enough light to see closer. The two cots had been slept on, and an empty basket of leftover food sat in the middle of the table.

The men went outside, and Gerald stomped out the burning branch. "Someone was here and not long ago." Butch looked at the men.

"You know, those wagon tracks outside make me think that Luke was put in a carriage and brought out here from town. This morning when we went to the bank, I bumped into one of the gals who works at the White Lily Saloon. I watched her drive out of town in a small carriage. You don't think that maybe she was helping someone rob Luke?"

"You may be on to something. A kidnapper would demand a lot of money, and the bank in Pine Hill doesn't keep a lot on hand. The man could have sent the girl into the bank to withdraw the money. No one would suspect she was in there to do anything unlawful." Sam thought for a minute and continued talking. "You know, Luke said that he keeps most of his money in Denver."

"It looks to me like we need to go to Blount Town and catch the next train to Denver," Butch said practically running back to his horse.

# Chapter 37

Lulu went into the train depot and purchased three tickets to Denver. Trace followed with a gun pointed at Luke's back. After they boarded the train, they sat in the passenger car near the back entrance.

The train had to make several stops at smaller towns during the eighteen-hour trip to Denver. It stopped to take on water, and passengers were allowed to get off if they so desired. There were two outhouses built on the side of the platform for personal convenience.

Luke felt as if everyone on the passenger car were looking at him. His clothes were dusty and wrinkled after being in the same ones for nearly three days. What he wouldn't give for a hot bath and shave. "You need to let me get cleaned up if I'm going into the bank. Everyone who works there knows me, and they'll certainly wonder why I look like a dirty hobo."

"You're just stalling for time. Ain't nobody going to take you to a hotel so you can get prettied-up to get your own money out of the bank." Trace practically had his own nose touching Luke's.

"Have it your way. I hope you'll have a good story why I look the way I do." Luke glanced at Lulu and gave her a smile. "Don't worry, miss. No one is going to harm you." She shook her head, swallowing hard.

"You'd better listen to me, Money Bags. If they start asking questions, you tell them to mind their own business. You don't have to tell them anything."

The conductor came in the passenger car yelling at the top of his lungs, "Denver."

The trio waited for other passengers to file out the doorway onto the platform. Just as Luke stepped in the doorway of the train, he spotted Jimbo and Harry, his two best friends from the mining camp. He stared at them and shook his head slightly, signaling them not to notice him.

\*\*\*

The two men immediately knew something was wrong by Luke's appearance and that cowboy, Trace, breathing down his neck. The girl was a stranger to them, but she wasn't Mary Grace. They stepped aside and allowed their friend to pass.

Jimbo and Harry watched the three walk past the train depot without stopping to wait for any luggage. "Harry, something's up. Luke would never be traveling with that Trace fellow. If the sheriff knew Trace was in Denver, he'd throw him in jail. Let's stay close and follow them. Remember now, not too close, because Trace knows us."

Luke glanced back and caught a glimpse of his friends following behind in a crowd of people. He tried to give them a smile and a nod, but he had to be careful. Trace would shoot to kill if he felt they were a threat. Walking faster, Trace led them to the First Bank of Denver.

Luke stopped at the front door of the bank and hesitated before entering. Trace was practically breathing down Luke's six-foot-four- inch frame, which looked kind of silly, but Luke didn't care and he wasn't afraid. "Good afternoon, Mr. Anderson." Luke said to his old friend who had purchased his gold mine. "How are you doing these days?"

"I'm fine son, just fine, but land sakes, boy, what have you been doing? You look like you've been digging in a mine again. You haven't found more gold, have you?" He laughed and looked Luke up one side and down the other.

"I don't have much time. I came in today to draw out a large amount of my money. I need twenty-five thousand dollars as soon as your clerk can count it out for me." Luke spoke loud, so the other clerks could hear him. This was something he never did. He always handled his business with another banker or with Mr. Anderson in his private office. Large amounts of money being withdrawn were always kept quiet.

Mr. Anderson led Luke and his companions into his office. Luke noticed a clerk slip out the back door. Hopefully, he'd get the sheriff. Mr. Anderson was a smart old man who had dealt with many bank robbers before; therefore, he probably used a signal to his clerks to go fetch the law.

*\*\*\**

Harry and Jimbo peeked into the bank and noticed that Luke, Trace, and the girl were in one of the private offices. Jimbo kept his hand on his revolver while Harry held tight to his cane. When needed, he had a single-barrel shotgun built into it. His new wooden leg worked wonders, and the cane helped him remain steady on his feet. They stood close to the back wall and kept an eye on the office door.

A flash of a man and then another came into view in the back room of the bank.

The clerk approached customers one at a time and asked them to quietly leave the bank for a few minutes. Everyone was cooperative, except Jimbo and Harry.

"We're Luke's friends and we're here to help the sheriff." The clerk realized if he tried to make them go outside, there would be a loud scene, and that would never do.

In less than ten minutes, Luke led Trace and Lulu out of the office. The sheriff waited until Luke stepped ahead of Trace a few feet before he called a halt to everyone. "Stand where you are, or I'll shoot the first person who moves," the sheriff shouted. "Trace Taylor, you are under arrest. Drop your gun or be prepared to die."

*\*\*\**

Luke took Lulu's arm and pulled her away from Trace. He hurried over to Jimbo and Harry and threw his arms around both of them. He didn't care who saw them hugging like womenfolk. He was thrilled to be alive and happy to see them. Mr. Anderson came out of the office and joined the men.

"So happy this ended well. I knew something was up the minute I saw you so—unkempt." Mr. Anderson laughed and patted Luke on the shoulder. Black dust flew from his clothes and Mr. Anderson said, "Man, were you lying down with dogs somewhere?"

"No, just lying on a nasty cot with a dirty, wool blanket."

Luke grimaced at his clothes. He wiped his hand down his pant leg and turned to the people in the bank.

"Thanks to you and your bank clerks. I will always remember this day." Luke turned to the employees of the bank. "Thank you, men, for your quick action in getting the sheriff." The men smiled and gave him a wave.

"Sheriff, this is Lulu—" Luke glanced at her.

"Lulu Mims. My name is Lulu Mims, Sheriff. Are you going to arrest me?"

Before the sheriff could answer, Luke jumped into the conversation. "No, he isn't going to arrest you. You didn't do anything wrong. You did take up with that cowboy before you knew him. I hope you learned a lesson from this experience. You could have gone to jail, or better yet, been killed. Be careful of the men you agree to help from now on." Luke spoke directly to the sheriff. "This lady helped save my life, and I will always be grateful."

\*\*\*

Jimbo and Harry were two happy men. They had missed Luke.

"Fellows, since you lost your café, I want you to come live with me. Mary Grace and I have plenty of room, and my brother and I are going to buy a herd of cattle come spring. I'll need a chuckwagon cook and helper."

"Shoot fire, man, I'll be glad to help. I'm sick and tired of sitting around with nothing to do but worry about all my money." Everyone laughed at Harry.

"Will Mary Grace be joining us on this cattle drive?" Jimbo asked.

"Not if I have anything to say about it." Luke laughed.

Luke placed his hand on Lulu's back and nodded for Harry and Jimbo to lead the way out of the bank. "Come, Miss Lulu, I need to send my wife a telegram to let her know that I'm alive. I'll rent us a hotel room where we can get cleaned up and then go have some dinner. I'm hungry as a bear." He turned to Jimbo. "Will you go and get us some tickets to Blount Town? I want to go home."

After two days of traveling, Luke and the others came out of the café. A few horses with riders passed by them. "Hey, fellows, that man riding ahead of the others looks like my brother, Butch." Luke stepped down into the street and whistled.

All the horses stopped, and the men whirled around in their saddles. Butch turned his horse completely around and jumped off. He raced to where Luke stood in the middle of the street, bouncing from one foot to another.

Luke was thrilled to see Butch and the other men, too.

Butch reached Luke, stopped, and stared at him. Suddenly he drew back his right fist and slammed it into Luke's jaw, knocking him onto his backside in the middle of the street.

Luke struggled to sit, shaking the cobwebs, and rubbing his bloody mouth.

Before Luke could stop him, Butch wound up to hit him again. All he could do was shield his face. Memories from childhood flooded back of other times Butch bullied him when he didn't like something Luke had done.

"Where have you been, boy?" Butch straddled Luke clenching his swollen fist. "You'd better have a good answer or I'm going to beat it out of you."

Jimbo jumped down off the boardwalk and stooped down beside Luke. "Give Luke a chance to stand," he said and helped his friend to his feet. "Who do you think you are? If you want to hit someone, hit me. I'm more your size."

"Jimbo, back off." Luke moaned, rubbing his jaw. "This is my brother, Butch."

"Your brother? Damn if I would claim him," Jimbo said and handed Luke his Stetson, then dusted his back off.

"Butch, let's get out of the middle of the street and go back inside the café. I'll tell you and the others what took place after I arrived in Denver." Luke grinned at Sam, who rushed over and patted him on the back.

"Man, I have been so worried about you. I knew something was up when you didn't come home." He walked ahead of Luke into the café.

After Luke relived the events of the last four days to the men, Butch apologized. "Mary Grace, Mama, and Pa are worried to death about you."

"Did anyone get my telegram from Denver two days ago?" All the men muttered to each other, shaking their heads.

"I sent one to Mary Grace to let her know that I was alive and would be home in two days. She may receive it later." Luke smiled and changed the topic. He thanked the men for searching for him. "One good thing that happened on this adventure. I found these two, Jimbo and Harry, in Denver." After introducing all the men to each other, Luke said, "Let go home."

# Chapter 38

Once home, the men stopped in front of the bunkhouse at Luke's parents' place. Everyone gathered with Mama and Pa to hear what happened to Luke.

***

Mary Grace heard the horses and she raced outside. Luke leaped from his horse and grabbed her up into his arms.

"Oh Luke, where have you been? You'd better have a good reason for disappearing for days, or I am going home to Pa this time, for sure."

"You can't go anywhere without me, remember? I own you," he said, grinning at her.

Patricia raced to Butch, and he picked her up and swung her around as he kissed her neck. Lowering her to the ground, she noticed his hand. "What happened? Why do you have it bandaged?"

"I'll tell you later." Butch turned Patricia around and pushed her through the back door. Lucy had eased over to Bill, and he pulled her into his arms. "I missed you," he whispered.

Ma waited until Mary Grace turned Luke loose and walked into his arms. "Son, I prayed you would be safe wherever you were. God is good." Luke held her tight. "Your Pa is in the kitchen waiting for you." Luke grabbed Mary Grace's hand and they went inside to let Pa see that his youngest was well.

Gerald punched Sam in the side. "It looks like we might have a double wedding. Look at those love birds." Bill and Lucy were sitting in the garden swing.

"Mary Grace, I have a surprise for you. Look who I brought home with me." Mary Grace twisted out of Luke's arm and screamed. "Jimbo, Harry, you came." She rushed into their waiting arms and hugged them both. "Oh my, where is Joe and Mike? Did they come, too?"

"No," Jimbo said sadly. "We rushed to get here to help you. You didn't give any details, so I left the boys with Marco, the deli owner, until I could contact him. I didn't know if we would be staying here, but we do have to make plans for the boys' future."

"I hope that you'll both stay and live with us. I'm sure the boys will be welcome. Lucy is here. She helps me in the house while Roberta helps in the kitchen." She took Jimbo's arm and gave it a squeeze. "Luke has a beautiful home with plenty of room. The boys will be a lot of help, too."

"Mary Grace," Harry grunted. "You said Luke's home. Is this not your home, too?"

Luke listened intently, waiting to hear Mary Grace's answer to Harry's question. "Of course, I just meant that Luke had bought this place after he left us in Denver."

After instructing Butch to tell Ma and Pa about his adventure with the bad cowboy, Luke took his new bride home, along with his two best pals from Crooked Creek.

Luke stayed outside but asked Mary Grace to show the men to their rooms. Once the two friends were reunited with Roberta, their cook in the café, the men were ready to settle in for the night. Luke's mansion had surprised both of them.

Jimbo whispered to Harry, "Luke has come a long ways from the mining camp."

Mary Grace instructed Roberta to show Harry his bedroom, while she took Jimbo up the staircase to his room.

\*\*\*

"You mean we're going to live in this beautiful house? It's fancier than any hotel that I have ever stayed in. Gee, I figured we would be staying in the bunkhouse with the other men." Harry's head was on a swivel. His eyes darted everywhere. The pictures on the wall, the lovely rugs on the shiny wood floors, the doodads sitting in the parlor.

"Now, you can live wherever, but Luke says you're both like

family to him, and family lives in the house. I hope you don't mind being on the first floor. Those stairs are a struggle for me sometimes.

"Thanks, old gal. Excuse me, Mrs. Tiller. I didn't mean to sound disrespectable," Harry said.

Roberta laughed. "None taken, Harry, old boy. Reminded me of our café days."

"How many people live in this house?" Harry asked as he limped behind Roberta.

"Let's see. Of course, Mary Grace, Luke, me, Lucy and now you and Jimbo. My son, Bill, and Sam enjoy living in the bunkhouse. I'll tell you, it's not like any other bunkhouse. It has nice beds, a fireplace, a stove, tables and chairs, rockers and anything else Mary Grace can put out there to make it like a home." She laughed and opened his door to his bedroom.

"Holy cow, look at this. I might never come out." Harry was in heaven as he stared at the big bed with fancy bedcovers.

"Breakfast is in the dining room between six and seven. We have a buffet. Just come when you're ready. Luke will go over the work schedule for the day. Everyone has a job here." She grinned and closed the door.

***

Luke had come back inside and saw Mary Grace standing at the bottom of the staircase. He hoped that tonight she was ready to become his bride, but he didn't want to play a guessing game. He'd wait for a sign from her.

"I'm so glad you're home, Luke. It has been nearly a week. I had waited in the dining room for your return. You said you had something you wanted to show me. When you didn't come home, Sam went to see Butch and he organized a search party for you. We were all so worried."

Luke took her arm and they walked slowly up the staircase to their bedroom. "I'm sorry. I was surprised to find myself in such danger. That cowboy friend of yours, Trace Taylor, was desperate for money."

"My friend? Yes, I suppose he was a friend, but that's all." She stopped and quickly turned to face him. "He wanted to be a little friendlier, but there was something I didn't trust about him," Mary Grace spoke softly. "He's the one who brought in the tainted beef which caused me and others to get sick, and we had to close our café." Luke pushed open the bedroom door and waited for her to enter. "Roberta and Bill had to leave Denver because no one would hire her as a cook."

Mary Grace didn't move out of the doorway. She realized that she had to change things between herself and Luke. Her heart was pounding, and it felt like it was in her throat. She felt herself blush, her body steaming all over. She couldn't meet the bold hunger he had in his eyes for her. "I'm going to get ready for bed. Please give me a few minutes of privacy before you come in," she whispered.

***

Luke smiled and gave her a little bow. "Anything for you, my lady." He walked back down the stairs and went into the parlor, strolled over to the table that held the decanter of brandy. He needed a stiff drink, but whiskey was too strong. He didn't want to rush her. After waiting about thirty minutes, he walked back up the stairs, slowly, and saw a light coming out from under the door of their bedroom. He entered the room. Mary Grace was standing in front of the fireplace.

"The room is warm enough. I don't feel we need to add more logs to the fire," she stammered. "What do you think?"

Luke strolled over to the fireplace and took the poker out of her hand. "The fire's fine just like it is."

"How's your jaw? I can't believe Butch hit you after all you've been through." Mary Grace reached up to touch his face but thought better of it.

"He was upset, sweetheart, and hadn't yet heard what happened to me. I don't have any teeth missing," he said, grinning at her.

***

Mary Grace stood in her modest, high-necked nightgown and walked over to the big four-poster bed. She adjusted the covers and fluffed the pillows." Luke watched her every move, and she could feel his eyes upon her. Then the trembling started.

Luke sat down on the divan and slipped off his western boots. He stood and unbuckled his belt and pulled out his shirt tail from his pants. Then he unbuttoned his vest and shirt. He removed his vest and then slipped off his shirt.

Mary Grace caught a glimpse of him in the mirror on the wall and blushed a bright pink. She was feeling a little faint. She wasn't a virgin, but she felt like one. The one night she spent in Luke's arms was like a dream, but tonight it was going to be a lifetime.

A small knock sounded at their bedroom door. Mary Grace hurried over to it and opened it. Roberta stood in the doorway with a tray that held brandy and two glasses. "I thought Luke might want something to help with the pain in his jaw," she whispered, but then grabbed Mary Grace and pulled her into the dim hallway.

"Listen to me, child. Your husband has been through a bad time these past several days. You are his wife, yes, his bride. He doesn't need to be sleeping on that divan any longer. Do I make myself clear?"

"How did you know he wasn't already sleeping with me?"

Roberta raised her eyes and looked to heaven. "Child, I'm an old woman, but I'm not stupid. I am in and out of your room every day."

Goodness, how many others knew that she was Luke's wife in name only? Surely Lucy didn't know, too. Her face heated up from embarrassment. But, she couldn't think of that now. "Roberta, thank you." She took the tray, and Roberta closed the door behind her.

"Luke, Roberta brought some brandy for you. She thought your jaw might be giving you some pain."

"It looks like she brought you some, too."

"Why do you say that?" Panic was in her voice.

"She brought two glasses." Luke cocked his head sideways.

"Yes, I'll have a glass. Maybe it will help me sleep."

"Sleep, yes. It will relax you a little bit," Luke commented sweetly.

After sharing their glasses of brandy, Mary Grace inched toward the bed. She pulled back the covers and crawled under them. After propping up the pillow, she watched Luke.

He blew out the lantern nearest to the door, then ambled over to the table near the divan. He blew out the candle. The only light in the room that remained was from the embers in the fireplace.

***

"Luke." Mary Grace's voice was so soft Luke wasn't sure he heard her. "Luke, come over here."

He eased to the side of the big four-poster bed and pressed his body into the mattress.

"You don't have to sleep on the divan. Come and get in bed with me." She lifted the cover.

Luke didn't dare flinch a muscle. He just stared at his lovely bride, with her long, blond tresses cascading over her shoulders, covering her breasts.

***

Mary Grace froze. He didn't make a movement to come to her. Oh, how she wanted to die. She was positive now that he didn't love her.

"Mary Grace." Luke placed his hands on his waist. "You know what is going to take place between you and me if I climb in this bed. Are you ready to be my wife in every way?"

"Are you going to just stand there and have a debate about what's going to happen or not?" Sitting straight up in the bed, she shrieked, "I'm sick to death of hearing that you can do what you want when you want with me because you won me in a high-stake poker game!"

In a flash, he slapped his hand across her mouth.

She stiffened, and her eyes opened wide.

Quickly, Luke pushed his pants and cotton underwear down around his ankles and gave them a kick out of his way. He jumped into the bed with a heavy sigh. "I have wanted to lie in this bed for weeks. It feels like heaven compared to that divan."

"Well, dammit! If I'd known you only wanted to lie in the bed with me, you could have gotten in here a lot sooner." Mary Grace slumped down further under the covers and pouted.

"Oh, my girl. I have more ideas than just lying here," Luke said with a chuckle in his throat. "Come here, my little bride, and let me show you how much I've wanted to be here." He pulled on her lovely gown and undid each button as if he were opening a treasure box. "I'll try not to hurt you, sweetheart." Luke pulled her into his arms and nuzzled her neck.

Chills flowed over her body and she held him so tight her fingernails were buried into his skin. After a few soft kisses and sweet words, she relaxed her grip on his arms.

***

Luke sat up on his elbow and looked at his beautiful bride whose lovely hair was the color of pale gold. A tightness settled in his chest and he was pleased the torment of trying to stay away from her was over. From the very first kiss, he knew in his heart this lovely girl would be his. Luke pulled her closer and then his large body captured hers.

***

Luke loved her! She was thrilled with Luke's vow not to hurt her. His lovemaking was so gentle and sweet she would remember it forever. Mary Grace giggled from nerves, but she was warm all over. Luke covered her face with small kisses, telling of his love for her with each touch. She'd longed to belong to someone and to have someone to hold her as if she was the most precious thing in the world. She knew she had won a piece of the moon.

She nipped at his lips, crying for all the lonely years she had spent alone after her mama died. Now, with Luke's love, she would never be alone. Mary Grace wiped his brows and pushed his black hair out of his eyes. "Oh, Luke, I'll love you forever and ever.

## Chapter 39

Early the next morning, Luke left his bride curled up in the bedcovers as he slipped out of the room. He asked Lucy to prepare a hot bath for Mary Grace and have it ready when she woke up.

A smile crept across her face, and she hurried upstairs to prepare Mary Grace's clothes for the day. She was thrilled that things had changed between her sweet friend and her boss.

***

All the men filed into the dining room, and Luke was happier than he had been in years. After Jimbo and Harry had each filled a plate of Roberta's breakfast, Luke asked them how they slept.

"I slept like a log," Harry said and Jimbo readily agreed. "I felt like I was in a palace like they have over the water in one of those foreign countries."

"How do you know of places like that, boy?" Harry grinned at his friend.

"Hey old man, I like to read. I read about all kinds of places, that is, when I have the time and of course, a book."

"Speaking of books, if, and when, we get those boys, Joe and Mike, here, they will need to attend school like Nellie. Right now, Patricia, her mama, is teaching her. I've heard that Pine Hill has a school. We'll need to check into that."

"So, Luke, you won't mind having two more people under your care? Those boys are good youngsters, and they need to get out of that busy city with all those wranglers coming through all the time."

"Why don't we go into town and send a telegram to Marco? I'll instruct Mr. Anderson at the bank to purchase them two tickets to Blount Town. I need to go into town and make sure that Taylor fellow is still locked up. I don't want him escaping and making any more trouble for me or Mary Grace."

"I'm ready to go anytime this morning. Jimbo and I didn't remember to pick up our bedrolls from the train depot. We'll need to purchase some more clothes, too." Harry glanced at Jimbo who was stuffing his mouth with a hot, buttery biscuit.

"Later, this evening, I need to talk with Butch about our plans to go to Abilene, Kansas, and purchase a herd of cattle. We won't have to drive them but a hundred miles from Abilene to here," Luke said.

"Shoot fire, son, that's a good idea. A hundred-mile trail drive ain't nothing with a lot of men," Harry said, laughing.

As they prepared to leave for town, Mary Grace came down the staircase. She was a vision of beauty in her new beige day dress with new brown boots to match. Luke propped his arm on the rail of the staircase and watched her glide downward toward him.

"Where are all of you off to? Maybe, I want to go, too."

"Mary Grace, if you get any prettier, I'm going to have to carry you away with me." Harry limped over to her.

"Harry, does your leg hurt you? You seem to limp more than before." Luke had taken her hand as she waited for Harry's answer.

"No, sweetheart, I'm just a little tired. After I rest, I'll be better. Don't fret over me." He turned and joined the others.

Luke raised Mary Grace's palm and placed a butterfly kiss in the center. "Harry is right. You are beautiful, and I am one lucky man." He wanted to take her back upstairs and continue with their lovemaking from last night.

"So, where are you going this morning?"

"To town. I need to check on that Taylor fellow, and we are going to send a telegram to Mr. Marco and have him send the boys. I'm going to ask Mr. Anderson to purchase two train tickets to Blount Town. While we're in town, we're going to check on the school. Nellie and the boys need to be in school, now that the weather is nice."

"All right, but next time, I want to go into town with you." Mary Grace smiled, walked him to the kitchen door, and kissed him goodbye. She floated back into the dining room where Roberta and Lucy stood waiting for her to appear. They both wore grins a mile wide.

"Well, we want to hear all about your honeymoon night, "Roberta said, smiling. "Well, I do, anyway. Lucy is too young to hear such details."

"Miss Roberta, for goodness sakes. I'll be eighteen in two months. I need to know something other than babies comes from the cabbage patch." Both ladies burst out laughing at the serious expression on the young girl's face.

***

Jimbo sent a telegram to Mr. Marco asking him to send Joe and Mike to Mary Grace's ranch in Pine Hill. Luke sent a note to Mr. Anderson requesting that he purchase two train tickets to Blount Town and deliver them to Marco's Deli for the two orphan boys.

Luke told Jimbo and Harry he really looked forward to meeting the young boys. While the men wandered around the dry goods store, looking for more clothes, they overheard several men talking about the old preacher. One of the men said it was sad that the old fellow fell over with a bad heart.

Luke had not had a chance to take his ma to Sunday services since he arrived home. He wondered if the townspeople would search for another man of the cloth to come and preach. Some communities had a traveling minister who came to town once a month. Luke hoped that the community would find a man to live here and be in the pulpit each week.

On the way back to the ranch, Luke told Jimbo and Harry what had happened to the old preacher. "I guess Ma will want to attend his funeral."

"Well, there's something to think over, son." Harry stopped his horse and spit a stream of tobacco.

"What are you talking about?" Jimbo asked. He twisted around in his saddle to listen to his old friend.

"If the preacher is gone to his great rewards, who's going to say the words over his grave?" Harry commented like he was talking about the weather.

Luke shifted in his saddle and pondered what Harry had mentioned. "Someone will step up and say something."

"I was just thinking. If there's going to be any weddings between those lovebirds on your ranch, there's gotta be a preacher man." Harry kneed his animal in the side and continued onto the ranch.

***

Mike Conners and Joe Singleton arrived in five days. Roberta and Mary Grace had cooked a special dinner to celebrate them becoming part of their family. Ma, Pa, Patricia, Nellie, and Butch all arrived along with Gerald and Arthur. Mary Grace nudged Luke in the side and whispered, "You need to ask the blessing."

"Why me?" he asked, whispering back for her ears only. "The oldest person here should say the blessing."

"This is our home, and you are the host. Do it, please." She smiled at the others while she whispered through her teeth at her husband.

"Luke," Mr. Arthur Turnbull grunted as he cleared his throat. The old man's Adam's apple bobbed up and down. "May I bless this wonderful event? I want to bless these two boys into our fold here on your wonderful ranch and bless this wonderful food."

"Please, I would love for you to stand here at the head of the table and say whatever you wish." Luke gripped Mary Grace's wrist and practically pulled her down in the chair next to him.

Everyone took their seat and quickly bowed their heads. The older man, who sat on the front porch daily with Luke's pa and played checkers, surprised the family with his beautiful words and knowledge of the bible verses he quoted. "Amen," he said, and all the others repeated amen.

"Mr. Turnbull." Ma couldn't hold back her inquiry into the old man's past. "You have never said what you did in your younger years. Were you a preaching man?"

"For many years, I was the preacher in Springdale, Colorado, about twenty miles north of Denver. After my wife passed away, from no fault of her own, I lost my faith, but this is not the time to discuss my sad life. This is a happy occasion, and let's keep it that way."

***

After the celebration, Luke asked all the men to meet in the bunkhouse so they could discuss a plan to form the trail drive from Abilene to Pine Hill, after they purchased the new herd.

Mike's and Joe's eyes were bright when they learned that they could go with the men. "You two boys are old enough to be a big help on the cattle drive."

"We'll all go to Abilene on the train and purchase several hundred head of cattle. The prices are lower there. The cattle are still pretty thin and not nearly as fat as they were before the war. Many of the older herds in Texas were either confiscated from the Confederacy or the Yankees soldiers. We will be purchasing a young herd."

"How will you feed that many cows while we're bringing them back here?" the younger boy asked. "I used to help feed cows on a farm and it ain't an easy job."

"That's a good question," Luke said and rubbed the boy's head. "After we buy the cows, we'll corral them in the stockyard until we're ready to start the drive here to Pine Hill. While on the drive, the cattle will eat the spring grass that is available and will drink from the creek beds. We will only be driving them about a hundred miles, but we can only travel about ten or fifteen miles a day. We hope to fatten them up while we're moving toward home.

"Jimbo, write this list down. I don't want to forget anything. Harry, you'll make a list of everything we need to purchase for the chuckwagon, and we'll do that while in Abilene. We want as much fresh food as we can get to begin with.

"Of course, we'll ship our own chuckwagon with us on the train to Abilene and drop it off at the livery. When we're heading the cattle out of Abilene, you can purchase our supplies. I don't want to take a chance that Abilene won't have a big, sturdy chuckwagon," Luke said, and Harry readily agreed.

"We'll need two flatbed wagons with sides built at least three feet high. When a mama cow drops her baby calf, we'll gather it up and put it in the wagon. We take turns milking the cows and bottle feeding the babies at least twice during the day. Mama cows will be able to tell her baby by its smell, and she will feed it her milk during the night. The littles ones can't keep up, and we don't want to take a chance of them dying on the prairie." Luke tried to explain the working ways of a cattle drive so the younger boys would fully understand.

"How many bales of hay do you think we'll need to buy while out on the trail? We can order the hay from a farmer and have it all ready as we pass by their land," Butch said. "I know a farmer who raises fields of hay and would appreciate the business in Dover, about fifty miles from home."

"How about you take care of purchasing the hay?" Luke said.

"Sounds like we got this trip all planned. Now, when are you planning on leaving? We'll be away from home for several weeks or longer depending on the weather. Should we hire some men to work our ranches while we're gone? Pa and Arthur will be here, but they'll need help with milking the cows and feeding the other livestock," Butch said. "Your ranch will need two or three men. You don't want to leave Mary Grace and Lucy all alone."

"Let's plan on going into Pine Hill in three days and line up some men to work for us while we're gone. We'll get the chuckwagon ready to take to Blount Town to put on the train. We'll have to make sure the four mules are in good shape, too. We'll be ready to travel by that time."

"You sure Mary Grace is not going to want to go with us?" Jimbo asked.

"Now, I didn't say she wouldn't want to go. I said she'll not be going. There's a difference." Luke laughed and went back inside the house to get ready for another wonderful night with his bride.

# Chapter 40

The men enjoyed their train ride to Abilene, Texas. Mike and Joe were excited young men as they arrived in the sprawling, dirty town of Abilene. There were old buildings and rough boardwalks. The smell in the air was enough to make a person gag. The streets were filled with piles of manure and wet, muddy holes. Long planks were placed across the street so people could cross from one side to the other. Large herds of cattle traveled right down the middle of the streets to the stockyards.

The rain had stopped when Luke rode up to the chuckwagon. All the men were riding their horses and would be surrounding the cattle once they were headed on the trail. Jimbo rode ahead of the herd, while Butch and Gerald rode drag. Mike and Joe rode on each side of the wide spread of cattle as they started moving them toward home.

Just as Luke got off his horse, Harry motioned for him to come to the back of the wagon. He'd purchased all the supplies and had placed many of them on the ground beside the wagon.

"Got any of the hot coffee left? I'll sure be glad to see the sun today so I can dry out this soaked hide of mine, "Luke said and leaped down from his horse.

Harry placed his fingers over his lips, indicating for Luke to be silent. Luke frowned but followed his lead. He motioned for Luke to listen to the surrey noise coming from under the wagon in the boot.

"What is it?" Luke mouthed to Harry.

"Hey, Luke," Harry called. "I think the boot under the wagon might have a raccoon or two in it. You know, they could have rabies this time of the year. Maybe I should shoot some holes in it to kill whatever's in there. Sure would hate to get bitten by a wild animal that's hunting for food."

Luke cocked his head and frowned at Harry. Whatever did he think was in there? Luke decided to play along. "Go ahead and shoot a hole or two, and we can light a fire and smoke it out. We don't want too many holes in the boot though."

Harry leaned down as close to the boot as he could and made a loud noise of cocking his shotgun. "Ready, boy? Watch out for whatever comes running out."

"Wait, don't shoot," a voice Luke recognized came from under the wagon. Mary Grace scooted to the end of the boot and stuck out her pretty face, smeared with sweaty dirt.

Luke got down on his knees and helped his disobedient wife to the ground. She straightened and brushed her long train of blond hair back over her shoulder.

"Help me," another weak voice came from under the wagon.

"My Lord, there's another stowaway." Harry bent low and said, "Miss Patricia, where did you come from?"

"She came with my lovely wife, who knew that neither one of them were invited to tag along on this trail drive. Am I right, dearest?" Luke stepped closed to Mary Grace while she took a giant step backward, away from those fierce eyes that were staring daggers into her.

"Now, Luke, I asked you over and over if I could come on this trail drive. You knew how much I wanted to come. So don't say that I didn't plead with you to let me."

"In a few words as possible, how did you get here in the bottom of the chuckwagon?" *This should be a good story.*

"It was no problem, really. I bought us two tickets for the train to Abilene and we just stayed out of sight from you and the others. When we arrived in Abilene, we hid while you purchased the cattle, and when you were getting ready to leave on the trail drive, we jumped into the wagon."

"I see," Luke said, staring at the smug look on his wife's face. Luke turned to Patricia. "What's your story, Miss? Don't tell me that you just couldn't allow my sweet wife to come alone." He twisted his head side to side and glanced up. Butch was riding into camp and leaped down off his horse when he saw the two girls standing in front of Luke and Harry. First he was surprised to see his fiancée, and then he was horrified to see her dressed in men's britches. "What in blue blazes is going on here? Where did these 'girls' come from?" Butch questioned the men.

"Where in hades do you think we came from?" Patricia screamed at Butch.

Butch stormed toward her, and she jumped backward. "You'd better prepare to run, woman, because I don't need any smart-ass answers. I asked you a question and you'd better lower that temper of yours before you regret it."

"Butch," Luke said, a little calmer. "Your new fiancée came along with my sweet wife. She wanted to make sure Mary Grace stayed safe on their trip. Am I correct, Patricia?"

Patricia glanced at Mary Grace. "No, I wanted to come on this trail drive, too. I've never had a chance to do anything away from home, even before I came to work on the ranch." She lifted her chin like she was an officer reporting to her commander, one that might be placed in front of a firing squad.

"Well, Luke. It looks like we have two new ramrods," Butch said, then strolled around Patricia, sizing her up. "Harry needs a lot of help cooking and cleaning for the men. Jimbo can ride with the herd instead of being Harry's helper." Butch glanced at his little brother to confirm his decision.

"Yes, Mary Grace, since you're here, you can help with the cooking every morning and help with the calves during the day and after supper. They need help finding their mamas, so they can be fed during the night." Luke waited for Mary Grace to complain, but no words came from her. "Mary Grace, I came into camp for a cup of coffee. Get me a cup, now," Luke spoke through gritted teeth.

"Now, Luke, you don't have to be so mean. Really, I am your wife, but I don't have to jump because you say so. I'm here to help and I will help because I want to, not because you demand it."

Luke took a step toward his wife, and she flew to the campfire and poured him a cup of hot coffee. She handed it to him with a sweet smile.

"What am I going to do with you?" With a crooked grin, he

took the coffee. She turned and marched back to the chuckwagon.

After Luke moved closer to the fire to get warm, he called to Butch. "Come along, Brother, and let's allow our new ramrods to get to cooking. I'm expecting a delicious lunch."

\*\*\*

Mary Grace's body was exhausted as she stretched out in her tent. Though it was midnight, sleep refused to come. She and Patricia had stayed up, walking the small, newborn calves out into the herd, seeking their mamas. Six new calves had been dropped the first day. She prayed there wouldn't be any new ones tomorrow. Milking cows and bottle feeding the babies was a huge job.

She lay on her side of the tent, waiting for Patricia to come, but she never did. Finally, her eyes grew heavy and she fell into a deep sleep. Early in the wee hours, she woke to find herself wrapped in Luke's arms. She ran her fingers through his dark hair, finding comfort in his strength.

\*\*\*

"We didn't get a chance to talk today," he said. She hummed and drifted back asleep.

Luke tucked her closer in his arms and fell asleep. He allowed his anger to fade because he was as pleased with his new bride as she was with him.

\*\*\*

Mary Grace felt wonderful this morning. Luke was snoring softly, so she slipped out of the tent. Harry was building the fire to start making the coffee. Rushing over, she grabbed some smaller limbs and placed them under the tripod. The fire flamed up and Harry pushed the big pot of coffee over the fire. "I'm going to whip up some honey buns for the men. They will cook in a skillet pretty quick," she said.

"Luke loves your sticky buns. Maybe he'll forgive you for not doing like you were told to do—stay home."

"Oh, Harry, please don't scold me, too. I wanted to be with all of you. It's been so long since I saw you and Jimbo. Things have been different since we left the mining camp."

"Aren't you happy with Luke?"

\*\*\*

Luke yawned and sat up. He'd patted the space next to him

and found it empty. Harry was talking to Mary Grace. He crawled to the edge of the bedroll and peeked out of the front flap. He was interested in hearing Mary Grace's answer.

"I love that man so much and I couldn't live without him, but he makes me so darn mad. He says he loves me, too but he owns me—not like a wife but like a piece of property. He won me from my pa. You've heard this before, right? Luke actually has a bill of sale for me, like I'm some prize horseflesh."

"Oh honey, he don't feel that way at all. I'm sure of it. Luke wouldn't keep you around because of a bet."

"I do know he loves me, and I guess I should forget about that stupid poker game, but it's really hard to forgive my pa. No man should do a thing like he did to me."

Luke crawled back into his bedroll and pondered Mary Grace's harsh words about that bill of sale. Not that he blamed her because twice he'd reminded her of it. He was going to have to do something about that crazy bet with her pa.

***

At the end of the day, Patricia and Mary Grace eased the tailgate down for the new calves to go find their mamas. They'd sat in the slow-moving wagon and bottled-fed the calves. It was a job, but Mary Grace enjoyed watching the calves suck the milk. Several of the calves ran directly to their mama, but two of them lingered and bawled. The calves' crying nearly broke Mary Grace's heart.

"Come on, Patricia, let's help these two locate their mamas. Their bags are full and these fellows are starving."

The two patted the behinds of the calves in and out of the cattle. The babes' bawling could be heard faraway, but no mother cow showed up to claim her baby. The sun had set, but the full moon guided the girls.

"We've traveled a good ways from the camp. I can't hear the men or see the campfire. Maybe we'd better guide these calves back the way we came," Patricia said.

"Guess you're right. Surely, their mamas will come and claim them shortly. They could be already waiting at the wagon like last night." Mary Grace shooed one of the calves forward. Suddenly she ran into Patricia, who stood like a statue.

"Who are you?" Patricia said.

THE GAMBLE

Mary Grace peeked around her and gasped. A painted Indian warrior, no more than twenty years of age, blocked their way. Colorful painted stripes covered his face, and his headband only had one feather. A knife poked out of a sheath and a small tomahawk hung off his belt.

"My Lord, where did you come from? I ain't heard of Indians being in this territory?" Mary Grace's question seemed to shock the young warrior. Perhaps it was her lack of fear.

"Go away," Patricia said, like she was shooing a buzzing fly.

"You both come with me, or I will scalp you," the young man said.

Mary Grace laughed. She'd always been taught by her pa never to show fear in the face of danger. Nor would she show this young man she was afraid, but Patricia had other ideas. She let out a blood-curdling scream.

The Indian socked her in the jaw, and she fell at Mary Grace's feet. The cattle shifted and bawled even louder from the scream.

\*\*\*

"Listen, fellows, that scream sounded like Patricia," Luke yelled to Butch. "Where's Mary Grace?"

"You go look for the girls, and we'll help try and stop the cattle," Gerald instructed Luke. "That screaming will cause the herd to stampede. If we don't hurry, they'll scatter all over the prairie."

Gerald leaped to his feet. "Let's ride, boys. We've got to turn them into a circle."

Butch lit a lantern and hurried down the trail where he'd last seen the girls caring for the newborn calves. He screamed their names, but the sound of the cattle's hooves and bawling drowned out his voice. Luke had jumped on his horse and rode into the middle of the herd.

\*\*\*

Mary Grace surprised the young Indian by kicking him in the groin. When he huddled forward, she jumped on his back and bit his neck and bare shoulder.

Screaming, he bucked backward and fell to the ground with Mary Grace's legs wrapped around his thin waist. "Off, you leopard. I'll kill you." Gasping for air, he tried to grab his knife.

Mary Grace bent forward and dug her fingernails into his arm.

Unprepared for a fight with this wild woman, he forced her off and backed away in quick, jerky steps, then spun and ran toward the clearing away from the scared cattle.

With a trembling chin, Mary Grace crumbled to the ground next to Patricia. She lifted her friend's head and patted her cheeks. "Patricia, wake up."

Patricia opened her eyes, which filled with tears, and she shrieked and batted Mary Grace away.

Mary Grace held her tighter until Patricia relaxed.

"We're safe? The Indians are gone?"

The sound of running footsteps. "Not quite yet," Mary Grace said. Then she let go of the breath she was holding when she saw Butch come running up to them.

***

"What happened?" he asked, as he lifted Patricia out of Mary Grace's arms.

"Indians, lots of Indians," Patricia cried into Butch's shoulder wishing she had not moved. Her head was pounding from the blow that she'd received. A sickness in her belly made her feel ill, and everything doubled. "Don't let them carry me away," she cried.

"Never, my love. I am here now," Butch said. As careful as he could, he carried Patricia into the darkness toward the camp.

***

Silence surrounded Mary Grace for the first time. The cattle had settled down. Many of the herd flopped down onto their bellies to rest.

Luke rode up to Mary Grace. Leaping down from the Black, he grabbed her and asked, "Are you alright?"

"Yes, I'm fine." She buried her face into his chest.

Gently pushing her away, he noticed the stains on her clothes. "Sweetheart, you're all bloody. Where are you hurt?"

"It's not my blood. It's the Indian who scared the bogeyman out of us." Mary Grace laughed at the puzzled expression on Luke's face. "I will be so happy to go home."

Once, back at the campfire, Mary Grace asked Harry if he would prepare a stiff tonic for Patricia to help her sleep. Butch carried it to her and struggled to get her to drink it, but he finally won her over.

As the men gathered around the campfire, Mary Grace told

them about the Indian warrior who came out of the darkness and wanted to take them back to his tribe. They smiled as she told them how afraid they both were, which caused Patricia to scream. "I didn't have a weapon, so I jumped on his back and held on until he threw me to the ground and ran away."

The men laughed, and Gerald said that he'd never known an Indian to allow a young girl to overtake him.

"He thought I must have been part leopard. It was so dark and the cattle were running wild, so he probably didn't know what he was dealing with. I just knew I wasn't going anywhere with him. My pa said to never show your enemies fear, so I didn't."

"Could you tell what kind of Indian marking he had on his body?" Gerald asked. "You can tell what tribe he came from by their paint. Are you sure he was alone?" Gerald kept glancing at Luke.

"I didn't see any more men, and no one came to help him. He just appeared out of the darkness in front of Patricia before we knew it," Mary Grace said.

"We're sure glad you took action to save yourselves. With the stampede of the cattle, we would never have found your tracks," Gerald said. All the men shook their heads and peered at Mary Grace with new eyes.

Jimbo stood and stretched his long lanky body. "I got one thing to say to you, Luke. Never make this little gal mad at you." He motioned for Mike to come on guard duty with him.

Mary Grace excused herself with a pail of hot water and went into her tent. She had to wash all the blood off her body and put on a clean gown to sleep in.

\*\*\*

"That Jimbo always has to have the last word about everything we talk about," Luke said to Harry.

"Well, son, this time he might be right. That gal sure can be a hellcat if she needs to be. That poor Indian probably had no idea who he tangled with." Harry smiled and limped toward the chuckwagon to go to bed. "Better hit the hay. Morning comes mighty early."

\*\*\*

Butch was sitting cross-legged in front of the tent Patricia was sleeping in. Mary Grace was inside getting ready for bed.

"Why aren't you in your tent for a few hours, big brother," Luke asked. Mary Grace sat and listened to the two brothers exchange comments.

"I promised Patricia I'd sleep in front of her tent. I've never known a gal so afraid before. She was lucky to have a brave woman like Mary Grace with her. So much younger than Patricia, too."

"I understand from Patricia that she's always lived in town. Mary Grace is a town gal too, but she's had to deal with a different class of people. Her pa owns the stage depot and a combination café-saloon in Crooked Creek. Mary Grace worked for him and had to learn to handle herself." Luke peered around the campsite. "I'm proud of Mary Grace. I don't know what I would have done if that Indian had harmed her."

Tears popped up behind Mary Grace's eyelids. Luke was proud of her. He wouldn't know what to do if something happened to her. Luke really did love her.

# Chapter 41

Pa, Ma, and Mr. Turnbull stood at the corral fence at their place and watched as the men led the cattle into the pastures. Mike drove a wagon, carrying about a dozen new calves into the corral nearest the barn.

"Oh look, Pa." Mama clapped her hands. "Aren't they the prettiest little things you've ever seen?" Pa glanced at Mr. Turnbull and laughed. "Women. They think everything that's small with four legs is cute."

"Hey, Pa." Luke pulled his horse to a stop at the fence. "How in the world did you get your chair way over here?" Luke was thrilled to see his pa outside.

"Mr. Booth's son-in-law from Chicago is visiting, and he said that I needed a ramp. He and Mr. Booth came over and built me two, one for the front porch and one for the back. Now, I can leave the house, but I still need a push to get back up the ramp," he said laughing. "Arthur, here, is a big help."

"I'll have to go over and thank both of the men for helping you with this project."

"Mr. Booth said he owed you, and no thanks is necessary. He found out that you paid all those men to help build his barn."

"You sure can't keep a secret in this community." Luke shook his head and rode into the middle of his new herd.

***

Mary Grace waved to Luke as she raced to their house. She

couldn't wait to get in the bathtub. She knew she smelled like one of the cows out in the pasture.

Luke rode up beside her and slowed his horse. "Howdy, beautiful. How about allowing a cowboy to give you a lift?"

Mary Grace stopped and smiled at her husband. "I don't know. I have an old, cantankerous husband who might shoot you for pestering me."

"If he's as old as you say, I can take care of myself."

Mary Grace loved the way Luke liked to tease. "Well, I'll chance that he won't find out."

Luke reached down and lifted her across his lap and nudged his horse toward the barn. "Whew, gal, you stink."

"Thanks, handsome. You sure know how to sweet-talk a gal." Mary Grace slid to the ground and practically ran into the house. Roberta was standing in the kitchen and laughed when Mary Grace came flying in the back door.

"Well, little miss stowaway, I'm surprised to see you're still in one piece. I thought Luke would probably have skinned you alive once he discovered you and Patricia," Roberta said.

"He wanted to, but I talked him out of it. Patricia handled Butch. Man, he was furious with her." She smiled. "Will you help me heat some water for a bath?" Mary Grace peered around the clean kitchen. "Gosh, I'm so happy to be home."

"Golly gal, you smell worse than one of those rovers that's been out on the range for weeks." Roberta wrinkled her nose. "Speaking of Patricia, how did she like her first trail drive?"

"I'll let her tell you about her experience." Glancing in the parlor, Mary Grace asked, "By the way, where's Lucy?"

"As soon as she heard that the men were back with the new herd, she shot out that door like her dress tail was on fire." Roberta grinned. "I'm afraid the old lovebug had bitten her and my son."

"Thought I saw those two making eyes at each other. You know, Roberta, Lucy has a birthday in two months, and she'll be eighteen. She's young, but she's had a hard life for a youngster. She'd make Bill a good wife." Mary Grace smiled. "Hey, there might be a double wedding. Butch has asked Patricia to marry him."

Lucy glided in the house, practically floating around the kitchen.

"Lucy, help me carry hot water up to Mary Grace. She needs a bath, and her hair will need to be washed." She didn't appear to have heard Roberta's request. "Uh, Lucy, please come down out of the clouds and help me."

"Oh, I'm sorry, Mrs. Roberta. What do you need me to do?" Laughing, Roberta instructed the lovely maiden to carry a pail of hot water up the stairs.

As the three women started up the stairs, Roberta asked, "Lucy, how's my son doing?"

"Oh, he's just wonderful." She sighed and moved into Mary Grace's room in a dreamlike state. Mary Grace and Roberta couldn't contain their smiles.

\*\*\*

Once all the cattle moved onto Luke's and Butch's property, the men drove them into the pastures. While still together, they assigned guard duties for each man. Butch didn't want any of the cattle to stray away from the rest of the herd until they were familiar with the area. The hands tossed loads of fresh hay around the pastures for cattle feed. Fortunately, a creek ran across the pasture land.

There was no way Luke would climb in a nice clean bed the way he was. He rinsed off in the freezing water trough and went into the bunkhouse. Thankfully, Harry had placed buckets of water on the stove. Luke washed himself from head to toe in a hot tub bath.

Gerald was in the bunkhouse lying on his bunk, fully dressed in his dirty clothes and snoring loud enough to scare the cattle. Butch stood holding his animal's reins while speaking with Jimbo and Mike who were taking the first watch. After saying good night to the men, Luke headed into the house with a dry towel wrapped around his neck.

It was drudgery to Luke to climb the spiral staircase to the master suite he shared with Mary Grace. Opening the door, he saw the lantern sitting across the room was turned down low. He also noticed there weren't any bed covers on the divan. Luke smiled and glanced at the bed.

Mary Grace had fallen asleep, propped against two pillows. She had not bound her hair on top of her head, and it flowed down her shoulders. She was the most fascinating young woman he had ever been around and the most beautiful. Each time he was near her, a desire to take her in his arms overcame him, and the heat rose through his body. One benefit of being married was Mary Grace herself. No matter what words had passed between them or what disapproving event had happened, he longed for the nights. She might pretend to avoid his advances, but she always turned to him. He knew she loved him.

Luke unbuttoned his shirt and pushed his underwear and pants down around his ankles. He stepped out of them and slid between the clean sheets that smelled like fresh air. He removed one of Mary Grace's pillows, disturbing her sleep.

"Mm, you smell so good," she said to Luke. She cuddled her head onto his shoulder, and he pulled her closer to his body. He couldn't deny that his body wanted this lovely woman, but he couldn't keep his eyes open.

\*\*\*

"Luke," Mary Grace whispered and turned his jaw to face her. A soft snore was her answer.

She cuddled closer, reached for the quilt, and pulled it over her sweet husband's shoulders. Nothing more needed to be said as both of them drifted off into a much needed rest.

## Chapter 42

Bill was sitting at the dining room table, watching Lucy's every move.

"For gosh sakes," his mom said, "let the girl work. I need her help with setting the food on the table. Just because it's Saturday doesn't mean there's not work to do."

"Oh Ma, I'm not doing anything." Bill and Lucy both blushed.

Mary Grace was walking down the stairs when Luke glanced up from the table and saw her. He hurried to the staircase and took her hand to help her step down the last three steps. Leaning close, for her ears only, he whispered, "I'm sorry about last night. You were so beautiful lying in bed, but I was dead tired."

"I was tired, too. I could hardly keep my eyes open while I waited for you."

"So, you were waiting up for me?" Before she could answer, he said, "I was hoping you were." He flashed a grin.

"You are waiting for me to tell you how much I want you. Well, you'll have to wait longer." She hurried into the dining room to sit next to Bill.

Luke followed and sat next to her while Lucy served him a cup of coffee. Lucy and Bill kept glancing from one to another, nodding toward him. "All right. Someone's going to have to tell me what's going on here." Luke stared at the young couple. Mary Grace's head popped up from spreading jam on her biscuit.

"What am I missing?" Roberta looked at everyone in the room. She slipped into a chair at the end of the table.

Bill cleared his throat. "Mr. Tyler, Lucy and I are in – love. We want to get married. Since she doesn't have any folks, and Mrs. Tyler is responsible for Lucy, I thought I should ask you. You being the man of the house and her boss."

Lucy's face pinkened. Luke glanced at Mary Grace, whose face glowed. "Well, Mrs. Tyler," Luke said. "Do you approve of this marriage?"

"Yes, I most certainly do. Don't we, Roberta?" Mary Grace pushed her chair back and rushed to Lucy, giving her a tight hug.

Roberta smiled and wiped away tears. "I couldn't be happier for both of them. I love Lucy like a daughter already."

"When do you wish to marry?" Luke asked.

"Well, Mr. Tyler, I wanted to wait until my eighteenth birthday, which is two months from now. That way I will be a woman."

Luke glanced at Roberta and Mary Grace. "Ladies, do you think you can make a wedding gown in two months?" The girls giggled and nodded.

"Maybe Butch and Patricia would like to get married at the same time. A double wedding." Mary Grace clapped her hands. "Luke, get Butch alone and ask him if he'd like to do that. He asked her, but they haven't chosen a date yet."

"Sounds like a big shindig. We can invite everyone in town. Let's make this a grand celebration." Luke stood and smiled. He walked outside, thinking this would be a great opportunity for the townspeople to see what he has done to the old Wainwright's place.

***

"I wish we had a church and a preacher," Mary Grace said. "It will be a shame not to have a long aisle for you to walk down and let everyone see your lovely white gown. You'd look just like a princess floating down it. Oh, and you'll have to decide who you want to give you away."

"I wouldn't mind getting married in this house and walk down the staircase into Bill's arms," Lucy said with a sigh and a glance at her intended.

Bill jumped up from the table. "Excuse me, but I have to get to work." When the back door slammed, the ladies laughed.

"Men. They don't want any part of planning a wedding. Just tell them the time and the place," Roberta said, shaking her head. "Speaking of the wedding gown, who among us can sew? I can patch, but that's all. The whole time Patricia was here, I never saw her with a sewing basket in her lap."

"I've never even threaded a needle. There was old Mrs. Whit who patched things for me and Pa. She has passed now." Mary Grace chewed on her thumbnail, then jumped up. "Just maybe we could hire Mrs. Gordon to help us make your dresses if she can get someone to help with the children for a few weeks. I'll send her a telegram and ask if she'll consider it."

"You know, we don't have a church but we could have one. We do have a preacher. Mr. Turnbull is a retired preacher, and I know he'd do the ceremony," Roberta said.

"What did you mean, we could have a church?" Mary Grace asked Roberta.

"That big white building sitting empty would make a great church. People would only come out onto your property once a week, and Arthur could stand in the pulpit and preach. I overheard a few ladies talking about how sad it is for the town not to have Sunday services. They said the mayor said there was no money to hire one or to make repairs to the old church building."

"That is sad. The church is really the soul of the town. I loved our little church in Crooked Creek. You know, Roberta, Luke has wanted to do something with that building. He even mentioned tearing it down." Mary Grace stared out the window and noticed the men standing around the corral.

"That's a great idea," Roberta said.

"The old building will need work. Oh, wouldn't it be grand if we had new shining pews on each side of the aisle. You know, the Catholic church in Denver is beautiful inside with its stained-glass windows and rows of pews." Mary Grace sat back down and refilled her cup with fresh coffee. "We could buy enough pews, but it wouldn't be practical to have stained glass windows," she said with a sigh.

"We aren't that far from town, and I think the townspeople and the ranchers' families would be willing to drive out here each Sunday. Tonight, I'll speak to Luke about what we've discussed this morning. I believe he'll like the idea of the building being turned into a church. He can talk Mr. Turnbull into preaching, if anyone can." Mary Grace had so much on her mind she didn't know where to start.

"What if the old building isn't ready in two months?" Lucy asked.

"Like you said, you could always get married here in this house." Lucy and Mary Grace giggled like school girls.

After dinner, Mary Grace and Luke strolled over to his folks' house. Butch and Patricia were sitting around the kitchen table with Pa and Mr. Turnbull. Mama was slicing everyone a piece of apple pie.

"Welcome, children," Mama said. "How about some apple pie and coffee?"

"No thanks, Mama, none for me. We just finished our dinner, too."

Mary Grace sat down next to Patricia and reached for her hand and squeezed it. "Luke has something to ask you, Mr. Turnbull." She glanced at Luke who looked like he could pinch her.

"You got something to ask me, son? Is this a private conversation?" His eyes darted from Luke to the rest of the family at the table.

"No," Mary Grace quickly answered. Luke smiled at his big-mouth wife and said, "Darling, since this is your idea, why don't you tell our friend what's on your mind."

All eyes flew back from Luke to Mary Grace. "All right. Mr. Turnbull, we all know you're a retired preacher. Luke wants to turn the big white building into a church. We know it needs work, but most of all we need a man of the cloth to preach each Sunday." It was out now, and Mary Grace took a deep breath. "We hope you'll agree to do this. The town can't afford to hire a new man, and the traveling preacher might only come once a month. We need a good man to deliver the Word of God each week. You'll receive a wage. All the money in the offering plate will be yours, and if it's not enough, Luke will donate more. Won't you do that, Luke darling?"

Luke raised his head with wide eyes. He drummed his fingers on the table. "I will do whatever it takes to make our new preacher happy."

Mr. Turnbull cleared his throat. "I don't know if I am up to doing this big of an undertaking. Will I have to serve the townspeople, like funerals, weddings, visiting the sick, and all the other things a preacher is expected to do?"

"We haven't thought about all that. We wouldn't want you to do something that would be a hardship on you." Luke gave his wife a look that said *be quiet.*

"Would you consider just preaching each week? And we really are in need of a preacher to perform a wedding ceremony for Lucy and Bill." Mary Grace gave him a sweet smile.

"We're gonna need a preacher to marry us, too." Patricia sat straight up and leaned forward at the table. "Butch said that maybe we could have a double-wedding ceremony with Lucy and Bill."

"Oh, I think that is a wonderful idea." Mama wiped tears from her eyes. "Oh, Arthur, I hope you'll agree to be the town's preacher. I have watched and listened to many of your blessings. You can do all of it, performing over funerals and praying for the sick. This will be a new beginning for you." Mr. Turnbull sat very still. "Pa and I would be willing to help you when needed." Mama glanced at her sweet husband who was improving each day because of his exercising. He had conquered getting in and out of his wheelchair.

# Chapter 43

After breakfast was over and the kitchen was clean, Mary Grace, Lucy, Patricia, and Roberta drove into town in Mary Grace's black carriage. She dropped the ladies off in front of the dry goods store before driving to the telegraph office.

After sending a quick note to Mrs. Gordon, pleading with her to come and help make two wedding gowns, she drove to the livery and left her carriage and the two beautiful black horses there. Crossing the street, she noticed two men standing in front of the boardinghouse. She stopped, lifted her palm to shade her eyes, and realized that one of the men was Josh Randall.

Frozen in place, the sound of galloping hooves reached her ears. A horse came racing down the middle of the street, nearly hitting her. Jumping back, she screamed.

Josh stepped off the boardwalk and hurried toward her. "Mary Grace, is that you? I can't believe it."

"It's me. What are you doing here in Pine Hill? This is a most unlikely place for you to show up—with your friend." Mary Grace nodded at the handsome, young man leaning up against a post.

"I had to leave Denver. My father was making all kinds of threats. After he realized you weren't going to marry me, he stole money from many accounts in the bank and said he was going to tell everyone that I embezzled it. After you became sick, I packed up and left in the middle of the night. My friend and I are on our way to New York City. We're traveling on and off the train so the sheriff will have a hard time trailing us."

"I'm sorry you were forced to leave Denver. I knew you were unhappy, but I had no idea it was because of me."

"Never you, Mary Grace. My father wanted me to marry you for your money, and I'm sorry I misled you. I've always wanted to get out from under my father's rule. After my mother left me with him, he's been a tyrant."

"I am sorry, Josh. I wish you success in New York. I'm happily married to Luke Tyler. He is good to me."

"I'm glad for you. Take care of yourself and don't worry about me. I was able to save enough money to travel and get away from Denver." He leaned forward, took Mary Grace's hand, and kissed it. "Good-bye, my fair lady."

Mary Grace stood watching Josh walk back across the street to his friend. She couldn't wait to tell Luke about Josh's father, the banker. He would need to contact Mr. Anderson, his own banker, and check on their money in his bank. Remembering the ladies, she hurried to the dry goods store and watched as the girls looked at the satin material. Lucy had chosen a piece that she liked because it was cheap. Mary Grace waited outside for the girls to finish.

"Mrs. Tyler," a young man called her name.

"Here I am, young man." She called back to him.

"I have a telegram for you from Denver." The young boy handed it to her and smiled. She reached in her handbag and gave him a quarter. "I can't believe I've received a note back so fast."

"Well, miss, our telegraph equipment is new. If the people on the other end can reach the customer, a reply can come quickly."

Mary Grace thanked the young man and hurried back into the store. "Hey ladies, I received a reply from Mrs. Gordon, though I wasn't expecting to hear from her for days. Let me read it." Mary Grace held the paper in the air and sat down on a barrel in the store. "Listen to this." Mary Grace read loud enough for Mrs. Rockwell, the store clerk, to hear the results of the telegram.

*Mary Grace,*

*Can come immediately. Lost our jobs at home. Need a home and job. Will arrive in three days in Blount Town.*

*Mrs. Gordon*

"This is wonderful news. She and her husband will be living

here. Mr. Gordon is a gifted carpenter. He can help us repair the white building and maybe make some pews."

As the ladies rejoiced that the seamstress and carpenter would be arriving soon, Luke came storming into the dry goods store.

He picked up Mary Grace from the barrel and ushered her outside onto the sidewalk. Luke frowned at all the people within hearing distance, then guided her into an alley and stopped directly in front of her.

"Luke, what's wrong?" She said and pushed at his hand that had a death grip on the upper part of her arm.

"Who in the hell was that man flirting with you and attempting to eat your arm off in the middle of the street? He got away before I could smash his pretty face."

"I can't believe you're jealous," Mary Grace said and spun to leave the alley.

Snatching her arm again, he forced her to face him. "I am not in a joking mood, missy. Who was the man?"

"All right. He was a banker's assistance in Denver who came around the café all the time."

"So, he was the other man sniffing after you, as Jimbo wrote me about."

"Jimbo wrote you that I had two men sniffing after me? My goodness, he could have written something nicer than that." Mary Grace shook her head and laughed. "Luke, Josh Randall didn't really want me. His father made him try and court me. His father wanted my money."

Luke frowned and looked away. "What is the man doing here in Pine Hill?'

"His father, a banker for Mr. Anderson, stole money from a lot of accounts and told Josh he was going to tell everyone that Josh did it. You need to write Mr. Anderson and check on our money."

"You're right. So this *hand eater* is leaving town soon?"

"Yes, Luke, he is." She laughed and held her hand to him. "Would you like to kiss my hand, too?"

"No, smarty, but I do want a kiss." He pulled her into his arms and kissed her rosy lips with such passion he left her standing in the alley weak in the knees

# Chapter 44

A long week passed, and the wedding plans were well on their way. Mr. Turnbull finally agreed to marry the two young couples and preach one or two sermons in the white building after it was ready.

Mr. and Mrs. Gordon were temporarily staying in Bill's room, while he agreed to bed down in the bunkhouse with the other men. Luke had Harry and Jimbo ride into Pine Hill to hire six new men to help with branding and riding guard during the days and nights. Three men would bunk down at Butch's home and the other three would live at Luke's. Harry did most of the cooking in the bunkhouse for the crew of men working at Luke's while Roberta and Mary Grace cooked for the family members only.

Luke hired several men to help Mr. Gordon with the white building's repairs and building the pews. Mary Grace and Roberta prepared a hot meal for them during the day, but the men returned home at night. Reverend Turnbull, a new name for Arthur, helped with small repairs, and designed a pulpit for Mr. Gordon to build.

Luke was so proud of his papa. He rolled his chair out to the corral while the men were branding the cattle. Then he rolled near the fire and kept feeding it to keep the pokers hot. His arms were strong and had begun to look like small logs. Papa was getting stronger every day.

Luke's ranch house and fields were a busy place. The ladies cooked and helped sew the lovely wedding dresses. A notice had been pinned up at the dry goods store, on the sheriff's poster board, and in the telegraph office inviting everyone to the double wedding.

***

Late one afternoon, Luke walked into the parlor. Mrs. Gordon was fitting Patricia and Lucy in their new wedding gowns. She quickly closed the parlor doors, blocking Luke's view of the gowns.

Luke froze and thought how beautiful Mary Grace would look in a dress like that. A dress she never had the chance to wear because of the hurried way that they had married. Mary Grace deserved to have a beautiful wedding, just like the one Patricia and Lucy were going to have. She was a young woman whom he was sure dreamed of walking down an aisle dressed in a beautiful white dress. He needed to speak with his wife. Luke took two stairs at a time up to their bedroom. He opened the door and slammed it into Mary Grace as she was coming out.

Twin spots stained her cheeks. She was so darn pretty dressed in her new pink gown. He hadn't meant to open the door and hit her with it. For a moment, he couldn't remember why he had hurried up to their bedroom. His thoughts were all scrambled whenever she was around.

He reached for her hand and said he was sorry as he pulled her into his arms and kissed her. Luke was the one to pull away first, leaving her looking like she wanted more.

"What do you want? Why aren't you out with the other men?"

"The other men?" he replied and trailed kisses down her slender neck until she was nearly out of breath. He couldn't get enough of her.

"Luke, its daylight. Now stop before someone sees us."

"You know, innocent little bird, men and women make love in the daytime, too." He smiled and tapped her on the nose with his knuckle. She waved his hand away and smiled at him.

He reached for her arm and led her to the divan. "Sit here with me for a moment." Luke took her hands in his. "Mary Grace—" Luke swallowed and smiled. He slid off the divan and kneeled on one knee in front of her. "Mary Grace, will you marry me? I love you with all my heart, and I want to make you happy every day of our life."

"But, Luke, we're already married, aren't we? Don't tell me

that you found out the preacher wasn't real!"

Luke placed his two fingers over her rosy lips. "I know we are married, but love, we didn't have a real wedding like Lucy and Patricia are going to have with Bill and Butch." "I want that," he said. "I want to watch you walk down the aisle to me. Would you marry me, again?"

"Oh Luke, I've always wanted to be a bride. I've always wanted to wear a long, beautiful dress. How did you know?"

"When I saw the dresses downstairs in the parlor, I knew that no one deserved to wear a dress like that more than you. We can have a triple wedding. But one thing I insist on more than anything. I want us to say our vows alone. Do you understand?"

"That will be wonderful. Each couple will have their special moment in the marriage ceremony. You think of everything. Thank you." She leaned into him and kissed him with all the passion of a honeymoon night.

"Hold on, girlie. Like you said, it is daylight." Luke jumped up and left the room.

\*\*\*

Mary Grace stood and whirled around in her bedroom. She was thrilled with Luke's formal marriage proposal. There could be a triple wedding ceremony. "Oh my, I must tell Roberta." Mary Grace raced down the staircase. "Roberta," Mary Grace ran to the kitchen where her dear friend was waiting. She leaned over with her hands on her knees, clearly out of breath from running.

"What's wrong, child?" Robert pounded Mary Grace on her back.

"Oh, the sweetest thing just happened between Luke and me. He proposed marriage to me." Tears brimmed in her eyes.

"But, you're already married. Why would he ask you again?" Roberta's brows formed a vee.

"Yes, we are, but he feels that I was cheated out of a big wedding ceremony, like the other girls are going to have. He wants us to remarry with them—a triple wedding."

"My, how sweet of your young man. This will be a glorious day for everyone who lives on the ranch. But Mary Grace, you don't have a dress. Mrs. Gordon can't make you a dress in two days."

"Oh, I forgot about the dress." Lowering her head she said, "I guess I'd better find Luke and tell him that we can't take part in the wedding ceremony." Mary Grace trudged out the back door.

As she entered Luke's mama's kitchen, Luke, Butch, and their papa were talking business in the parlor. They seemed to be in a deep conversation, so she sat and visited with Maureen, Luke's mama.

"Tell me, Mary Grace, what's wrong. I can tell something is on your mind," Maureen asked. She patted her daughter-in-law's hand.

"Your wonderful son wants us to say our wedding vows again with the other two couples. We both forgot I don't have a wedding gown, and Mrs. Gordon cannot make me one in two days. She does have some satin and lace left over but not enough to make me a dress."

Maureen jumped up and hurried down the hall to her bedroom. After a few minutes, she stood in the doorway of her room and called for Mary Grace to come. Once Mary Grace entered her bedroom, Maureen lifted a white gown out of an old trunk that sat at the end of the bed. "This is my wedding gown. I never had a daughter to share it with. It's in perfect condition but could use more lace on the bodice and maybe a longer train on the back. I was about your size when I married Luther, believe it or not. What do you think?"

"It's glorious, Mama," Mary Grace responded, not calling Luke's mama her given name. "I would be honored to wear your dress. May I try it on now?"

In less than an hour, the two ladies were standing in Mary Grace's parlor with Mrs. Gordon. "Do you think you could add a few things to make this a more modern gown for Mary Grace?" Maureen asked.

"Yes, I have material and I'll start on it now. Get undressed, child, and let me get your measurements and envision how I'm going to re-design this beautiful garment. Oh, what a wonderful day—a triple wedding."

# Chapter 45

Luke and Butch, along with Gerald and the new hired men, worked from sunup to sundown with the herd. All the branding was over, and the new calves were corralled in a small pen whenever the men found one dropped out in the pasture. The men were planning on fencing the back part of the pasture, but they were going to wait until the wedding celebration was over.

Six dozen chickens and two strutting roosters were purchased after the men had completed the henhouse and chicken yard. A dozen sows waddled around a big pen behind the chicken yard. The place was beginning to look like a working farm and a ranch combination. The men sowed the ground close to the kitchen, so the ladies would have a kitchen garden. Vegetable bushes bloomed already.

While the men were working hard outside, the three women along with several hired ladies from town were busy cleaning the inside of the white building. Mrs. Gordon sewed while Mr. Gordon and a couple of townsmen built pews and other pieces of furniture needed for the inside of the church.

Mary Grace had hired two household maids—an upstairs maid and one to work downstairs. Roberta was the overseer of the kitchen and the meals for the family and household staff. Lucy continued working as Mary Grace's personal maid, and she helped serve the meals in the large dining hall. Two ladies came from town three times a week to wash and iron for the household.

Luke was proud of how smoothly his household ran. Mary

Grace ran a tight household, but everyone loved her even when she had to reprimand someone. She was a gracious hostess to anyone who dropped by uninvited.

All the townspeople were invited to the triple wedding ceremonies. Roberta and Maureen had hired ladies to help cook and deliver food to Luke's ranch for the wedding reception.

Mr. Gordon came to the house and told Luke that he was afraid the white building wouldn't be ready for the wedding but would be a grand place to hold the reception. "We don't have enough pews ready for everyone to sit, but there will be plenty of places for ladies to sit between dances. We've built enough tables and benches for the guests to sit and eat at the reception."

Luke thanked Mr. Gordon and said that the couples could be married in his house and everyone could walk or ride over to the white building. "I know how hard you and your men have worked, but I believe young Lucy really wanted to be married here in the house." Mr. Gordon smiled and hurried back to work.

In the late afternoon, the day before the wedding, Luke told the girls about the change of plans for the ceremony. They laughed and said that they were fine with the change.

"I hope I don't fall on my head coming down that long staircase," Patricia said."

"Don't worry, Butch will catch you, honey," Roberta commented, and the girls giggled. Luke hurried to escape the silly brides.

The whole family had been invited to Luke's home for a pre-wedding supper. Another long table sat in the parlor next to the dining room because all the hired hands and housemaids had been invited to join in the celebration.

Roberta, Harry, and Jimbo had outdone themselves with the delicious food. Ham, deer steaks, beef roast, and all the trimmings were served.

After a lengthy blessing from Reverend Turnbull, the couples explained where they were going after the wedding. Butch said he and Patricia were taking a weeklong trip to Denver. Bill said that he and Lucy were going to go up to her bedroom. Everyone laughed and Harry slapped him on the back.

Luke looked around at everyone sitting at the table and he said, "If you think that's funny, you can laugh some more because

Mary Grace and I are staying home, too." Mary Grace blushed while everyone laughed more.

Luke raised his hand to stop everyone from laughing. "I plan to take my beautiful bride-to-be on a long vacation when I feel that we can get away from the ranch." He glanced at Mary Grace and gave her a wink.

Before everyone left the table, Roberta signaled for everyone to listen. "I have an announcement to our three grooms. When you say good night to your bride-to-be, you cannot see her again until she's ready to walk down the aisle to meet you at the altar. It's bad luck if you break this tradition."

Everyone laughed, patted the men on their backs, and wished them good luck. Luke took Mary Grace by her arm and whispered, "Meet me at the bottom of the staircase in thirty minutes."

She raised her eyebrows but didn't ask. She nodded and watched him walk out of the dining room. Mary Grace ran upstairs and undressed. She brushed her hair out and let it hang down around her shoulders, slipped off her dress, and put on a nightgown with a matching robe. Mary Grace powdered her chest with a lavender scent and unbuttoned her robe enough for him to see the top of her cleavage. With a pinch of her cheeks to give them a rosy glow, she hurried down to the bottom of the staircase and waited for him to come.

***

Luke had been standing in the parlor and watched his young bride rush down the staircase. She stood and posed, looking like she had just arrived.

He walked to her and said, "What are you trying to do to me? Mm, you smell wonderful and look like you're all ready for the bridal bed." He glanced down at the open robe and grinned.

"Oh, you. I do not. Why did you want to see me tonight before we retire for the evening?"

"I want to give you a wedding present," he said, while holding a mahogany box.

"But Luke, you have already given me a wedding gift. You gave me the fancy black carriage and two beautiful horses."

"I know, but this is a different wedding."

"Wait here. I have a wedding present, too." Mary Grace grabbed up her gown and robe while rushing into the parlor and pulled out a desk drawer. She hurried back to Luke. "Here," presenting him with a small black box. "Open it."

Luke placed the box he had for Mary Grace under his arm while opening the small box. A shiny pocket watch sat on green satin.

"Do you like it?" she asked.

"No. I love it. I will always treasure this gift. I'll wear it tomorrow."

"Now, for my wedding gift." Mary Grace smiled and held out her hand.

"Mary Grace, I hope you will like this," Luke said, wishing now that he had bought her a piece of jewelry.

She reached for the box and flipped up the latch on the front. Lying in the box was a piece of white paper. She lifted the paper and turned it over and over again. She glanced up at him, her brows forming a furrow.

"It's the bill of sale I had for you. I want you to have it, so you'll feel free from me."

"But, it's only a plain piece of paper with no words written on it."

"I know. After I won the bet, your pa took a piece of paper and started to write out a bill of sale for you. I took it away from him and folded it in my vest pocket. I told him that I didn't need a bill of sale. I only wanted you to be my cook. Told your pa that you could leave any time if you weren't happy."

"All this time, you never had a real claim on me? You didn't own me?"

"No, I didn't own you, but after a time I wanted you. There's a difference," Luke whispered.

"Yes, there's a difference. Thank you for setting me free. I shall keep this bill of sale to show our children one day." Mary Grace kissed Luke on the cheek and slowly walked up the staircase.

## Chapter 46

The wedding day was beautiful. It was as if God created a special one for the three brides. Unfortunately, the three brides were full of nerves. One minute, Lucy was crying while Patricia snapped at one of the housemaids.

Roberta instructed Lucy to go to her room and Patricia to go home and relax. "This is going to be a long afternoon," and under her breath, she whispered *and night*, but she didn't want to upset Lucy anymore.

Mary Grace was marking off all the things that needed to be taken care of. She was issuing orders like an Army first sergeant, and everyone was jumping at her commands.

Jimbo had been assigned to meet Lucy at the bottom of the staircase and escort her to Bill at the homemade altar. Gerald was going to walk Patricia to Butch while Harry was going to escort Mary Grace to Luke.

Mrs. Gordon had surprised everyone by being able to play the beautiful piano that sat covered in the corner of the parlor. She would play a few soft pieces of music while the guests and the mothers were being seated. Then she'd play the wedding march when time came for the brides to appear at the top of the stairs.

With a signal from one of the housemaids, Mrs. Gordon began playing softly while Reverend Turnbull walked from the outer room and took his place next to Pa Tyler, who was serving as best man to all three grooms.

Nellie, Patricia's eight-year-old daughter, came down the

staircase with a halo of yellow flowers in her hair. She looked like a little angel in her ankle-length, soft yellow dress with puffed sleeves. She passed out long-stem daisies to the ladies as she walked to the front where Butch stood waiting with his pa by his side, sitting tall in his wheelchair.

She walked over to the side of the preacher and stood. Maureen followed behind Nellie, wearing a lovely green dress that matched her eyes. She walked up to Butch and kissed him and then took a seat in the front row. She smiled at Nellie, assuring her that she did a good job.

Patricia stood at the top of the staircase, and the congregation turned to see the beautiful bride wearing a lovely, white satin dress with lace trim covering the bodice and long lace sleeves. Her tears hid behind a sheer white, tulle veil.

As Gerald, dressed in a new black suit, walked Patricia into the parlor, comments abounded about the bride's beautiful gown. He walked her to the altar and smiled at Butch.

Mrs. Gordon stopped playing and turned to listen to the preacher.

"Welcome family and friends to this glorious event today. This is my first triple wedding, and I am proud to perform the wedding ceremony for these three young couples. Two couples coming together for the first time, and one couple renewing their previous vows. Before the first ceremony begins, I want to say a few words about love and marriage. I would like to quote a scripture from our good book about love." He held his worn black Bible up for the congregation to see. "Please bear with me," he said and cleared his throat.

"'Love is patient, love is good to each other. It's not proud. It does not disgrace the other, it is not self-seeking, it is not easily angered.'" He took out his hanky and wiped his mouth. The reverend eyed the guests, then he continued with the Bible verse.

"'Love protects, always trusts, hopes, and always takes care of each other.'" He glanced up, and his voice lifted. "'Love never fails.' First Corinthians 13:4 to 8. One more short verse, 1 Corinthians 13:13. 'And now three things are important in a marriage: faith, hope, and love. But the greatest of these is love.'" He coughed and signaled for everyone to bow their heads. "Let us pray. *Gracious heavenly Father, we pray that you will bless these young couples as they come together as one. Amen."*

He turned to Mrs. Gordon, and she shifted around on the bench and began playing the wedding march.

Butch reached for Patricia's hand, and Reverend Turnbull spoke, "Repeat after me. 'I, William Luther Tyler, take thee, Patricia Nell Thompson, to be my lawful wife, to have, and to hold, from this day forward, for better, for worse, for richer, for poorer, in sickness and in health, until death do us part.'"

Then he turned to Patricia and asked her to repeat after him, and she did in a loud, clear voice.

"Now join hands and repeat after me," Reverend Turnbull said. "'With this ring, I thee wed.'" Butch slipped a ruby ring on his bride's finger and then it was Patricia's turn.

"I now pronounce you husband and wife. You may kiss the bride." Butch lifted the pretty veil and kissed her until the men began to hoot. Everyone laughed and clapped.

Butch, grinning like a drunken donkey, guided his bride to the chairs decorated with flowers and white sheets to watch the other ceremonies.

Mrs. Gordon played soft music as Roberta walked down the aisle, dressed in a lovely peach-colored dress covered with white lace. She joined her son, Bill, and gave him a kiss. Then she took her seat next to Maureen.

With the sound of the wedding march, Lucy took her place at the top of the staircase. Jimbo walked to the bottom of the stairs and waited for the pretty young girl to reach him. She was dressed in a long white satin dress with a high neck and a lace bodice with lace sleeves that almost covered the top of her hands. Like Patricia, she wore a sheer white tulle veil that helped conceal her quivering lips.

\*\*\*

Lucy held a death grip on Jimbo's arm. He wasn't sure if she felt that he might run or if she would be the one to escape. She was a beautiful bride. Jimbo led her to Bill, who reached out for her hand as she neared him. Both of the young couples' hands were shaking, which caused a few giggles from some of the congregation.

\*\*\*

Lucy took Bill's hand, and the couple stood in front of

Reverend Turnbull. He spoke loudly, "Repeat after me. 'I, Bill Tiller, take thee Lucy Marie Smitten, to be my lawful wife, to have, and to hold, from this day forward, for better, for worse, for richer, for poorer, in sickness and in health, until death do us part.'"

Then he turned to Lucy and asked her to repeat after him, and she did in a soft voice that sounded like a weak kitten.

"Please repeat after me." The older man looked over the congregation and attempted a smile. "'With this ring, I thee wed.'" Lucy watched Bill's shaky fingers push a small gold wedding band over her finger. Then it was Lucy's turn. Once the ring ceremony was over, Reverend Turnbull said in a loud clear voice. "I now pronounce you husband and wife. You may kiss your bride."

Bill reached for Lucy and gave her a peck on her rosy lips. The congregation laughed and clapped. Several ladies wiped tears from their eyes as the couple rushed to take their seats next to Butch and Patricia.

***

Mary Grace heard the wedding march, so she walked to the top of the staircase. As she took the first step down the stairs, one of the housemaids raced to her and smoothed out the long white train that flowed from the back of her gown.

As she took a few more steps, Mary Grace realized that Harry wasn't standing at the bottom of the stairs. Her pa stood gazing up at her. He was dressed in a new black suit and his bald head shone like it had been buffed. She had never seen him look so handsome.

When she reached the last few steps, her pa took her hand. "Oh pa, I never dreamed you would come, much less be willing to give me away."

"Your gambling man did. He asked me to come, and here I am," he replied. "I have a gift for you. Please turn around and allow me to put it around your neck." He reached into his suit coat pocket and pulled out a string of white pearls. "These pearls were your mama's that her mama gave her the day we married. I saved them for you."

"Oh, Pa," she said and fingered them around her neck. "Thank you. Now I feel that she is really here with me—us, today." Tears flooded her eyes.

"None of that, gal. Your man will think that I said something ugly to you."

The wedding march had begun again. Mrs. Gordon was leaning back on the piano bench to see what was keeping Mary Grace.

Mary Grace reached up on her tiptoes and kissed her pa. Her heart was overflowing with love for him. She stepped back and took her pa's arm and walked to the entrance of the parlor. They continued down the aisle. She was radiant beneath a sheer piece of white tulle. Lifting her eyes toward Luke, she grinned at the man she loved more than life.

\*\*\*

Luke stood at the altar with a fresh haircut and a crisp white shirt tucked under a new black suit coat. He tried to stand straight, with his feet straddled, and one knee kept locking and unlocking. Luke had never felt so insecure, and he didn't like the feeling one bit. He was beginning to regret this idea of his to remarry.

Once Mary Grace and her pa reached him, Moon leaned down and kissed her. "Be happy, baby girl." Taking his daughter's hand, he placed it in Luke's palm.

Luke's blushed beneath his summer tan. He clasped Mary Grace's soft hand. Moon took his seat beside Gerald and Jimbo. Luke wanted to look at Mary Grace, but he resisted and stared straight ahead at Reverend Turnbull.

\*\*\*

The old reverend's third ceremony, Turnbull was suffering from fatigue. Maybe he shouldn't have agreed to take on this big job, he thought. He needed to get this wedding over so he could sit down.

Once Luke and Mary Grace stood in front of him, he said, "Repeat after me." He proclaimed this louder than the last two times. "'I, Luther Clark Tyler, take thee, Mary Grace Winters, to be my lawful wife, to have, and to hold, from this day forward, for better, for worse, for richer, for poorer, in sickness and in health. I promise to love, cherish, honor and obey her, until death do us part.'"

"I will," Luke declared. A thought flashed through his mind. He didn't remember hearing the last sentence in the other ceremonies.

Reverend Turnbull faced Mary Grace, cleared his throat, and

said, "Repeat after me."

***

Mary Grace listened and repeated every word of the wedding vows until the preacher got to the last part where he said, *obey*. Mary Grace stood silent, refusing to look at Luke, but she leaned forward and whispered to the older man, "take the obey part out."

The preacher didn't understand but glared at her for a moment. Finally, realizing what she meant, he cleared his throat again, and began once more. "Mary Grace, will you love, cherish, and honor this man, *et cetera*." He waved his hand at the couple.

A big smile appeared on her face and she said, "I will." The congregation began to mumble among themselves.

Before the preacher could continue, Luke held up his right palm to stop the preacher. Frustrated, the older man leaned his head toward Luke, and growled, "What now?"

"Repeat the vows again, and add *obey*." The congregation who were close enough to hear the whispered words began to giggle at the battle of wills taking place before them.

Reverend Turnbull, red-faced and trying to hold a grip on his anger, whispered, "What is heavens name is going on here?"

Luke motioned to him to repeat the vows again, adding back the word.

With her backbone stiff and biting her bottom lip, she faced Luke. He was staring straight ahead without a trace of expression on his handsome face. Sighing and lowering her shoulders, she hated to make a scene, and she could tell she wasn't going to win this argument. Still, she had to know. She looked him in the eye, "Why? Is that what you want—me to obey you? I thought the bill of sale meant you didn't own me."

She watched the grin spread on Luke's face. "I don't, and I'll always treat your fair. I just want you to trust me."

Reverend Turnbull sighed, looked to the heavens, and said something under his breath.

Mary Grace stared at Luke for the longest time. Then she nodded and repeated the vows with the word *obey* in it.

The preacher rushed through the ring ceremony and finally announced, loud and clear, "In the name of our Lord and Savior, I now pronounce you husband and wife. You may kiss your bride."

Luke faced his bride, and taking both of her hands in one of his, he lifted her chin with the other one. "Whatever am I going to do with you?"

"Kiss me, boss man. Just kiss me."

The End.

A note to my readers:

I begin to write one night, to take my mind off being sad, and it worked. Your acceptance of my stories have lifted my spirit for the last seven years. After I complete a story, I feel sad that I won't be communicating with my new friends, whom I gave birth to and watched them grow.

But, you, as my reader, give me great joy when you purchase my soft-back book or a kindle copy. Your wonderful comments about my book on Facebook or an Amazon's review brings a smile to my heart.

I would love to hear from you. My social contacts are listed below:

Lindajk@cox.net
Facebook.com
Facebook Blog: https://writerlindasealyknowles.com
Goodread.com
Amazon Author Page:
https://www.amazon.com/author/lindasealyknowles

Made in the USA
Coppell, TX
30 May 2020